"I'll answer the rest of your questions once you're dressed," Kaitlyn told Jake emphatically.

He gave her a pleased grin. "I still have that effect on you."

She groaned aloud. "You and your oversize ego," she muttered. "Look at you, Jake. Any woman would drool."

"I'm not talking about any woman, Katie. I'm talking about you. And me. We were damn good together in bed. We still would be."

He knew instantly he'd pushed her into realizing what she did not want to admit even to herself. She straightened. Her blue eyes directed her fury at him.

"If you go down that road, you'll go alone."

Dear Reader,

It's no surprise that Intimate Moments is *the* place to go when you want the best mix of excitement and romance, and it's authors like Sharon Sala who have earned the line that reputation. Now, with *Ryder's Wife*, Sharon begins her first Intimate Moments miniseries, THE JUSTICE WAY. The three Justice brothers are men with a capital M—and they're about to fall in love with a capital L. This month join Ryder as he marries heiress Casey Ruban for reasons of convenience and stays around for love.

Popular Beverly Barton is writing in the miniseries vein, too, with *A Man Like Morgan Kane*, the latest in THE PROTECTORS. Beverly knows how to steam up a romance, that's for sure! In *Wife, Mother...Lover?* Sally Tyler Hayes spins a poignant tale of a father, a family and the woman who gives them all their second chance at happiness—and love. *Reilly's Return* also marks Amelia Autin's return. This is a wonderfully suspenseful tale about a hero who had to fake his own death to protect the woman he loved—and what happens when she suddenly finds out he's really still alive. In *Temporary Marriage*, Leann Harris takes us to the jungles of South America for a tale of a sham marriage that leads to a very real honeymoon. Finally, Dani Criss is back with *For Kaitlyn's Sake*, a reunion story with all the passion you could wish for.

Let all six of these terrific books keep you warm as the winter nights grow colder, and come back next month for even more of the most excitingly romantic reading around, right here in Silhouette Intimate Moments.

Yours,

Leslie J. Wainger
Senior Editor and Editorial Coordinator

Please address questions and book requests to:
Silhouette Reader Service
U.S.: 3010 Walden Ave., P.O. Box 1325, Buffalo, NY 14269
Canadian: P.O. Box 609, Fort Erie, Ont. L2A 5X3

FOR KAITLYN'S SAKE

DANI CRISS

Silhouette®
INTIMATE™MOMENTS®

Published by Silhouette Books
America's Publisher of Contemporary Romance

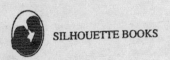

SILHOUETTE BOOKS

ISBN 0-373-07822-6

FOR KAITLYN'S SAKE

Books by Dani Criss

Silhouette Intimate Moments

Sheriff's Lady #490
For Kaitlyn's Sake #822

Silhouette Romance

Family in the Making #1065
Family Ties #1112

DANI CRISS

has wanted to write romance since she first read Jane Austen's *Pride and Prejudice*. In high school she dabbled in poetry and short stories, though she has finally found her true love in novels.

She squeezes her writing time between working as an office manager and taking care of her family. She lives in Kansas City with her husband, Dan, her two lovely daughters, Crissie and Sara, and Timmy, their dog.

To the Princess and the Puter,
two lovely young women.
May all your dreams come true.

Prologue

You lied to me. You didn't work late.
I came by to see you, but the office was closed.
I don't like being lied to.

The message was scrawled in red ink on a piece of her agency's stationery, the letters huge on the ivory paper with the rainbow-colored logo for Memories To Go Travel.

The note was unsigned, but Kaitlyn Adams didn't need a signature. Nor did she need convincing she had a genuine problem on her hands.

He'd been asking her for a date every day since he'd come in two weeks ago to talk about a trip. Last night had been no different. Again she'd politely refused, coming up with yet another made-up excuse for not having dinner with him. Something about the man had made her uncomfortable from the start and now she knew her instincts had been right.

What was she going to do? she asked herself, still not

picking up the note he'd placed in the exact center of her desk.

Rubbing her arms against the chill she felt, she glanced around her tasteful office. Nothing out of place. Nothing missing. The only thing out of the norm was this cryptic message he'd left behind.

How had he gotten in? The thought of his having access to her here at any time made her stomach knot with fear. She sat down and whirled her chair around to face the window behind her, gazing out at the morning's cloudless blue sky. Outside, birds chattered and chirped, their songs competing with the noise from the riding mower engine. Grass grew, leaves waved in the hot August breeze, water trickled over the rocks in the courtyard fountain beyond the second-story office window.

A world so at odds with what was going on inside the building.

Shivering again, she picked up the phone and dialed her closest friend.

"I know. You're looking for that head count on the engagement party you're throwing for us on Friday," Shelly Preston said, not giving Kaitlyn a chance to explain otherwise. "It's so good of you to do this. Rob hasn't given me a number yet, but I'll get it before lunch or I'll strangle him. Police detective or not."

Kaitlyn felt fear climb her spine. Is that what the writer of this note had in mind for her? Strangulation. The threat, though veiled, was unmistakable.

"Actually…" She paused, the words she needed to say sticking in her throat. Saying aloud what had happened made it seem even more frightening.

"What is it, Kaitlyn? You sound…upset. Is it the party? You're doing this on such short notice. We decided to get married only last week."

She latched onto that excuse until she could pull herself

together. "I do need to tell the caterer how many to plan for...."

"I'll get Rob on it immediately. Let's have lunch and go over the number of guests. I've got some other wedding ideas I'd like to run by you."

"All right," Kaitlyn agreed, looking forward to a few moments without fear. "Um, Shelly, when you talk to your fiancé, you might tell him I'm looking into an alarm system for the office. Maybe he could give me a couple of names...."

"One name," Shelly said emphatically. "I can tell you there's only one person he'll recommend—his buddy Jake Riley. Has his own company. Riley Security Services. Call him. I've been dying for you to meet him."

Kaitlyn's heartbeat tripped. This was not a name she wanted to hear. "Jake Riley? How does Rob know him?"

"They met on a case three years ago—about the time you and I met—and they've been friends ever since, just like we have."

"But surely Rob knows someone else who could—"

Shelly laughed softly. "We've been wanting to get you two together for...let's see... I met Rob two months ago, fell in love with him about a week after that," she said on another bubble of laughter, "then about a month ago we finally began introducing each other to our friends. We haven't managed to get you and Jake together, though. We figured that would happen at one of the wedding events, but your calling him for an alarm system beforehand will be great."

Kaitlyn groaned softly. In her mind there was nothing great, or even good, about this. While on one level she knew Jake was one person whose expertise she had complete trust in, on another level she didn't want to deal with him again. He wouldn't be the solution to her problem. He was a complication she didn't want. A danger of another kind.

Chapter 1

He was here, the lover she'd left five years ago. Seated behind her desk, Kaitlyn took time to collect her thoughts. But apparently two days of stewing about this moment—worrying about seeing him again, wondering whether they would be able to deal with each other, fretting whether he would even want to see her again—two days of chasing the questions around in her mind hadn't been long enough to prepare herself, and she doubted a few more minutes were going to make facing him any easier.

Jake Riley hadn't changed a lot in appearance. He still was a commanding presence with his dark hair cut short and almost military in style, his wide-shouldered, rigid-backed, six-foot-two stance and his sharp-edged features—the straight line of his nose, jutting chin, squared-off jaw, piercing midnight eyes. There was not a wrinkle in his charcoal suit, and how he managed that in the middle of an August heat wave was beyond imagining.

Seeing him again brought back a rush of unwanted memories—memories that should have died from neglect. Then why were they still here, taunting her, mocking her, tempting her beyond reason?

Not a good omen. Kaitlyn closed her eyes and breathed deeply in an effort to achieve a level of calm that would allow her to deal with him without old emotions getting in the way. The calm eluded her, just as her peace of mind had since she'd found that note on her desk Tuesday morning.

Wednesday—yesterday—her admirer hadn't come into her office as he had every day for the past two weeks, but had walked the hallway several times, pausing to give her a pointed look whenever he happened to catch her eye. A silent warning? A threat? Whichever, she couldn't take any more of it. This morning she'd called Jake's office, deciding that difficult or not, she would have to deal with him. She needed that alarm system installed.

She stood up, squared her shoulders, then opened her office door.

His eyes fixed on her immediately, his gaze hot and so intense she took an involuntary step backward. Her breath caught. Her heartbeat tripped as her planned greeting was lost in her mind's confusion. She'd expected he might feel some lingering anger over the way she'd handled leaving him, but was that all he felt? Were there traces of desire in the heat in his gaze as it swept over her from head to foot? Anger she could handle, but the other...

He took several purposeful strides toward her. She retreated farther into her office. He followed, closing the door softly and firmly behind him. Her back was against her desk before he came to a stop, a bare breath away. The scent of his aftershave, spicy and sharp, teased at her nostrils as it always had, drawing her into a whirlwind of sensations.

Too easily the memories returned. Memories of lying in his strong and possessive embrace. Feeling his heat as he made love to her. Experiencing the depths and heights of passion that instinct told her she would never find with anyone else. In all these years, she'd never even tried.

"Hello, Katie," he said.

How could his voice be rough and satiny at the same time, and how, after so many years, could it still affect her this way, the sound of it surrounding her like an embrace? It would be heaven to throw herself into his arms, but he'd nearly destroyed her once before with his need to overprotect and his strong, dominating personality.

Reason broke through the sensual fog he created. She pushed against his chest until he finally moved back, giving her barely enough room to escape behind her desk. The wood between them, she could at last find her voice.

"Hello, Jake," she said, managing somehow to sound firm when she felt as steady as Jell-O. Just being near him was almost too much for her senses. How could she be so weak? She raised her chin an assertive notch that hopefully hid the fact that butterflies were somersaulting in her stomach.

Jake placed both hands on her desk and leaned forward, deliberately narrowing the distance between them. He wanted to make her sweat—even if it was just a tiny bit—for the way she'd walked out on him. Not very professional of him, but he only now realized he'd been carrying this grudge for five years. Seeing her, he wanted to vent all that rage he'd felt the day he'd come home and found she'd left, with only a cryptic note saying she had to leave while she could.

"Imagine my surprise when my secretary told me you'd called," he said, noting her breathing was rapid and shallow. Her navy blue eyes were huge in her lovely and now-pale face. He had her practically cornered there behind her desk and the computer table—a tactic he knew she hated. But he figured he owed her a little something for all that her leaving had put him through. She hadn't given him a chance to say his piece back then.

"I'd hoped that your temper would have cooled by now," she said, her spine straightening, stiffening. Her delicate chin raised several more defiant notches. "Maybe I shouldn't have called you...."

He felt the muscle in his jaw clench. "You let me go to work believing—expecting—that we would make up when I got home."

"You always had a habit of assuming you knew what I felt, no matter what I said to the contrary."

That seemed to give him pause, Kaitlyn thought as he slowly straightened. When she'd finally worked up the courage to make the appointment with his secretary this morning, she'd hoped that five years had been long enough for him to forget the past. But then, it hadn't been long enough to kill the embers of desire within her that he could ignite so easily.

Working with him wasn't going to be smooth sailing. But she needed his expertise, needed that extreme attention to detail of his. During the eight months they'd lived together, that particular trait had caused her to lose her temper more than once. Now, though, she was nervous enough to appreciate it. She didn't want Craig Fallon breaking into her office again.

Somehow she had to work with Jake, without getting weak-kneed and without dissolving into a pool of longing at one heated glance. And without the past anger getting in the way.

"If you're willing to put your anger aside," she said, sitting in her chair, "we have some business to discuss. Otherwise, I'm sure Rob Donovan or one of his buddies on the police force can recommend another reliable security firm."

He must have read the resolve in her gaze, because he slowly backed off and eased his tall frame into one of the chairs on the other side of the desk. She finally managed a full breath.

"I'm sure Rob could find you someone else to install your security system," he said evenly, "but you don't settle for just anyone. You know me, know how I work. I'm thorough—"

"You're also demanding, difficult, stubborn, deliberately intimidating, authoritarian, and the list goes on. We don't work well together."

"Then why did you call me and not someone else?" He leaned forward in his chair, his dark gaze probing hers.

"Because when it comes to your work," she said quietly, "I trust you. But I won't deal with you, Jake, if the past keeps getting in the way."

He continued to study her. "Intimidation isn't your style, but difficult, demanding, stubborn…"

True, Kaitlyn mused. She could be all those things, in spades. It seemed that all her life she'd had to fight to be able to stand on her own, to have her abilities recognized and respected. Her father's expectations had been impossibly high, and his criticism loud and clear when she didn't measure up. He'd regularly stepped in and taken over a task rather than allow her to complete it in what he called her "usual inept way." She'd had to work hard to develop any self-esteem at all and she would fight to hang on to what ground she had gained.

"You're right," she admitted. "We are a lot alike in temperament. Neither one of us wants to give an inch. I supposed that's the main reason we couldn't get along."

"Except in bed," Jake responded, needing to make that one crucial point.

She gripped the arms of her chair. "That's why I had to leave before you got home," she said softly. "You could always make me want you so easily, and once you had me where you wanted me, I would agree to anything. I can't go down that road again."

Had he actually been such a manipulative bastard? Jake wondered, but even as he asked himself the question, he knew the answer. He'd always known what he wanted and he was never afraid to push hard to get it. It appeared he'd pushed too hard.

In Katie's case, though, his motives had been pure. He'd wanted to take care of her—as he'd always taken care of the people closest to him. Wanted to have her depend on him, need him, lean on him. She'd called him pushy and overprotective, domineering, and said the only thing she'd needed from him was room to stand on her own. It appeared that hadn't changed.

She'd phoned him—rather than press Rob for another name—because she needed his help, he told himself. That couldn't have been easy for her and he hadn't made it any less difficult.

"All right," he said, getting up from the chair to extend his hand to her across the desk as a gesture of peace. "Let's start this meeting over. My secretary said you wanted advice on a security system. What happened?"

She blinked as she returned his handshake, her hand tiny in his, and still he felt the urge, the need, to protect this particular woman. A need as strong as ever. Though he knew she would resist as much as before.

"What do you mean?" she asked.

"You always hated my 'gadgets and gizmos,' as you called my security systems. Said they made you feel like a prisoner in your own home. I figure something drastic had to happen to change that."

Drastic? Kaitlyn had forgotten how very astute the man was. How much did she want to tell him? It had to be enough to satisfy that damned curiosity of his, yet not enough to activate his overprotective streak.

She would have to come up with a convincing story, something unrelated to the note she'd received. If Jake knew about the break-in, there was no telling what he would insist on doing to look out for her. Escorting her to and from home every day. Following her everywhere she went. Always being no more than a short reach away. She couldn't have him that involved in her life, especially not now that she knew how vulnerable she was to that old chemistry between them.

She needed to come out of this meeting with an alarm system, nothing more. That would be enough to make her feel some degree of safety until the intruder in her life moved on to another interest. More to the point, she needed as little contact with Jake as possible. That, she knew, would be the safest course of action for her.

"At the Chamber of Commerce meeting the other day, several other business owners were concerned about break-ins," she stated, figuring this was the best way to convince Jake her reasons were minor and not enough to warrant much concern on his part. "I've worked hard to get this business off the ground. I have to look after my interests. So, I put aside my resistance to a little electronic protection."

"And you want me to believe that's all there is to your reasons for calling *me?*" He settled back in his chair, crossed his legs, then carefully adjusted the crisp crease in his pants.

Kaitlyn didn't miss the subtle message. He was prepared to stay planted in that chair until he'd gotten everything he wanted from her.

Damn him and his "we do it my way" method of operating. She could argue, insist the matter was none of his business, but probably to no avail. She could save herself a lot of trouble and just show him the note. There was the hint of a threat—enough to have her scared, jumping at shadows. It would be a huge relief to tell someone, but telling Jake would pull him even further into her life—a dangerous thing unless she could bring her hormones under control.

Jake remained silent as she got up and walked over to the window. She was upset. She didn't want him here, yet she'd called him and not someone out of the Yellow Pages. Something had frightened her enough that suddenly having him in her life was better than the options.

Those had to be some high-stakes options. During the months they'd lived together, their fights had been frequent and always over the same thing. She wanted to stand on her own, to build, achieve, succeed. He'd wanted to make the way easier for her. Whatever knowledge he could impart, she'd accepted gratefully, and occasionally she'd even taken his advice. But mostly his help, as he called it, was far too hands-on, too up close and personal, to suit her.

But she needed his help now. The only question in his mind was how much help? Would an alarm system be sufficient? He had to make sure. He'd already failed someone he cared about—his youngest sister, Candy. He wouldn't fail again.

He watched Katie toy with a strand of her red-gold hair. She wore it long now, softly curled, pulled back on one side to show off one sexy ear. He remembered nuzzling her ear as a prelude to making love, kissing her lovely shoulders hidden under that short-sleeved, pale green jacket she wore, holding all of her five-feet-nine inches against him as he ran his hands over her slender frame. Interesting that he could recall each detail so clearly. Interesting and unsettling.

"Katie," he said to change the course of his meanderings, "what happened?" He noticed how she squared her shoulders before turning from the window to face him.

"You're going to be hardheaded about this," she said sharply. "You're going to make me say it, aren't you? I've grown up, Jake. I've realized that you were right about a person protecting what's hers." She paused to glare at him. "Want me to say it again? You were right."

"That's not what I meant."

"Isn't it?" she demanded.

He wasn't buying this offended routine of hers. It was a

smoke screen, an attempt to put him on the defensive. There was something she didn't want him to know and it was obvious she wasn't going to give him any details to deal with. He would have to be patient—something he'd always found difficult where she was concerned.

"All right," he said, holding up one hand in a pretense of surrender. "I apologize. For the way I acted when I came in here and for pushing you just now."

"Apology accepted," she said a bit warily.

"Surprised, Katie?" he asked when she continued to stand there as if braced for a fight.

"I expected to have to go another couple of rounds at least."

He gave her a wry smile. "Being in business for myself has taught me to pick and choose my battles and to tread easy with some clients." He got to his feet. "How about showing me around the office?"

"I've got work to do," she said, sitting down at her desk. "You've pretty much seen all there is to see. There's the outer office and this one, the front door and this door to my right that leads into the back hallway. If you have any questions, Mary can help you."

"Mary being your assistant?"

She nodded, then pointedly pulled some files out of her desk drawer. Jake took the not-very-subtle hint and left. In the other room, he introduced himself to Mary Rowland and took a moment to explain his purpose for being there, then went to counting the number of sensors and boxes he would need and planning how best to run the wires.

Katie had pulled it all together, he decided, noting the blue-gray speckled carpet, the ivory-and-dusty-blue papered walls, the elegant cherry-wood furniture. *Look successful from the start.* He'd taught her that, those long nights they'd lain awake and talked about starting their own businesses. Look successful to attract the type of clientele you wanted.

She'd done it. That didn't surprise him. What did catch him off guard was that it hurt to think she'd done it without him. Very unsettling to say the least, he decided, jotting down some final notes about the parts for her alarm system.

"I'll have a crew here first thing in the morning to start the installation," he told Mary, wondering if he shouldn't go in and have a final few words with Katie. It would be the polite thing to do.

"I'll sure feel a whole lot better when it's in," Mary said fervently.

At that, warning bells went off in Jake's head. He glanced sharply at her. "You will?" he asked quietly.

"Sure. I mean, I know the creep isn't interested in me, but I just don't like the thought of him breaking in to leave notes on Kaitlyn's desk."

Breaking in? Leaving notes? So something *was* going on. But what? This sounded serious.

Memories of Candy and the man who'd stalked her flooded back. She'd nearly died because Jake hadn't picked up on the signals fast enough—a costly mistake and one he would never repeat. Better to err on the side of caution.

Katie obviously wanted him to install the alarm system, then disappear from her life as quickly as possible. Well, a person didn't always get what she wanted. He needed to learn how potentially dangerous this situation might be and he couldn't do that from his office.

Part of him wondered at the strength of his need to protect her when she apparently didn't want him involved. A bit of perverseness on his part, probably. Katie's stubbornness had always riled him and it seemed that hadn't changed. But, damn it, sometimes a woman needed a man to look out for her.

He flipped to a fresh page in his notebook and prepared to lie through his teeth if necessary to find out exactly how much and what kind of danger she was in.

"Katie gave me the details about this break-in once, but

my briefcase was out here and I didn't have my notebook to jot them down." He glanced at the small window between the two rooms.

Kaitlyn's head was bent over a folder while she spoke to someone on the phone. Perfect, he thought, giving Mary his most winning smile.

"She appears to be busy," he said. "How about I just go over the details again with you? I want to be sure I didn't miss anything."

Mary was only too happy to help. "Sure," she said eagerly. "He got in here either late Monday night or early Tuesday morning before Kaitlyn and I came in."

"Did he take anything?"

"No, he just left that—" she shivered "—note on Kaitlyn's desk."

"Was the note frightening?"

Nodding, Mary shivered again. Out of the corner of his eye, Jake could see Kaitlyn calmly carrying on with business as usual. He could cheerfully wring her beautiful neck. She'd called him in to provide an alarm system and, as she used to do with unpleasant events in the past, then put the problem out of her mind to concentrate on other things. She had to know she'd only put a Band-Aid on the situation, but she would forget about it until reality hit her in the face a second time. It was her way of coping, he supposed, her way of keeping the fear at bay. However, he was apt to worry himself crazy over her safety.

"I suppose the police took the note to check it for fingerprints," he said slowly.

Mary shook her head. "She didn't call the police. I was tempted to do it myself, but Kaitlyn had enough to deal with without having to find a replacement for me. There are times you just don't cross her, and after almost a year of working with her, I'm learning when those times are."

Jake chuckled, knowing exactly what Mary meant. But how could Kaitlyn not have called the police? At the least she could have mentioned the incident to Rob Donovan. What was going on with her?

"So she still has the note," he mused aloud, half statement, half question. If he could get that note, he could take some matters into his own hands. Providing she hadn't done something stupid like throw it away.

"Actually, I saw her put it in our safe," Mary stated innocently. "I'll get it for you."

Jake couldn't believe his luck, but he wasn't going to question his good fortune, not when it was handing him a means of looking out for Katie in spite of herself. He watched as Mary strolled over to the closet and up to the small safe inside. She pushed a strand of her soft brown hair out of her face as she worked the combination and then, once the door opened, extracted a piece of paper. The sheet was unfolded, indicating that perhaps she and Katie might have spared the few fingerprints the man may have left behind.

"Thanks," Jake said absently as he carefully took the paper from her. His entire concentration on the handwritten words scrawled angrily across the page, he read the message and the implied threat to Katie. She'd tried to dodge a date with the man and he'd cared enough to make sure she was telling him the truth, then he'd taken the next step to let her know he'd caught her in the lie and was angry as hell about it.

Katie had to be scared about this, yet she would allow Jake to do only the bare minimum to protect her. The past all over again. She'd been in her last year of college when they'd met and had insisted on going to night classes by herself, walking the dark campus rather than letting him drop her off and pick her up after his shift as a police detective. She'd been robbed twice in her job delivering pizzas before she would listen to him and find less dangerous employment.

He should drop the matter. She'd asked him for an alarm

system and he should leave it at that, shouldn't get involved. She'd walked out on him once, and seeing her this morning, he'd realized that he still had some of the fallout to deal with. He didn't need to put himself through this wringer again.

But, damn it, he couldn't just walk away. No matter how unwise, no matter what he would have to go through when it was over, he couldn't shake the need to do what he could to protect her. Whether she wanted it or not.

As she heard the office door close, Kaitlyn dared to glance out the window dividing her office from the other room. Jake was gone. For the first time since he'd walked in, she took a deep breath and relaxed her tight shoulders.

Dealing with him hadn't been such an ordeal after all, not once he'd gotten all the anger out of his system. In fact, he'd been fairly reasonable. He'd also been as virile as ever, and thirty seconds in his presence had been enough to awaken her senses to that masculine sexuality. The old chemistry was still there, amazing as it was, but this time she was smart enough to resist.

Not that there was anything to resist, she mused, staring at a blank computer screen. He hadn't even poked his head in the door to say goodbye. Which was well and good, she chided herself. Whatever they'd shared was finally over. So where was the feeling of elation that should be washing over her about now?

With a sigh, she pushed back her chair and strode into the other room. He'd talked to Mary for quite some time, she decided, checking her wristwatch. Maybe she should find out what they'd discussed about the alarm system.

"Did he tell you when he'd get it in and running?" she asked Mary.

"First thing in the morning," Mary answered with one of her brilliant smiles. "He's going to put the main box in the closet, then there'll be a keypad out here and one by the back door. He said to be thinking of a number for the code, something we'll both remember easily.''

Kaitlyn grinned. "How about the date I hired the best assistant in the world?"

Mary beamed. "Thanks. That's really sweet."

"Yeah, well, one day I'll be able to show my appreciation for your conscientiousness with money as well as words." She breathed in relief that everything about the matter with Jake was going off without a hitch. "Meanwhile, I'll let you get the phone," she said as it rang.

She turned toward her own office and was almost to the door when Mary finished her conversation and hung up.

"Not one of the corporate offices I visited this week asking for travel information, I assume," she said, a bit disappointed. Business was good enough to pay the bills, with a little left over, but she was hoping to pick up a couple of major contracts.

"No, it was Mr. Riley," Mary said.

"Jake? What did he want?" Kaitlyn wondered aloud.

"He said to tell you that he has a crew available today. They'll be here later this afternoon to get started on the system. It should be 'operational,' he said, before we leave tonight."

Kaitlyn frowned, aware of a sense of unease niggling at the edges of her mind. "What's the big rush?" she mused aloud.

"The break-in, I suppose," Mary said with a shrug.

Kaitlyn's breath caught. "What about the break-in?"

"You were busy and he wanted to make sure he had everything written down, so he and I went over all of it together. He took the note with him."

Kaitlyn felt her world spinning out of control and heading for a crash of major proportions. Jake had the note.

Chapter 2

Damn it, Kaitlyn thought, pacing her small office. Jake couldn't get what he wanted from her so he'd quizzed unsuspecting Mary. Of all the sneaky, wily tricks. He'd even managed to get that note in his big hands.

What was he going to do with it? she wondered, forcing herself to sit in her chair. Take it to the police? She'd already called the police. Tuesday morning, after she'd talked to Shelly. The officer she'd spoken with had told her that she could file for a restraining order, providing she had documentation that this man was harassing her.

She had the proof—or rather, Jake did at the moment. But the idea of filing for a restraining order had terrified her. It would be admitting that the situation was serious, that she was being stalked—something she wasn't ready to do. The guy was just hanging around her office and he wouldn't break in again once the alarm was installed. That avenue closed, he would grow weary of her giving him the cold shoulder and would leave her alone. She refused to believe the situation was any more serious than that. Jake, though, was one to anticipate the worst.

Would he go straight to Rob with the note? She groaned softly. She hadn't wanted Rob involved. He had enough cases to solve and a wedding a month away. She hadn't wanted to add to his workload or take away from what little time he and Shelly had together.

Kaitlyn pounded her fist on the arm of her chair. It had probably never occurred to Jake to ask her how *she* wanted the matter handled. In typical fashion, he'd decided what needed to be done and hadn't bothered to consult anyone. He was like a tank, plowing over everything in his path to get to his goal.

His intentions were always the best. That's why she'd often found it difficult to stand her ground with him. He came by his need to protect honestly. He'd been taking care of the people he loved since his father died in a construction accident when Jake was eleven, leaving his mom with three children to raise. He was the eldest and the man of the house.

Once he'd graduated from the police academy, his mother had allowed him to make all the major decisions for the family. His sisters, especially Candice, had consulted him on everything those months she'd lived with him, and Kaitlyn imagined they still did. He was accustomed to being the one in charge, to having people follow his advice and obey his commands.

That's the part she couldn't take—his methods—she decided as she picked up the airline tickets she had to deliver that afternoon. She recalled how it had been between her parents. Her mother had been fragile, insecure, deferring to her husband's judgment on everything, down to the way a military wife should dress and comport herself around the top brass and their wives.

She'd been totally dependent upon him, and during the times his orders had separated them, she'd looked to liquor to get her through until he was back to tell her what she should do. Soon she needed to have several drinks during the course of the day in order to get her through until he came home each evening. Then one day he'd packed his bags and walked out, leaving Kaitlyn to deal with her devastated, helpless, alcoholic mother.

Kaitlyn's father had totally dominated her life, as well, giving orders, demanding immediate obedience. He'd told her what to wear, what to say, how to act—and punishment for disobeying orders was severe. She'd worked hard to break out of that cycle. She couldn't make the dreadful mistake of giving up her ability to make decisions for herself, and under no circumstances would she end up like her mother.

Calling the police was just the beginning of Jake's interference in her life, she was sure. She delivered the tickets and made several cold calls to prospective clients, then drove back to her office on Quivera Boulevard, all the while wondering just how many encounters with him this ordeal would bring. She'd hoped for one and only one when she'd phoned his office this morning. One trip down that hormone-laden memory lane was about all she could take.

But fate was not on her side, not today, she decided, walking into her office just before five o'clock to find Jake there with Rob Donovan and a fingerprint technician. With a quick glower at Jake, she led him and Rob into the other room, stopping inside the doorway as Rob explained that the forensic tech would dust everything in the room. He would undoubtedly leave behind a film of white on every surface, even the arms and backs of all the chairs. It would take a good two hours of cleaning to get rid of it. Kaitlyn groaned inwardly at the thought.

Just then Shelly breezed in, cheery as a canary, her yellow hair feathering around her pixie face. "Ah, the gang's all here. Good to see you, Jake," she said with an obvious wink at Kaitlyn. "Jake said he and Rob were going to take you to dinner. Did he tell you I invited myself along?"

Kaitlyn's smile was more grimace than grin. "No, we hadn't even discussed dinner yet, but then, Jake likes his surprises."

Shelly hooked her arm through her fiancé's and studied the other couple. "Do I detect a few sparks flying between these two?" she asked him.

Rob rolled his pale blue eyes. "This morning Jake told me they once lived together for several months."

"They've known each other all along?" Shelly questioned in surprise. She looked at Kaitlyn. "You sly thing. You never said a word about that when I mentioned that Rob and I were hoping to get you two together."

"I don't envy you," Rob said, giving Kaitlyn a sympathetic smile. "Shelly's going to want to hear every single detail."

Standing across the room from Kaitlyn, Jake could practically hear her blood boil. Her eyes had narrowed and she had a death grip on her purse strap—probably imagining it was his neck she was wringing. Fortunately his installation crew arrived at that exact moment. He got them lined out and his three dinner companions out of the office without a hitch. The fact that Kaitlyn didn't protest the driving arrangements—Rob and Shelly in Shelly's car and he and Kaitlyn alone in his Lincoln Town Car—meant she had something she wanted to say to him, he knew.

He didn't want to do battle with her this time around. Before, they'd always been itching for a fight, but he'd learned a few things in the past several years. Such as it was easier to catch flies with honey. He had to convince her she needed his help and he couldn't do that if she was in a blind rage. He had to make her see the potential for danger. Apparently she hadn't labeled the situation as a stalking, but Jake had been in police work, then in the security field, far too long to call it anything else.

Back in his early days driving a beat, his sister had been involved in another situation very similar to this one. He'd taken a wait-and-see attitude and Candy had nearly died because of it. Things in Katie's situation could turn ugly and she needed someone who could protect her.

But there was another danger to contend with, he decided once he'd let her in on the passenger side and had slid in behind the wheel. As he drove south on Quivera Boulevard, her light, delicate scent wafted through the big car, tempting him to do something foolish like pull her into his arms. All afternoon he'd been thinking about this morning and how, if only for a second or two, her eyes had been lit with hunger.

It had been that way the first time he saw her at the Quick Mart, her red-gold hair pulled back in a sexy ponytail, her thin, curvy shape defined in tight shorts and tank top, her walk sassy and mesmerizing. She'd snagged his attention immediately. One-thirty on a Saturday morning in what was not exactly the best part of Kansas City, she'd decided she needed chocolate milk more than she needed sleep and had consequently gotten herself caught in the middle of a holdup.

He and his partner at the time had been staking out the place and Jake had managed to pull Kaitlyn out of the line of fire. Then, feeling the aftereffects of the icy fear that had gripped him when he'd realized she was in peril, he'd lectured her about why a female alone shouldn't be making late-night jaunts after groceries. In response to his forceful advice, she'd poured the half gallon of chocolate milk over his head.

The next day he'd shown up on her doorstep and both of them had soon given in to the volatile chemistry between them. In the end, they hadn't been able to make it work, except perhaps in bed—there they'd meshed perfectly. He still remembered. But outside of the bedroom—

"Will this be just dinner, or does it come with an inquisition?" she asked, breaking into his thoughts.

"According to Shelly this is supposed to be a working dinner. We're supposed to discuss wedding arrangements."

"Then why are you tagging along?" she queried, suspecting the worst.

He smiled over at her as he swung the car onto College Boulevard and headed east. "I'm the best man."

And she was the maid of honor. This was the worst possible situation. She groaned. "Jake, this isn't going to work. You know that. Rob is your close friend and Shelly is mine. We can't mess up this wedding for them."

"Agreed," he said, thinking that this wedding might provide the leverage he needed to get her to work with him and not against him. At least it would give him plenty of excuses to keep his eye on her. "We'll have to find a way to get along."

"You're still angry," she observed aloud. "About the way I walked out."

He shook his head. "I was, but after I left your office and cooled off, I came to the conclusion I was more angry with myself. I thought about our conversation that morning and realized you'd tried to explain why you had to leave, but as usual I didn't let you."

Kaitlyn mulled that over. Something about the way he owned up to his part in their separation touched a chord. "You weren't the only one to blame, Jake. I never was very tactful or diplomatic about how I stated things."

"And I was even worse than you." He sighed. "The point to all this is that we can't let our past differences ruin this 'moment of bliss' for Rob and Shelly. Truce?"

She studied him for a few moments. "Think this one will last longer than any of our others?"

"It has to. Besides, this time we have a wedding to motivate us."

Kaitlyn nodded and was quiet for several seconds, absorbing this new development. "Best man?" she finally muttered at the disturbing thought of the amount of time she would have to spend with Jake. The parties, the photo sessions, the celebration dinners Shelly had planned, the fittings, the rehearsals, the ceremony and reception, and heaven only knows what else was bound to come up.

She turned to see him smile, the grin deepening the lines that bracketed his firm mouth and the tiny crinkles that accented those dark, penetrating eyes of his. How could he be so happy about this situation when he knew it would throw them together several times over the next month?

Didn't he remember their shouting matches? The time he'd come back to their apartment and found his clothes in the hall? The time he made fun of her lack of cooking skills and she dumped a bowl of cold, pasty spaghetti on his head? How they'd had to set their box spring and mattress directly on the floor because the wood slats in the frame would often give out during their lovemaking?

Heat rushed through her at that last memory. She wanted to back out of her duties as maid of honor, but she'd made a commitment to her dear friend and couldn't let Shelly down.

She would have to control her runaway longings, and that would be easier said than done, she realized as Jake ushered her into the restaurant, his hand at the small of her back. He eased his large frame into the booth beside her. He was too close. Kaitlyn could feel his body heat. To her dismay, his nearness was as unsettling as ever. When Jake was around, the desire to lean into his solid strength had always been—and apparently still was—difficult to resist.

But resist was something she had to do. She'd fought long and hard to establish her independence and her confidence in herself. She would not surrender either one to any man the way her mother had.

She put her purse on the seat between them, then looked up to find Shelly grinning at her.

"I believe I *do* detect some friction between these two," she said to her fiancé, sliding into the booth. She didn't sound the least bit worried about that friction causing problems at the wedding.

Kaitlyn opened her menu, though at the moment she didn't have much of an appetite. She decided on a grilled-chicken salad, then once the waiter had taken their orders turned to Shelly.

"Let's talk about the wedding," she said, hoping she could steer the conversation in this direction.

Shelly shook her head. "We'll take care of that later. Right now, I'm more concerned with this guy who broke into your office. Rob told me about it on the way over here. Why didn't you say something before?"

Kaitlyn shrugged. How could she explain that talking about it made it seem so much more frightening? She wasn't ready to deal with the fear yet.

"Nothing against the marriage plans, but I'm more concerned with this guy, as well," Jake put in. "What's his name? How much do you know about him?"

Kaitlyn decided she would have to answer his questions eventually. The man was terminally persistent. May as well get it over with. Jake would just keep at it until she would be ready to scream in irritation. The only way to end the interrogation was to answer his questions.

"He said his name was Craig Fallon. Two weeks ago he came into the office to ask about an Alaskan cruise special," she said. "He stayed and talked for almost an hour."

"Did he book anything?" Jake asked.

She shook her head. "That didn't bother me. I figured he was in the 'where do I want to go and what can I afford' stage."

"Did he ask you out then?" Jake inquired.

She shook her head. "Not then. I didn't think much about him at the time, until he came back at closing. That's when he asked me out. Something about his coming back made me feel very uncomfortable.''

Jake's left eyebrow arched questioningly. ''Uncomfortable? How do you mean?''

''Well, this time he was so insistent. Didn't want to take no for an answer. He said he'd noticed I hadn't had lunch,'' she added with a shiver.

''He knew you hadn't had lunch?'' Jake demanded sharply. ''You failed to mention that to anyone.''

''I'd forgotten about it. I mean, it bothered me a little at the time—'' She paused as the waiter set their plates and a basket of French bread on the table.

''A little?'' Jake queried as the waiter walked away.

''All right,'' Kaitlyn said, picking up her fork, ''a lot. But I told him no and he finally quit pushing, so I figured I was simply overly tired and letting my imagination run amok.'' She drew in a shaky breath. ''Then he showed up the next day, once when Mary went to lunch and again midafternoon when she went downstairs for a break.''

''As if he knew when you'd be there alone,'' Jake mused aloud, cutting into his Kansas City Strip steak. ''Is that still going on?''

She nodded. ''Mary doesn't leave me alone very often, though. She's been bringing her lunch back to the office and taking her breaks at her desk. This hasn't been much fun for her, either.''

''It'll probably get worse,'' he told her softly.

Deep down Kaitlyn knew that, but it wasn't what she wanted to hear. She wanted him to reassure her that the alarm system would be enough to deter the man from breaking into the office, enough to give him the message she wasn't interested. Instead of comforting, Jake's words had her painting a pretty grim mental picture of what she would have to deal with if he was right about the situation.

''Worse? No one will ever accuse you of being a ray of sunshine,'' she snapped at Jake, taking refuge in her annoyance over his handling of the matter. "The man will get tired of being turned down and will move on to someone else."

The two men exchanged glances at that, but neither one spoke his thoughts. They all finished most of their meal in silence, then ever the detective, Rob pulled a notebook and pen out of his jacket pocket and jotted something down. "Give me the guy's last name again and his address," he said, glancing up from the page.

"Fallon is his name, but I don't have an address," Kaitlyn answered, pushing her half-finished salad away. The return to this conversation had effectively killed what little appetite she'd had.

Jake growled softly. "And of course you didn't bother to ask," he said, helping himself to the rest of her salad and another slice of bread.

Put in this context, not asking did seem like a dumb move on her part, but she wasn't about to tell Jake that he was right. "I figured he was just curious at that moment and I didn't need to know where he lived. Then when I realized he was hanging around just to talk, I was more interested in getting him out of my hair so I could get back to work. When he came back after we'd closed up, all I was concerned with was making him understand I wasn't going to have dinner with him. Asking where he lived would have been a bit counterproductive."

"What does he look like?" Jake demanded.

"Blond hair, blue eyes, good-looking, a little under six feet tall, average build. I'm guessing he's around thirty years old."

"Could cover a good portion of the men who live in Kansas City," Jake muttered. "What does he do for a living—does he work in the building? If not, how can he hang around to know that you don't often take a lunch break?"

She shrugged. "I don't know."

She didn't know, because she'd never asked, Jake realized. He barely refrained from swearing and from lecturing her on the wisdom of asking for details in such a situation. A woman alone had to pay attention to everything. He'd drummed that into his mother's head and his two sisters'.

But what he considered looking after the people he cared about, Katie regarded as domination and overprotectiveness. She'd walked away from him once before over the issue. He couldn't let that happen again, not until he knew for sure how much danger she was in.

"Katie," he continued cautiously, "most people think stalking is a celebrity crime, but in reality it can—and does—happen to anyone. This situation could turn dangerous. You tend to minimize things up to the moment reality slaps you in the face."

"And you look at going outside to get the morning paper as a potential catastrophe," she countered. "I'm not taking things lightly, you know. Otherwise I would have found someone else to install the damn alarm."

Jake took a deep breath in an effort to hold on to his temper. Losing it would accomplish nothing; it would only drive her away at a time when she needed his help. He couldn't let that happen.

"Katie," he said quietly, "you have to realize that an alarm system alone may not be enough."

Again not what she wanted to hear, Kaitlyn thought. But she couldn't ignore the reality of the matter any longer. Truth was, she was far more frightened than she wanted to admit even to herself. It would be a comfort to put things in the hands of professionals, even if one of them was Jake Riley.

There was strength in that chiseled profile of his. Integrity. And passion. The man didn't do anything by halves, not even eating. Not that there was a spare pound on that tall, solid frame of his. She'd bet her favorite navy pumps that under the charcoal suit he wore, his body was as rock solid as it used to be. Something she had no business re-calling.

But her mind seemed to have a will of its own. She remembered the feel of his strong arms around her, holding her at night, keeping her safe, making her feel wanted. Re-membered the heat of his kisses and longed to know if he could still set her on fire. Something else she had no busi-ness imagining. She sighed quietly and tried to force her attention back to the unwanted conversation.

"Jake is right," Rob put in. "It may not be enough. This situation is all too weird."

Shelly nodded her agreement.

"You need to take all the safety precautions you can," Jake informed her, pausing while the waiter removed their plates and left the check. He took out his credit card and laid it on the tray on top of Rob's. "I'm hoping you'll consider an alarm system for your condo."

She glanced at him in surprise. "Condo? How did you know…"

He shrugged. "Rob told me. I've already had a look at the place from the outside. I only need to see the inside, then I can get the parts together and get the system installed tomorrow."

Which meant Jake thought the man might show up on her doorstep. That was a bit too much reality to absorb in one day. And having Jake at her house tonight was more than her emotions could handle. She needed a breather, time to collect her wits and bring her emotions under some sort of control.

"I'll think about it tonight and let you know tomorrow," she told him. "I assume you'll be at the engagement party after work tomorrow night?"

"Of course. But we ought to get started—"

"I need time to think about this, Jake." She looked at Shelly. "Do you have that revised number of people you're inviting to the party so I can tell the caterer?"

Shelly nudged her fiancé. "Did you narrow down that list today like you said you would?" she asked him.

He pulled a piece of notebook paper from his breast pocket and handed it to her. "These are the guys who said they could make it. Does it meet with your approval?"

She read it over carefully, nodded, then quickly counted up the number of names on the list. "Sixteen, plus significant others," she told Kaitlyn. "Too many?"

She smiled at her friend's concern for her finances. "Not at all. Andrew gives me a wonderful discount because I use his catering service so much."

To Kaitlyn's relief, the conversation turned to topics that concerned tomorrow evening's party and the wedding details yet to be taken care of. Tux fittings were scheduled for Sunday afternoon. She and Shelly agreed to go shopping for dresses Saturday after she closed the travel agency office at one o'clock.

In many ways she envied Shelly and Rob, being in love, wanting to spend the rest of their lives together. But as a military brat she'd seen too many failed marriages, including her parents'. When things fell apart there was too much heartache and too many bitter feelings left behind. She could only hope things would turn out better for her friends.

Chapter 3

Jake sat back in the dainty-looking wrought-iron chair and observed the guests milling around in the Hollowbrook Estates clubhouse. Rob had a number of friends on the police force and Shelly had invited a fair number of people from the public defender's office. The party was in full swing and everyone was determined to enjoy the great food and good company. Everyone except Kaitlyn, that is.

She was putting all her energies into ignoring him. He had no one but himself to blame. He should have sent an unmarked car to patrol the area around her house last night, but he hadn't figured on her being awake and looking out her kitchen window. She'd spotted the Riley Security Services logo on the vehicle's door and had called him this morning to give him what for over it, then she'd slammed down the phone before he could reply.

He watched her supervise the caterer and the bartenders, and gently remind Rob and Shelly a couple of times of their duties as guests of honor. She mingled with the people, smiling through the fatigue she certainly must have felt, seemingly oblivious to the many admiring glances she received. The neckline of her teal blue dress showed off her lovely collarbone and the column of her neck. The hem stopped just below her knees, displaying her shapely calves to perfect advantage and making more than one man's imagination run amok. Stirring those memories Jake had thought dead and buried.

She was a vision, her dress skimming her slight curves, her hair falling across her shoulders in a tumble of soft, red-gold curls. But she was also angry with him. Time to clear the air, he decided as he got to his feet. He caught another glimpse of her as she attended to every detail of the party and avoided the one issue she had to realize was the most important—them. Or at least how they would deal with each other to keep her safe. He had to convince her to let him help her. This was one thing she could not do on her own.

He set his empty beer bottle on a tray by the bar, then walked purposefully over to where she stood conversing with an older couple, certain she wouldn't want to appear rude in front of guests. They had to settle things between them and here at this party would be the most practical way to do that.

He smiled, then extended his free hand to the gray-haired man. "Jake Riley," he said by way of introduction.

"Frank Preston," the other man said, returning Jake's handshake. "This is my wife, Ruth."

"Preston. You must be related to Shelly," Jake continued. "Her parents, perhaps?"

"Her aunt and uncle," Frank corrected.

"Well, I hope you'll forgive my barging into the conversation like this, but I was hoping to convince Katie to dance with me."

"Exactly what she should be doing at such a lovely soiree," Ruth said, patting Kaitlyn's arm.

Jake's grin widened. "Will you excuse us, then?"

"Of course," she said with a wink to Kaitlyn. "You go dance with your handsome young man, dear. I'll call you Monday about Egypt."

Jake didn't miss the way Kaitlyn clenched her teeth at the other woman's referring to him as her "young man," but he figured this wasn't the time or place to comment on that. Baiting her into an argument was not the way to gain her cooperation, and under the circumstances that was essential.

His first instinct had been to push her into accepting his help, but he knew the direct-and-demanding approach would net him nothing where Kaitlyn was concerned. One sideways glance at the ramrod straightness of her spine told him she would resist that tack as much now as she ever had.

Still, she needed help, and she would have his, with or without her knowledge. They'd once shared something very special. He wouldn't turn his back on that or on her.

"Egypt?" he asked, inclining his head toward the dance floor as the older couple walked away. "You can actually send people that far away and bring them back?"

"Yeah, with my magic wand," Kaitlyn replied. "I could even send you somewhere…Siberia, maybe."

She turned away, treating him to a tantalizing view of her backside as she sashayed over to the buffet table instead of the dance floor. He knew a cold shoulder when he received it, and not being the type to beat his head against the proverbial brick wall, he generally took the hint. But he was never able to back off with Kaitlyn. That haughty, aloof attitude of hers was as much of a challenge, and a turn-on, as ever. He hoped that someday before he passed on to the next life, he would understand why this particular woman made him frustrated enough to grind his teeth and filled him with desire at the same time.

He followed behind her, loading a plate for himself as she dropped dabs of food on hers. Food had never been a priority for her. She was walking down the buffet line—bypassing the majority of the best goodies—only because it was the one sure way to avoid a few minutes with him on the dance floor.

"Does this mean you're not going to dance with me?" he asked as she led the way over toward an empty table, the gentle sway of her hips as mesmerizing as ever.

"You're a little slow on the pickup, but you get the message eventually."

She set her plate on the table and glared up at him, her chin thrust temptingly toward him. He'd better resist taking that chin in his hands if he didn't want to end up alienating her altogether.

"We need to talk, Katie, not fight," he said, holding her chair.

"It doesn't work that way with us."

"It didn't back then, but this time has to be different," he told her, needing to make the distinction between who they'd been and who they were now. It was important to him that they not spend what little time they might have together doing battle, and not just because they would have to work together to keep the situation under control. He was afraid he was letting his feelings carry him away again—but then, he had a hunch it would always be that way where Katie was concerned. Especially if she was in danger.

Kaitlyn studied him for a long moment, then nodded once. She'd learned to pick and choose her battles carefully, and while having Jake back in her life was not something she wanted, she feared she would have to deal with it. Reality was, she would probably need his help if Craig Fallon didn't become interested in someone else soon.

She toyed with the pasta salad on her plate as she considered her words. "What makes you think things can be any better between us this time around?"

"We have our friends' wedding to think about, remember?"

She nodded. "You're right. But, Jake, we're the same people we were five years ago. When it comes to security, you have your ways of doing things without discussing your agenda or your reasoning behind it with anyone, especially me. I can't deal with those methods and that will get in the way every time we're thrown together."

He bit into a meatball and chewed thoughtfully, as if he, too, were selecting his words with care. Kaitlyn supposed that was a start at trying to get along with her.

"Katie," he finally said, "let me ask you this. Why were you awake, pacing the floors and looking out windows, most of last night?"

"I couldn't sleep," she quickly replied.

He stared down at her for a long moment. "Don't be difficult," he said when she didn't volunteer any more information. "You know what I'm getting at."

She did, and she knew that trying to evade answering him would get her nowhere. "All right," she said on a frustrated sigh. "I was nervous…"

"Afraid," he corrected emphatically. "Why is it so difficult for you to admit you're afraid?"

"Because it accomplishes nothing. Fear paralyzes a person at the very time she most needs to take action." Her mother had always been afraid.

"A healthy dose of fear also makes a person cautious," he stated quietly.

It could also leave her afraid to make a move, to trust herself. "Why should I concern myself with caution when you have enough for half the people in this room?" she retorted. Then, realizing she was letting him, as well as her lack of sleep, get to her, she pushed her plate aside. "I guess this truce isn't going to be easy."

"We'll manage." He stabbed another meatball and chewed with enjoyment. "You aren't eating."

Kaitlyn shrugged. "I don't have much of an appetite."

"You never have. At least you won't fight the battle of the bulge," he said, letting his gaze glide over her frame, starting with her face and sliding downward, lingering here and there as it traveled the length of her.

She frowned at his frank perusal, even as the warmth of his gaze shot through her, threatening to make her melt as it always had in the past. She couldn't have that. This man had a way of making her forget all her priorities.

"Careful, Jake," she said. "Don't let your overactive libido get carried away."

"As I recall," he said in that seductive voice of his, "yours had no trouble keeping pace with mine."

"But I do not repeat my mistakes," she said, her body heating as the memories of the frantic passion they'd shared filled her mind—memories that were too strong and should have been long gone. Time to change the subject to one a bit safer.

"About last night…" she began.

"I told you this morning I won't apologize for sending that car out to your area," he said, his jaw beginning to clench.

"I wanted to tell you that I was grateful."

"Grateful?" One dark brow rose. "You have an odd way of showing it."

"By raking you over the coals when I phoned this morning, you mean?" She flashed a rueful smile. After she'd seen the car for the fourth time and realized it would be in the area all night, she'd finally gotten some sleep. "What you don't seem to be picking up on is the fact that my anger is with your methods, not with what you did."

"My methods," he repeated thoughtfully. "You mean that if I tell you what I'm going to do, you won't fight me on anything?"

She laughed softly. "Not on your life will I give you that kind of carte blanche."

"Can't blame me for trying," he said with a shrug and a grin. "But seriously—"

"Seriously, I've decided I'd like a price on a security system for the condo," she told him, smiling as he helped himself to the pasta salad and meatballs she'd left on her plate. He'd cleaned his own and was now working on hers with gusto.

"I thought I'd have to do some pretty fast talking to get you to consider that," he said.

Her eyes narrowed. "I'm independent, Jake, not foolhardy when it comes to my safety. And, no matter how difficult you are to deal with, I feel more comfortable having you and not some stranger install the system. I figured that maybe the guy saw the crew putting in the system at the office. I didn't see him once today," she said, her voice the tiniest bit hopeful.

Jake peered down at her, seeing the dark circles under her eyes that her makeup barely concealed, and for the first time he could read the traces of fear in her gaze. He could have kicked himself. Katie wasn't dense. In fact, she was very astute. If she didn't dwell on the big picture and how dangerous the situation might become, it was because she was feeling vulnerable—something she hated even more than his bluntness.

He laid his hand over hers. While her skin was temptingly soft, she was cold. Her dark blue eyes were wide. Again he wanted to kick himself for not realizing how very upset she was.

He patted her hand. "Tell you what, in the future I'll try to remember that you're not taking this lightly. Think that will make dealing with me any easier for you?"

She studied him for a long moment, gauging his seriousness. Finally she nodded. "It would certainly be a start," she replied.

Jake took her hand in his and gazed solemnly into her eyes. "Whatever happens, we'll handle it. Trust me?"

Kaitlyn breathed deeply, as if to collect herself, then nodded again. It was herself she was afraid to trust. She was too susceptible to this man's charm—something she would have to control now that he was back in her life for whatever time they would have together.

"Does the nod mean you'll let me help you?" he asked, breaking into her thoughts.

She sighed. Jake's help was an oxymoron. He didn't assist—he took over. She couldn't have that. She'd worked too hard to get where she was. But she recognized she was out of her league. Somehow she would have to work with Jake, maintain her independence and keep her hormones in line. The last would be a challenge in itself.

"I should check on things..." she said, pushing her chair back and getting to her feet.

"First you two have to dance," Shelly insisted, coming up to lock her arms through theirs. "The deejay wants everyone in the wedding party to dance. He's going to play our song—Rob's and mine, that is," she said with a little laugh.

There was no graceful way to get out of it, Kaitlyn realized as Shelly ushered them to the dance floor. Once there, she released them to rush into her future husband's waiting embrace.

Kaitlyn looked up at Jake and he smiled at her, one of his rare and devilish grins that crinkled the fine lines of his face and lit the depths of his midnight eyes. He took her hand in his, placed his other hand at the small of her back, then tugged her closer and settled her firmly against the length of him. She felt the rock-solid plane of muscle, was wrapped in his body heat. It was all so achingly familiar. She wanted to lose herself in the sensations, the memories. Wanted to sag against him and absorb the strength of him. Wanted *him,* she knew as his eyes filled with warmth and desire.

She wanted to run, but she needed to be right where she

was, in his arms. She longed to kiss him, but she knew that doing so would be the riskiest thing she'd ever done. The dreamy saxophone notes swirled in her head, clouding her judgment, blurring reason, awakening her senses. She felt the cloth of his jacket brush her cheek. Smelled the woodsy and male scent of him. His breath, hot and enticing, fanned through her hair and along her face. His hand gently held her next to him as he moved them to the rhythm of the music.

What could it hurt to enjoy the feelings and sensations only he could bring to life? Just for a moment she wanted to pretend that nothing could come between them, that nothing ever had and she was free to give full rein to all the longings coursing through her. For just a short while she wanted to feel fully and truly alive and female.

He might never be able to hold her this way again, Jake thought, and he was going to make the most of what little time he had with her. It wasn't sane to resurrect all the memories and savor them, but he couldn't stop himself. Her softly rounded contours fit him as if she'd been molded just for him. Her hair and creamy skin smelled of wildflowers, light, delicate, feminine. Her eyes held a desire he remembered so well.

He trailed a fingertip down her cheek and lightly across her full lower lip. Her mouth opened, in surprise and a silent plea for more. He could barely hold himself back. He wanted—needed—to kiss her so badly. To taste the nectar of her mouth once more. But even as he longed for her, he knew once would never be enough and that giving in to the need pounding through him would be to put himself in the line of fire again. She would leave him one day, as sure as the sun would come up tomorrow. Already he was sure that pain would be even greater this time around.

The music stopped and he slowly released her. She looked up at him, need battling sanity in the depths of her eyes. For both their sakes, he took a step backward and inclined his head toward the table they'd left.

As Jake pulled out her chair, the caterer walked up to her, dropping a hand on her shoulder when she'd sat down. "How do you think it went?" he asked her.

"You outdid yourself as usual, Andrew," Kaitlyn replied. "The future bride told me she'll be contacting you about the wedding reception."

"Then we can figure the food for it will be excellent," Jake said.

Andrew beamed at the praise, then looked down at her plate and smiled. "It must have been good if Kaitlyn ate. For a change, I won't have to wrap up something for her to take home." Not giving either one a chance to correct him, he handed her a small white envelope.

"What's this?" she asked.

"Hopefully a compliment on the party," he said with a laugh. "Someone asked me to give it to you while we were setting up. I should have brought it to you long ago, but we've been busy."

"No problem." She slid a finger under the envelope's flap.

"Well," he said, nodding to Jake and giving Kaitlyn a smile, "you leave the rest of the details to me. We'll do the cleanup and lock things up on our way out, just like always."

"Thanks, Andrew. I don't know what I'd do without you." With her lack of kitchen skills, Kaitlyn would never have been able to pull together the many parties she'd thrown for clients and friends.

As he walked away, Kaitlyn pulled the card out of the envelope, then read the words to herself. "Once our friends are married, you can start planning our wedding. I'll call you when I've set the date. It should be soon. Craig."

Her breath caught. A shiver raced down her spine. She stared at the note, knowing things with him had just escalated to a new and more frightening level. She'd never had one night out with this man, had refused all his invitations to have dinner or go to a play. Now the man was planning their wedding. As Rob had said last night, this was all too weird.

She looked up at Jake, not knowing where else to turn. He gave her a sharp glance. Wordlessly, she handed him the note, listening as he read it aloud. Hearing it was even more chilling than reading it.

Frowning, Jake studied Kaitlyn closely. She was whiter than white, her dark blue eyes huge in her lovely face. She was scared to death.

He swore in a vehement whisper only she could hear. "Damn it, Katie—"

"Don't swear at me, Jake Riley."

Not now, her fear-filled eyes pleaded with him. Jake swallowed his anger, reminding himself that losing his temper would accomplish nothing other than to push her away at a time when she needed his protection. He'd figured he would give her some space and hopefully she would let him be there for her. She was turning to him for help. He couldn't blow it now.

"Don't get testy on me," he said.

"Then don't use that 'the little woman can't think for herself' tone with me. Jake, what am I going to do?"

He took a deep breath, noting she used her anger with him to keep the fear at bay. Funny how he would have to notice the vulnerability behind the panic in her eyes.

"Get that security system installed. First thing tomorrow," he stressed, his eyes searching the room for any male fitting the description she'd given him. He found no one, but then, Andrew had indicated he'd been given the note much earlier and had only now gotten around to handing it to Kaitlyn. The creep was probably long gone.

"You will start taking every conceivable precaution," he told her firmly.

She nodded without protest—a sure sign that she was numb with shock. Jake clenched his jaw. He wouldn't put up with this sicko terrorizing Kaitlyn. Somehow he would put a stop to it. Soon. He wouldn't fail this time, as he had with Candy.

"Where are you going?" Katie asked when he pushed back his chair.

"To give this to Rob. He can have this one checked for fingerprints, too. Maybe he'll find something better than the partial he found on the first note. And I want to talk to him about getting a restraining order." As he started to stand, she caught his arm.

"Jake, wait—"

His jaw clenched tighter. He leaned closer, towering over her. "Now, listen. This," he said, waving the note in front of her face, "puts a totally different slant on the situation. He wants you and he's through playing games."

"Believe it or not, I managed to figure that out myself!"

"Then think about this. The guy is not rational. There is no way to predict what he will do. You're way out of your league here and you'll do as I say—"

"Oh, cut the macho bull," she retorted. "I'm not disputing your expertise or my need of it at the moment."

"Then what—"

"This is their engagement party. With their careers, their time together will be interrupted too often. I want them to have this evening. The fingerprints will still be there in the morning."

"I'll give it until the party's over. No longer. I want to know what kind of wacko this Fallon is and if he has any kind of record."

"In the morning," she said firmly. "Please, Jake. I'll defer to your judgment on everything else. However, you let Shelly and Rob have this night. Agreed?"

Jake had delayed taking action in Candy's case and was damned lucky she hadn't been killed. He wouldn't take any chances with Katie. But looking into her eyes, he knew she wouldn't budge on this. She was scared, yet she would put her friend's happiness first. And she would fight him fiercely if he went against her wishes.

That left him little choice on this particular issue. But there were others. Like protection for tonight. This note from Fallon made it clear the man was unstable. There was no telling what he could do next. Jake was not leaving Kaitlyn alone in an unsecured house and he was not putting the matter up for discussion.

Jaw clenched, he caught her wrist and tugged her to her feet. "Get your purse," he ordered.

"The party—"

"Is winding down. Rob and Shelly can see to the guests who are still here and Andrew said he would clean and lock up." He gripped her wrist tighter, letting her know he meant business. "I want to get started on that alarm system. Immediately."

Her chin came up. She studied him through a narrowed gaze, but soon backed down and went to do as he'd told her. Jake wondered whether it was fear of Fallon or of his temper that had her complying. Whichever, he decided, watching her walk away, her shoulders slumped, he didn't like seeing her defeated. It left a definitely sour taste in his mouth.

Chapter 4

In short order, Jake had them out of the clubhouse and into their cars, then he followed behind her Honda Accord as she threaded the winding streets back to her condo. She pulled into the garage and he parked his Lincoln Town Car in the driveway behind her.

The alarm system was just one of the many lifestyle changes Jake was certain to insist upon, Kaitlyn was sure. How far did she dare let him go? she wondered, reading the frustration that was so evident in his strong profile. He would undoubtedly want her to leave everything up to him, to place her welfare completely in his very capable hands.

She wouldn't object if it involved her physical security alone. But there was so much more at stake, such as the need to feel strong, independent, in control of her own future—things that Jake had never been able to understand. Things that had made living with him impossible. With a weary sigh, she turned toward the door leading into the kitchen.

Jake pulled his briefcase out of the trunk, gathered the

bottle of Chablis and the two bottles of beer the bartender from the clubhouse bar had given him, locked his car, then followed her into the house, pausing a moment to make sure the garage door was closed.

"Do you bring booze on all your estimate calls?" she asked as he set the beer and wine on the long butcher-block countertop.

"I've had a rough week and figured a couple of beers would go down real nice. I brought the wine for you, thinking you might enjoy a glass. Got a corkscrew?"

Kaitlyn decided she could do with a glass. She was taut and more tense than she'd been when she made the decision to start Memories To Go Travel. Though she still shook when she recalled the note in Jake's suit pocket, she had to admit that much of her current nervousness had to do with his being there in her home, standing in her kitchen, looking tall, all-male and more tempting than a double-fudge brownie sundae.

She handed him the corkscrew, half-entranced by the fluidity of his movements as he opened the wine. Once he'd filled her glass and handed it to her, he looked into her eyes.

"You doing okay, Katie?"

She breathed deeply, allowing herself to voice her biggest fear. "He knows where I live. Doesn't he?"

Jake wanted to hold her, pull her into his embrace and promise her he would make everything all right. But he stood his ground, unsure of how she would react. More uncertain of how he would handle the contact. The attraction he felt for her hadn't waned all these long years apart. But he was wiser now. Wise enough to see that their natures hadn't changed. That a relationship with this particular woman wouldn't work a second, third or fourth time around.

Her walking out had hit him hard. One morning he'd been making plans for the future, ones that included her and a pack of redheaded kids, then that evening he was all alone and wondering how he would pull himself together. He wouldn't go through that pain again.

"It's very likely he knows," Jake told her. "You're going to have to make some tough decisions."

"About what?" she asked, her shoulders braced, her back against the counter as if for support. She took a sip of her wine and breathed deeply.

"You need to send him a very clear message that you want him out of your life," Jake told her. "Starting with a restraining order. We can see a judge first thing Monday morning."

"Will that keep him away?"

Jake sighed, not liking what he had to tell her. "It could make him decide you aren't worth the trouble of going to jail, but most likely it'll tick him off royally. Stalkers rarely pay attention to a piece of paper telling them to stay away from their targets."

Kaitlyn shivered at his words. Much as he hated having her afraid, Jake had to lay all the cards on the table for her to see. No longer could he let her deny that she was the target of a stalker.

"But if it won't keep him away, why go to the trouble of filing for one?" she asked.

"Legal recourse. The police will have a file started on him. They can arrest him if he hangs around your office, follows you around, anything he does to disobey the judge's orders. Eventually they might be able to put him away for a long time."

"Eventually?" she squeaked in sudden alarm. "Jake, you make this sound as if it'll go on for weeks. Months."

Or longer. His silence told Kaitlyn everything she didn't want to hear. This was going to be a long, drawn-out ordeal, with her playing the lead role. Center stage. Craig Fallon was going to turn her world inside out, make her life a nightmare.

She'd never felt more vulnerable in her life, more at another person's mercy, and she didn't like the feeling one bit. Fallon was calling the shots. All right, she thought, sipping her wine, he might be pulling the strings, but that didn't mean she had to dance to his tune.

"I may be the target," she said, looking Jake square in the eyes. "But that doesn't mean I have to play the victim, does it?"

Giving her a nod of approval, Jake tipped the neck of his beer bottle to the rim of her glass. "I'm glad you're thinking that way. It will make my job that much easier."

Jake's job. She didn't want to consider the extent of his involvement in her life just yet. She had enough to absorb without adding him and her confusing feelings for him into the equation. Being around him, it was too easy for her to be vulnerable, too easy to turn everything over to his sharp intelligence and willing, strong shoulders. He made it so easy to be weak—a luxury she couldn't indulge in.

"The alarm system," she said, pointing to his open brief-case on the kitchen table. "Shall we get started on the estimate?"

With another nod, Jake took out his tape measure, a note-pad and pencil and started his work at the entrance from the garage. She watched, sipping her wine, as he thoroughly went through the nooks and crannies of that area and every room after that, listened as he explained some of the features of the system and services she would have. And, she secretly admired his body and wondered why his particular brand of virility drew her so strongly.

She needed temporary protection—the physical kind. She did not need a temporary affair, no matter how exciting the package. And being with Jake had always been exciting. He could take the sharp side of her wit and give it back in good measure. Their verbal battles had been charged with energy and underscored with a passion so intense it left them both exhausted.

Watching him as he finished measuring the bedroom windows, she realized that those days she was with Jake, she'd been truly and completely alive. She'd felt a passion she hadn't known was missing in her life until now.

Must be a formerly unknown masochistic side of her that made her feel this way toward a man who was the essence of everything she couldn't live with, she decided, sipping the last of her wine.

"You've got great taste in decorating," he said, breaking into her musings.

"Hmm?"

"This bedroom. The whole house, in fact. Did you do it yourself?"

She nodded and gave him a pleased smile that Jake realized was the first genuine smile she'd given him tonight. He liked it. And he did like what she'd done with her home. Her taste leaned to the cherry wood and brass with an Oriental touch that said elegance and class in a very subtle way. His own preference was for the oversize and comfortable, but he had to acknowledge that his apartment could do with a bit of Katie's kind of style.

"Shall we go into the living room and I'll spell out all you're going to get?" he asked, jotting down the last measurement.

What she would get extended beyond security for her home. That would be just the start. But Jake wouldn't go into those details tonight. Right now she was apt to resist further attempts on his part to keep her safe, so he would have to use subterfuge in order to keep his eye on her without her knowledge. It was not the way he normally did business, but she would have his protection one way or another. He knew how very bad this situation could get. He doubted she fully appreciated what happened to many stalking victims. He wouldn't let her down the way he had Candice.

"Give me a minute to change out of this dress," she told

him, tucking a strand of her silky hair behind one lovely ear.

"I like looking at you in that dress," he protested. To emphasize the point, he let his gaze once again roam over her curves, softly outlined by the clingy material, reminding himself to no avail that he was enjoying the sight much more than was wise. Why was it that where she was concerned, wisdom always took a back seat to desire?

Jake's eyes filled with that languorous heat Kaitlyn had noticed in them several times this evening. Once more, she felt the warmth reach out to wrap around her, making her wonder what it would be like to be in his arms again. Making her long for just that.

It was the stress of getting that damned note, she knew, that made her momentarily crave the safety of a pair of strong arms around her. It was an ironic twist of fate that Jake—the only man whose embrace could make her feel safe and cherished—happened to be here. And it was the wine that had her resistance to temptation weakening rapidly.

She set the empty glass on the corner of the sleek, polished dresser, then gestured toward the door. "Save the leers for someone who might succumb to them."

"Ah, Katie," he murmured, coming to stand in front of her. "You shouldn't chastise a man for something he can't help."

He was so close she could feel that heat she wanted to lean into. He touched her cheek, as if he truly couldn't help himself, much as she couldn't keep from absorbing the tenderness in his light caress. His deep brown eyes darkened to the color of midnight. Just when Kaitlyn thought he would bend down to kiss her, just when she decided that's what she wanted, desperately needed, he pulled away.

"I'll carry your glass out to the kitchen," he said, taking the first step toward the door, leaving her wanting to turn back the hands of time for just a moment. "Mind if I finish that other beer while we go over everything?"

She shook her head, then as he went back into the living room, she shut the bedroom door. What was she going to do about the way this man made her feel? she asked herself as she grabbed a pair of jean shorts out of a drawer. She was her own woman now. She made her own choices, relied on herself, didn't have to clear her agenda with anyone, and that's the way she liked it. She doubted Jake would. A leopard didn't change his spots, after all.

He'd been about to kiss her a moment ago; she was sure of it. But at the last minute he'd pulled away, as if he knew as well as she that they could never make it work between them, no matter how wonderful that would be. Jake wanted a woman who would lean on him. She wasn't the leaning type. Jake was strong, liked wielding his authority, giving orders and seeing them followed. She wouldn't allow herself to be dominated by anyone as her father had tried to control her.

With a small sigh, she hung up her dress, slipped into the shorts and a T-shirt, then walked into the living room, settling herself on one corner of the low-slung sofa. Jake came out of the kitchen with the beer in one hand and her refilled wineglass in the other.

She accepted the glass, though debating whether to drink any more, since she already felt fuzzy around the edges. She'd skipped lunch, then had been too upset over her discovery that she was still attracted to Jake to eat dinner. Maybe she ought to go to the kitchen and see if there was anything to snack on. But she was entirely too comfortable to move.

"You'll get new doors and more solid locks on all of them—" Jake began once he'd settled into the chair across from the sofa.

"Whoa, I understand the bit about better locks, but why do I need new doors?"

"The ones you have are hollow and could be kicked in too easily. You'll get something solid, and you can even pick the style. We'll replace the back, front, the one from the garage and the bedroom."

"The bedroom? Let's not get ridiculous about this."

"This is the basic stuff," he insisted. "If an intruder enters the house, you need to be able to barricade yourself in one room until help comes. That's usually the bedroom. You have a telephone in there so you can call for help."

"Barricade…" Kaitlyn swore. "Jeez, Jake, this isn't doing a hell of a lot for my peace of mind. Can't you sugarcoat some of this?"

"You wanted to know about the bedroom door. I told you."

"Yes, but can't you break it to me gently," she protested, her voice more shrill than she liked. He was treating this as if danger were imminent. She just wasn't ready to face all the frightening possibilities he was laying out. "You're talking about turning my house into a fortress and all the guy's done is—"

She came to an abrupt stop, remembering the irrationality of that note Craig Fallon had asked Andrew to give her. Jake waited with that trademark patience of his—the very patience she generally managed to wear thin.

"Katie," he finally said when she picked up her wineglass with a shaky hand and took a drink from it. "Honey, in only two weeks, the man went from meeting you, asking you for a date you refused, to telling you to plan the wedding. That's not the mind of a reasonable man."

"Maybe it's his idea of a sick joke," she ventured, though she knew all too well that Jake was right. She just wished this whole ordeal were over.

He studied the ceiling for a long moment. Kaitlyn knew he was trying to hold on to his self-control and regretted that she was pushing him into possibly losing his temper. However, she couldn't face the harsh realities he was painting. Not all at once. Her life was changing in ways she didn't want to envision.

Jake ran a hand across the back of his neck, massaging the tightness. "This is sick, but it's no joke," he said emphatically. "Rob is having Fallon's name run through the computers to see if anything comes up on him—"

"What do you mean?"

"He may have a history of stalking. We need to check that out to see what we're dealing with."

"Then there is a chance he'll turn his attention to someone else," she said, latching onto the glimmer of hope.

"There's a slight possibility that someone else will catch his eye and he'll lose interest in you soon, but we can't bank on that. You can't bury your head in the sand about any of this."

Kaitlyn pressed her fingertips against her eyelids, then pinched the bridge of her nose. She had a doozy of a headache. "As usual, you're telling me what you feel I have to hear, whether I want to hear it or not." She sighed. "But I have to admit, you're being unusually diplomatic about it. I didn't expect that."

"Yeah?" He chuckled wryly. "Once I was in business for myself, I soon discovered I had to 'adjust' my style of dealing with clients."

"You mean other people resent being bullied by you as much as I do?" she asked, laughing.

"Funny," he grumbled good-naturedly. "Back to security," he told her, opening his briefcase amid the travel magazines that cluttered the coffee table. "For the sliding patio doors, we'll use shatterproof glass. For the basement windows, we can go with the shatterproof glass or decorative wrought-iron bars."

"The glass. I'll already feel like enough of a prisoner in my own house without having to look at bars."

"You won't be a prisoner," he stated emphatically. "You'll be safe."

"And probably penniless," she said dryly. "State of the art isn't cheap."

"Is money a problem?" he asked, making her smile at the way his protective instincts extended even to the financial.

"Not now, because I'm careful with my money." Anyone in business for herself had to watch her cash flow carefully.

"I do a certain amount of pro bono work. For several battered-women's shelters," he added when she raised an eyebrow. "I can always—"

"That's nice of you to offer." And very like him to donate his time to someone who needed his protection. Jake was the knight on the white charger, rushing to the rescue. She had to remind herself she needed to do her own saving. "You should give the freebies to those who really can't afford to pay you. How did you get into that, anyway?"

"I installed a system for a battered-women's shelter a couple of years ago. Met some of the women, realized they were trying so hard to break out of that cycle of violence, decided I'd like to do what I could to help." He rubbed his neck once more. "It's some of the most emotionally draining work, having to protect these women from the men who supposedly love them. In too many of these situations, things turn really ugly. You haven't had a previous relationship with this Fallon character, but the potential for things to become violent is there."

"Violent." She sighed again. "Can't you leave me some illusion that this will turn out to be quite innocuous?"

"That's a *de*lusion. Now back to the money issue. We can do twelve months, zero-percent-interest financing if you need."

"I won't let you do that, but I will take ninety days same as cash. How much are we talking?" When he named an unbelievably low figure, she shook her head. "Get real, Jake. I pay my own way in this or it's no deal."

"Don't go stubborn on me, Katie. I'll go cost, no higher."

Deciding from the tone of his voice that she would have to live with that, she stretched her legs out on the sofa and sipped at her wine. As long as she was on the sofa and Jake stayed many feet away in his chair, she would be safe from herself and her longings to have him hold her.

"I'll have a crew here in the morning and they'll stay until it's operational," he continued.

She frowned. "Tomorrow? It's Saturday. Won't you have to pay them overtime?"

"Let me worry about that."

Wriggling farther down into the sofa cushions, she gave him a small laugh. "That's Jake. Always ready to take on the worries of the world."

"I'm not waiting until Monday to get the system up and running. There's no discussion on that."

Another ultimatum that she would have to live with. She could argue, but realistically she needed that system in as soon as possible for her own peace of mind. She would just have to make certain that Jake's bill covered the cost of the overtime.

She studied him over the rim of her glass as he continued jotting notes in his bold, southpaw scrawl—his strong hands, the straight line of his nose, the blunt edge of his prominent jaw, his eyes intense, his high brow knit in concentration. He must have shaven before the party—shaven away the heavy five-o'clock shadow that had always given her skin that delicious scrape as he'd made love to her in the evenings and early mornings.

The remembrance nearly made her choke on her wine. She coughed.

"You all right?" he asked, glancing up at her.

She nodded, forcing her thoughts back to the reasons he was here in the first place. She drained the last swallow of wine, as if the liquor could fortify her to deal with this whole terrifying situation.

It didn't, of course. *"Fortification does not come from the bottom of a bottle."* How many times had her father shouted that to her mother? How many times had her mother pleaded with him to understand the difficulty of dealing with the rigors of their military life—the rituals she was forced to observe with senior officers' wives, the moving from place to place, the being alone for long periods? Her mother had never mentioned the stress of trying to please a man whose standards were unattainably high, though.

Kaitlyn set her empty wineglass on the coffee table next to Jake's briefcase. "The thing is," she said, "seeing this Fallon, talking to him, you'd think he was perfectly normal."

"That's often the case," Jake said softly. "It's their thinking that's skewed, not their appearance."

"Yes, but Craig looks, well, he looks like every woman's dream date. He's blond, blue eyed and gorgeous. He's clever, you know, witty. He does all those old-fashioned things like standing up when a woman enters the room, holding the door for her. He's got this perfect manicure, for crissakes."

"Think of it like that flashy sports car you used to say you'd have one day. The body lines are flawless, the paint and chrome shine to perfection, there's not a speck of rust or a dent or ding anywhere. But the wiring's shot."

He sat back in his chair as she slid farther into the sofa, wriggling into a very comfortable position, staring thoughtfully at the ceiling. The mental image of Craig Fallon's handsome face materialized. With a shiver, Kaitlyn blinked it away and turned her gaze to Jake, his frame dwarfing the low-backed chair he slouched in.

"Whatever happened to that white Porsche you were going to have?" he challenged.

"I decided that right now I needed to go for the lower-priced luxury and dependability," she said dryly. "With the travel industry's ups and downs, that Porsche may have to remain just a dream."

She folded her arms across her abdomen and, because she couldn't hold them open any longer, closed her eyes. She felt warm and wonderfully lazy. Liquid. Safe.

"I'm going to make some calls," Jake told her, sounding very far away. "Get things set up for the morning."

"Hmm," was all she could manage.

She was dimly aware that he'd gotten up and walked into the kitchen to get the phone, and just before she slipped into sleep, she concluded that his deep voice was a very comforting, and sexy, sound.

Jake awoke with a start as someone cuffed his upper arm, hard enough to bruise.

"Katie?" he mumbled, his eyes snapping open.

"Wake up, Sleeping Beauty," she said from very close by. "Some watchdog you are."

She perched on the arm of the chair, very near, very wide-awake, her mood obviously not the best. She looked sexy in the morning, her hair slightly tousled, her T-shirt wrinkled, her face still soft with the remnants of sleep. Damn but he wanted her with an intensity so strong it was all he could do to control it. He wriggled out of his slouch and into an upright position, wincing at the crick in his neck from the uncomfortable chair. Elegance had its drawbacks.

"I must have fallen asleep," he muttered, though there wasn't the slightest chance she would buy that story.

"Right." She snorted. "Just after you neatly folded your trousers and got blankets and pillows for both of us. You sly, shifty, sneaky snake."

She'd had enough time to work up to a full head of steam, Jake realized. He'd figured she wouldn't appreciate his staying overnight, but he hadn't wanted her to be alone in the house and he hadn't wanted to do battle over his need to be here. So he'd plied her with wine on an empty stomach, bided his time until she fell asleep, then set his mental alarm clock to awaken him with the sun, figuring he'd tell her he'd taken her key last night and had let himself in that morning. It was more dishonest than he liked to be, but the situation called for it. The problem was she'd awakened before him. How could he have slept so soundly?

He caught her wrist before she could complete another punch at his upper arm, yanked to pull her into his lap, then instantly regretted the move. With her fanny positioned over a certain part of his anatomy, she struggled to get free of his light hold on her. The wriggling was torture and pure ecstasy.

"Honey," he began through clenched teeth, "if you have any recollections of what it was like in the mornings when we lived together, you'll sit still."

With a soft gasp, Kaitlyn went stock-still. Oh, she remembered, all right. And her body responded just as it always had. She wanted to run her hands through his thick hair, over the morning beard that covered his jaw. Wanted to snuggle against his unyielding chest, to experience once again the power and passion of his kisses. Wanted him to make love with her.

Some things apparently would never change. But other things had to, starting with his method of operating in secret around her.

"Let me up," she demanded softly.

"I rather like having you here this way—on my lap and docile."

He began to nuzzle the top of her head. Images and erotic memories trapped the breath in her lungs, made her body heat soar. She heard his muffled groan, then suddenly his arms went from cradling to caressing. He found the hem of her T-shirt and eased a hand under the material, tracing the column of her lower spine with hungry fingertips. When she felt him fumble with the back hooks of her bra, reason asserted itself.

"Stop, Jake," she protested with the little strength she could summon as he nibbled at her earlobe, his warm breath feathering across the side of her face.

He groaned again. "I'm not sure I can," he murmured. "I know I don't want to."

"Let me help you," she told him, slamming the base of her hand into his shoulder.

"Ow! That wasn't necessary." He set her on her feet, then massaged the spot she'd pounded.

"Jacob Alexander Riley, you have absolutely no business spending the night here," she rasped, glaring down at him, those deep blue eyes of hers flashing fire.

Jake resigned himself to the fact that there wouldn't be any lovemaking this morning, and to the fact that he would have to face the consequences of her being the first to wake up. Here, guarding her, was where he'd wanted—needed—to be last night, and he would not apologize for that.

"Katie, after that last note, I felt you needed protection—" he began.

"Have you ever heard of the 911 system? Or were you afraid that in a crisis I might forget the number?"

He chose to ignore her sarcasm. "What if they couldn't respond in time? I decided I would prefer not having that on my conscience."

"*You* felt, *you* decided. *You* never once considered including me in your plans, did you?"

Because he'd feared she would fight him tooth and nail over it. "You were exhausted. You hadn't gotten much sleep the night before and you fell asleep before I could tell you last night—"

"Fell asleep before you could tell me," she scoffed, throwing his words back in his face. "You never intended on telling me your plans, did you? That's why you brought the wine.''

Jake knew he would have to be honest with her. "I didn't tell you because I figured this is what I would get—a fight—one that you wouldn't win," he added firmly.

Suppressing an angry growl, Kaitlyn turned away from him, snatched up the blanket he'd covered her with last night, then began folding it. Somehow she had to get her temper under control. Losing it around Jake was a knee-jerk reaction she had to get over. While his methods and his prehistoric attitude might not be to her liking, he'd given up his comfortable bed to watch over her, and she imagined that on some level she'd known he would be there and so had slept peacefully. She draped the folded blanket over the low arm of the sofa, then sat down and faced him.

"Okay," she said on a deep sigh, "maybe you would have gotten a fight. Or maybe not. I don't know how I would have reacted had you asked to stay. You never gave me that option. I resent being treated as a brainless twit.''

He moved to sit beside her on the couch. When he spoke, his voice had softened. "Katie, that wasn't the meaning behind my actions. Security is my field—''

"And this is my life. I demand that I be involved in all decisions concerning it," she stated, stabbing his chest with her index finger.

"I hate it when you do that." He pushed her hand away.

"I hate it when you try to run my life. You're big, bold, authoritative, and damned near everyone is intimidated enough to let you have your way.''

"Everyone but you. Whenever I try that approach with you, I end up ducking for cover.''

She gave a wry laugh. "You're the only person who ever made me angry enough to throw things." She breathed deeply. "But, Jake, we have to change the way we deal with each other. Agreed?''

"Change in what way?" he asked warily.

"I need you to realize that I can make responsible decisions concerning my welfare. You have to be honest and up-front with me or I'll find someone who will."

That threat had its desired effect. His jaw clenched and his eyes darkened and narrowed. "Kaitlyn—" he began in a tightly controlled tone, using her proper name—a sure sign she was pushing him. "I will not have you going to someone else for help."

"'Help' is the key word here. It implies that you will work with me, keep me informed of what's going on, discuss your thoughts with me before you make any decisions. Before," she stressed, "not after the fact. You abide by my terms or—"

"Don't threaten me with finding someone else. You don't pin your safety on a name you find in the Yellow Pages. Your safety is important to me."

It was said without fury but with enough emphasis to give her pause. To make her wonder whether he was speaking strictly professionally or very personally. She wasn't certain she wanted to know the answer to that.

"And your involving me in decisions about my fate is important to me. Do we have a deal?" she asked, holding out her hand to him.

He stared at it long and hard before finally wrapping both of his around it. Not in the handshake she expected, though. Instead he traced a pattern across her knuckles with his thumb—a move designed to short-circuit her thinking. It was very nearly working, too.

"Last night you said you would defer to my judgment regarding your safety," he reminded her very quietly.

She snatched her hand away. "I said that to get you to let Rob and Shelly have their evening together and you know it. You can't hold me to—"

"I have to, Katie. I have to know that *if*," he stressed, "*if* things get ugly, you will listen to me."

"Follow your orders without question, you mean." It was her turn to growl. "That's playing dirty."

"Only because you've made it clear you might do something foolish and dangerous."

"Like going to someone else—"

"Which you're not going to do because you know that if you need protection, you can depend on me. Right?" He gently tugged her arm when Kaitlyn tried to get up and walk away. "Come on, Katie," he cajoled where she'd expected him to bully. "Give me your word on this."

Her word was not something Kaitlyn gave easily, and when she did, she kept it. Jake knew that, damn him. Just as she knew that she could trust in his expertise. It wasn't his skill or his willingness to go to any length necessary to protect her that annoyed her, only his methods. But perhaps there was something she could do about that.

If only she could snuggle against him.

Her breath caught again at the renewed need to do that very thing. He looked so damned tempting, clad in his V-neck undershirt and briefs, the shadow of his morning beard heavier, his hair mussed invitingly, the strong lines of his face softer and gentler. If she were to make love with him now she knew how it would be—tender, lazy, playfully passionate. It took all her strength to summon her resolve and bring her thoughts back in line.

"All right," she said slowly. "I'll give you my word that I will follow your instructions if things get ugly, *providing* you give me yours that you will not operate behind my back, that you will be honest with me, that you will discuss things with me, and…" She poked him in the chest one final time. "You will listen to and consider my wishes."

"Katie, this is my field—"

"You're starting to repeat yourself, Jake."

Jake narrowed his eyes in irritation. This conversation was not working out exactly the way he'd planned. He didn't like not having total control, in this instance particularly. In a crisis situation there wasn't time to explain your reasons to a client and wait for approval. You had to act first and analyze later. When protecting his clients, he demanded ultimate and unquestioning authority to operate as he saw fit, or he told them to find someone else.

Katie wouldn't give him that much leeway. But with her he couldn't—wouldn't—put her safety in anyone else's hands. He would have to compromise and hope he didn't regret it down the road. She was leaving him no other choice.

"All right," he muttered tightly. "But I don't like this one bit."

The all-too-triumphant smile she gave him made Jake extremely uneasy. As if he'd overlooked something crucial, something that would come back to haunt him at a time when he could least afford it. He rubbed the back of his neck, hoping that fatigue had him imagining things.

"Go grab a hot shower to work out the kinks," she told him, getting to her feet. "I'll start the coffee."

"Coffee?" he asked suspiciously.

"I have it in the house and I'll even make some for you." She pointed to the bedroom. "Use my shower."

Obediently he got to his feet. Once he was on his way to the bathroom and she was in the kitchen, Kaitlyn allowed her pleased smile full rein. She put grounds in the coffeemaker and filled it with water, hardly daring to believe her luck. Yes, she'd had to agree to follow Jake's orders if things got ugly. However, in what was a rare stroke of good fortune for her, he'd failed to define "ugly," and that left her with a lot of room to maneuver.

Chapter 5

Jake Riley fresh out of the shower was even more dangerous to Kaitlyn's senses. His bare chest was a distraction a saint couldn't ignore. How she wanted to touch him. Feel that soft, dark hair under her palms as she brushed her hands over his broad, muscled torso and down to his waist. Determinedly she forced her thoughts, and her gaze, to stop there where his towel began.

"Thanks," he said as she handed him a mug of coffee. He looked past her shoulder to the coffeemaker. "Have you developed a taste for the stuff?"

"Not really. I do a lot of entertaining here at the house. Travel parties where we focus on a particular trip, what there is to see and do, what the customs are if it's outside the country. That's why I have the big-screen TV in the rec room downstairs—to better display the travel videos."

He leaned back against the counter, crossing those long and powerfully built legs of his at the ankles as he settled comfortably to listen to her. But Kaitlyn wasn't comfortable at all. The towel parted an inch at the bottom hem, displaying a tiny bit more of his outer thigh, enough to make her body heat rise a few degrees. There was too much intimacy and too much masculinity in the room to suit her, and too many memories of the passion they'd shared all those years ago.

Finally she paused in her monologue about travel films, unable to stand the torment of looking and not touching another second. "Clothes would be nice, Jake."

He gave his appearance a cursory glance to make sure he was somewhat decent. "They're in the car."

She blinked. "You have a change of clothes in your car?" Had he been planning all along to stay the night here when he hadn't even known Craig Fallon would be at the party or that he would give her that note? How could that be?

"Take it easy, Katie. There've been times that I've met with a client and decided immediate physical security was necessary," Jake explained quickly before she could get the wrong idea. "Those times I can't get home for fresh clothes, so I keep a shirt, a change of underwear and a razor in a bag in the trunk."

She was squirming, unsettled, he realized, all because he was in her kitchen first thing in the morning, drinking her coffee, wearing nothing more than a pale green bath towel. He could read it in her wide eyes and in the way her pert breasts rose and fell with her rapid breathing. It did wonderful things to his ego and equally painful things to his libido.

"I'll go get the bag," she offered, holding out her hand. "Where are your car keys?"

"That's all right. Tell me more about these parties. How many people do you usually have over?"

"Three or four couples. Occasionally five. Only people I've dealt with for a long time."

"Then Fallon hasn't been here?" Jake asked softly. He

hated reminding Katie of the weirdo, but it couldn't be helped.

"No," she said on a shaky breath. "Now, if you don't mind, I'll answer the rest of your questions once you're dressed," she told him emphatically.

He gave her a pleased grin. "I still have that effect on you."

She groaned. "You and your oversize ego," she muttered. "Look at you, Jake. Any woman would drool."

"I'm not talking about any woman, Katie. I'm talking about you. And me. We were damn good together in bed. We still would be."

He knew instantly he'd pushed her into realizing what she did not want to admit even to herself. She straightened. Her eyes shot blue fury at him.

"If you go down that road, you'll go alone." She whirled around toward the living room, halting abruptly as the back doorbell rang.

"That should be Dallas Steele," Jake said, making no attempt to move away from the counter. "He'll be in charge of the crew putting in your system."

Her anger with Jake only slightly under control, Kaitlyn yanked open the back door. A brown-haired version of masculinity strolled in, casting her a lusty grin as he looked her up and down.

"Well, hello-o, darlin'," he said. "Aren't you a gorgeous sight in the morning?"

She gave him a frosty glare that didn't dim his cocky grin in the least. He placed a bakery box on the counter, then turned to Jake. His eyebrow shot up as he took in his employer's state of undress.

"Hey, Boss, I hope my, uh, timing—" he began.

"Is fine. There's nothing going on here," Kaitlyn snapped, shoving the door closed, then stalking out of the room. As she passed the two men, she muttered that it was men and not children who should be seen and not heard from.

Jake's chuckle didn't sit any better on her mind than his comment about…them. There was no them. There couldn't be. But she'd sure wanted there to be. She'd wanted to walk up to him and wrap her arms around his neck, to drag him off to her bed and never let him go. His comment about them in bed was right. There they were a perfect fit. So perfect that she'd never been with anyone else, knowing nothing or no one could compare with the match she and Jake made.

The trouble was, she realized as she closed the bedroom door solidly, when they were not making love, Jake would overpower her with his need to take care of her.

She got into the shower, recalling how it had been between them. Jake was strong, physically and emotionally, and she had cared for him much more than she'd thought she could care for anyone. It would have been so easy to let him take over, make her decisions for her. He was thoughtful, tender, caring, and most of their clashes would not have occurred had she put herself in his capable hands.

But each time she'd considered doing just that, she'd thought about her mother and how she'd allowed her husband to control her life and how devastated she'd been when he'd left her. She'd never been able to function on her own.

Kaitlyn had come very close to letting Jake Riley detour her progress toward self-sufficiency, and it was very unsettling to realize that she needed all her willpower to keep from throwing it all away for another fling with him, another chance at heaven in his arms.

She finished her shower, toweled off and dried her hair, all the while berating her hormones for eternally kicking into overdrive around the man. She slipped into a print skirt and a sleeveless yellow blouse, made her bed, spent as much time as she could on her hair and light makeup, all to avoid having to go out there and face Jake and what he did to her senses.

When she could delay no longer, she grabbed her brief-case out of the spare bedroom she used as an office, carried it into the kitchen and set it next to her purse and keys.

Four people now sat around her table, enjoying coffee and doughnuts—Dallas Steele and three others, one of them a young blond-haired woman about Kaitlyn's age. Jake, as devastating in a suit and tie as he was in a towel, introduced the woman as Dev, the young man with the round glasses as Nate and the dark-haired man as Max Slater, their computer whiz.

Dallas jumped to his feet and held out his chair for Kait-lyn. "Here you go, darlin'. I've got it all warmed up for you."

"Are you this obnoxious all the time or just in the morn-ing?" she asked him, pleased to see a look of shock replace his smug grin.

The other three hooted with laughter. "It's about time someone put the egomaniac in his place," Dev said, giving Kaitlyn a wide grin.

Smiling at the friendly put-down and the camaraderie among the four, Kaitlyn snatched a chocolate doughnut out of the box, then collected her purse, keys and briefcase. Jake grabbed another doughnut and his briefcase and started after her. She came to a dead stop, one hand on the doorknob.

"I'll ride with you," he said, inclining his head toward the garage.

Kaitlyn needed to assert herself. Now. She needed dis-tance from Jake. Time to think. Time to figure out how to bring her longings for him in line. She couldn't do that when he was a mere glance away. "Thanks, but I can find my way to the office on my own."

"That's why I'm letting you drive."

Letting her drive? Oh, but the man had nerve. "It's kind

of you to allow me to drive my own car to my office," she
said sharply. "The question is why you feel you have to
tag along."

"Because Rob Donovan is meeting us there at ten." He
grinned. "No sense taking two cars."

She gave a growl of frustration as she pulled the door
open, then led the way into the garage and over to her navy
blue Honda. Jake wondered how much of her present sniping had to do with frustration of the sexual kind.

Comforting to think he wasn't suffering alone, he mused
as she negotiated the Saturday-morning traffic east on 119th
Street and north on Quivera. Again her light scent wafted
through the small car, teasing his nose, testing his resolve.

He knew full well they weren't suited for each other.
What he wanted from Katie—what he realized he still
needed from her—was for her to come to him, let him help
her fight her battles. Five years ago, he'd wanted to do the
fighting for her, but since then he'd learned not to crowd a
person.

He wanted Katie to consult him, to let him advise and
help her. But she couldn't do that. She needed to do everything on her own—as if she still had something to prove
to her domineering father. Or perhaps to herself. Being with
her this time around, he was sensing that Katie Adams had
her own personal demons to slay. Alone.

With an inward frustrated sigh, he finished his doughnut
just as she pulled into the lot of a three-story brick-and-
mirrored-glass building. She checked her mouth in the rearview mirror; then, satisfied there were no chocolate
smudges, she got out of the car.

Kaitlyn was very aware of Jake, her tall shadow following her into the building. She'd been very aware of him in
her car. Too much so. The fact that she had absolutely no
control over this attraction was unnerving. She didn't have
a clue how to change that, but she would have to come up
with something. Soon. Or go crazy with longing.

As they headed toward the wide marble stairs to the second floor, Kaitlyn noticed how he catalogued every bit of the building they walked through, committing it all to memory, then muttering about the lack of any form of security at the front door or in the spacious foyer.

"The guy's probably in his office," Kaitlyn told him. "Probably watching the monitors or something."

"Meanwhile, anyone could get in this place," Jake grumbled.

"That's right," she gasped with mock fright. "Office staff. Clients. Customers in the food court. Really dangerous people."

"When are you going to start taking this seriously?" he demanded, catching her arm to bring her to a stop at the foot of the stairs. "When Fallon shows up with a loaded automatic?"

Her eyes widened, then she squared her shoulders. "I doubt that's likely to happen." She yanked her arm free and started briskly up the stairs.

Jake caught up with her on the second-floor landing. "You met him two weeks ago and last night he decided you're engaged to him. What's he going to decide two weeks from now—that if he can't have you, no one will? I've seen it happen over and over again."

She came to an abrupt stop. Though her face was suddenly drained of color, she glared up at him. "You couldn't bully me into submission," she told him with quiet fury. "So you're trying to scare me into it, instead."

"I'm simply making you aware of the potential—"

"Give it a rest, Jake. I know exactly what you're doing. A cowering client is a clinging client and that's the way you want things to be. Well, I won't cower and I won't cling."

It took a moment for her words to register in Jake's mind. Before he could form a halfhearted denial, she was heading down the hall. How the hell she could move so fast in those high heels was beyond him. He picked up his pace, reaching her as she slowed her steps in front of the glass office door with Memories To Go Travel emblazoned in vivid yellow, blue and red.

"Katie, listen—"

"Save your breath. We both know I'm right."

Kaitlyn opened the door to her office and stepped inside, nodding to her assistant, whose smile was as bright and friendly as always. This time, though, Mary was more interested in the man who walked in behind Kaitlyn than in greeting her boss. The girl's hazel eyes lit up with curiosity.

"Didn't expect to see you again," she said warmly to Jake.

Kaitlyn scowled. "Since you seem to enjoy his company, he can sit out here with you." With that she sauntered into her inner office and shut the door softly.

Jake stared at the glass panel in the door and the closed miniblinds, wondering how long it would take for Kaitlyn to cool off. From their interaction this morning, he guessed she didn't hold on to her anger as long as she would have before. However, he'd backed her into a corner with his scare tactics and that was a ploy she hated.

It occurred to him once more that she might not be as tough as she let on, that behind the biting words, the stabbing glares and the battle-ready stance, there was that vulnerability that she refused to show. No matter what it cost her emotionally, she would hide her fear, especially from him.

What direction would their lives have taken had he made this realization when they'd lived together?

By the time Rob showed up, Kaitlyn's temper had cooled, thanks to the physical work of cleaning up the mess the police and then Jake's crew had left behind. Between helping with phone calls, she'd dusted and run the vacuum, polished the furniture, then had looked for spots she'd missed the first time around. All the while she was aware that Jake was in the outer room, giving her some space.

Something the old Jake would never have done. How many times in the past had he pushed and prodded until she'd caved in or until they were both fighting mad? It appeared they'd both done some maturing over the past few years. But it was also apparent Jake's methods weren't going to change. He got what he wanted, one way or another.

Maybe it was for the best that he wasn't letting her cling to false hopes, she decided as she saw him hand Rob the note. This was serious business. The sooner she faced that harsh reality, the better.

"Grab yourself a cup of coffee, Rob," she said, opening the door between the two rooms.

"Thanks. Yours is a hell of a lot better than the crud they have at the station. Want a refill, Jake?" he asked, holding up the pot.

Jake held out his cup, then once the coffee was poured, the two followed Kaitlyn into her office, Jake shutting the door behind them.

"I'll get the lab on the prints as soon as I get back to the station," Rob said, dropping into a chair. "McDonald didn't find much on the first note. Doubt he'll find much more on this one Jake gave me this morning. Still don't have anything from the computer on this guy, either. Too many people out on vacation right now."

"It would help to know if he had a record," Jake added. "We could make the judge aware of priors when we get that restraining order Monday morning."

Kaitlyn sighed. "Next time I meet someone, I'll be sure and get his life history," she bit out.

Rob's brow arched at the sharpness in her voice. He threw a glance at Jake, who merely shrugged.

"Sorry," she said. "I'm a bit testy this morning."

"Understandable." Rob took a drink from his coffee

cup. "I didn't see anyone hanging out in the hallway. I take it our fellow's not out there."

Kaitlyn shook her head. "I didn't see him yesterday, either." She'd begun to hope he might be gone from her life, but then Andrew had given her that note. Could the man really be planning their wedding details? A very chilling thought.

"Well, I'm sure he'll show up before long," Rob said. "These weirdos don't usually just go away."

"When he does show up," Jake put in, "we'll have gotten that restraining order and can have him arrested."

"A few times in jail would make him change his mind, you'd think," Kaitlyn mused aloud.

"Unfortunately," Rob said, "that's not always the case. But don't worry, Jake and I will be looking out for you. You've got my pager number in case you need to reach me, right?"

She nodded.

He finished his coffee, then stretched as he got to his feet. "Shelly reminded me to thank you for that party last night. We had a great time. She's phoning the caterer and the deejay this morning to see if they're available for the wedding reception." He turned to Jake. "I'll call as soon as I find out anything about this guy."

Jake walked him to the door, then once Rob was gone, he turned to face Kaitlyn. "I wanted to apologize for the way I acted on the way up here," he told her. "I guess my methods could stand some improving."

He looked so genuinely contrite, so sorry for having upset her. He'd had her safety on his mind, nothing more. How could she not forgive him?

"Yes, they could," she agreed, giving him a small smile. "But I understand why you did what you did." She decided she needed to make peace with him. After all, they would have to work together. "I wanted to tell you that I slept really well last night."

He eyed her suspiciously. "I noticed. I, on the other hand..." He reached up to massage the back of his neck.

Kaitlyn laughed. "I owe you a neck rub."

"I'll take you up on that later." His eyes were all soft and warm again for an instant, then they turned serious. "I know there's a security guard somewhere on the premises. I'm going to see if I can find him, inform him of the situation. You should be all right here with Mary, but do me a favor and don't go anywhere by yourself. Okay?"

"All right," she assured him. "Security's office is on the first floor. One of the rooms on the north side."

She was being surprisingly cooperative, Jake thought as he walked down the hall toward the steps. If it were anyone else, he wouldn't have questioned his good fortune. But this was Katie, the woman he'd once known so well, so completely. She was trying to see matters from his perspective. Perhaps he'd be wise to try harder to see things from her point of view before he lost her trust.

Without that he would fail for sure, as he'd failed with Candy. This situation had some striking similarities. Candy had met a man at a party. She'd been nineteen and the man twenty-three. It had been Jake's first encounter with a stalker and he hadn't reacted quickly enough to the things his sister told him. He'd nearly lost Candice. He wouldn't make the same mistake with Katie, he vowed.

He found the security guard in room 105, watching morning cartoons, but at least the man looked fit enough to run the length of the building without passing out. And the man was helpful and concerned when Jake explained the situation. He agreed to keep his eye on Katie's office, to escort her to and from her car as many times a day as necessary, and more important, he promised Jake a full report at the end of each day.

Deciding the man was competent despite the cartoon watching, Jake headed back up the stairs to Katie's office. As he started down the hall, he detected movement out of

the corner of his eye. Someone was in the hallway and had
ducked into the doorway of an office when he'd heard Jake
coming.

Jake worked to keep his steps even and unhurried despite
the panic he felt. His heart thumped double time. He passed
one office, then a second, slowing slightly as he neared the
one across from Katie's. The man pretended to study a
computer services poster, but Jake knew the guy was
watching him. He was blond haired, good-looking, average
build, just under six-foot.

Nonchalantly, Jake strolled past the man. Then suddenly
he spun around. He grabbed the man by the arm, wrenched
it back. Fallon cursed vehemently. Jake shoved him up
against the window, pressing his face into the glass.

"You lousy, son of a—" he started to say.

"Shut up!" Jake rammed his body into the man's, leaning hard against him. He wanted the creep put away for a
long time, but so far the only proven crime the man had
committed was loitering. Not an arrestable offense. Rob
would say his hands were tied until the restraining order
was in place or until the man was caught actually trying to
hurt Katie. Jake was not willing to wait for that to happen.

He reached for Fallon's wallet and flipped it open. He
realized Kaitlyn and her assistant had heard the commotion
and had come out to see what was going on. He tossed the
wallet to Katie.

"Take out his driver's license and make a copy of it,"
he told her.

She blinked a couple of times in surprise, then hurried
to do as he commanded.

"Is this the creep?" he asked Mary.

She nodded.

"Get security up here," he ordered.

She raced for the telephone.

Jake put his mouth against Fallon's right ear. "Now, you
listen to me—"

"Get off me, you bastard."

Jake grabbed the man's collar and whirled him around, then pinned him against the glass. "You are going to stay away from this building," he snarled. "You are going to stay away from her house and away from her. She tells me she sees you anywhere, I'll hunt you down and break you into little bitty pieces. You got that?"

The guy didn't answer. He was staring at Kaitlyn, who'd returned with the wallet. Jake pressed his arm into the man's throat. When he gasped, Jake knew he had his attention.

"You understand what I said?" Jake demanded.

Fallon only glared at him, hatred burning in his eyes. Jake pressed harder, until Fallon's eyes glazed over.

Kaitlyn grabbed his arm. "Jake, stop." He didn't respond. "Jake," she shouted, pulling at his arm. "You're going to kill him."

Jake heard footsteps racing down the hall toward them, then a deep voice commanded, "Let him go, Mr. Riley."

Jake dimly realized the security man was also trying to pull him off Fallon. Slowly he released his prisoner, shoving him at the guard. He took the wallet from Katie and rammed it into Fallon's back pocket.

"Get him out of my sight," Jake growled at the guard.

He turned to Kaitlyn. She was breathing hard. Her eyes were huge in her pale face. He took her arm and led her back into her office, closing the door, then pulling her into his arms before she collapsed.

"Are you all right?" he asked against her hair. It smelled like heaven.

"I thought you were going to kill him."

He'd wanted to. With a strength that stunned him. The thought that Katie was in danger had overridden everything else.

She was trembling. So was he—with the knowledge that her stalker had been close by, that he'd shown up the mo-

ment Jake had left the scene. And with the nearness of her.
He was holding her again—something he'd never dreamed
would happen. But here she was, in his arms, looking up
at him, her eyes full of concern and caring.

She fit as perfectly as ever. Felt small and fragile in his
embrace. He wrapped his arms more tightly around her,
rested his chin on the top of her head and drank in that
perfume of wildflowers and sunshine. She sighed, laid her
head on his shoulder. Her arms went around him.

What was she doing? Kaitlyn asked herself. She
shouldn't be holding him, shouldn't let him hold her so
tightly she could feel every plane and contour of his
rock-hard chest. Pull away. That's what she should do. But
this was where she wanted to be. She felt safe, cherished,
things no other man's embrace could make her feel. He
stroked her hair with infinite gentleness. His warm breath
fanned through the strands.

"Katie," he said softly, "I'm sorry if I frightened you."

"You did," she told him, her voice still shaky.

"I saw him standing there in that doorway and I thought
maybe I could scare him into leaving you alone." And vent
some of his frustrations on the creep.

She gazed up at him, the fear in her eyes replaced with
what looked suspiciously like admiration. For him? Was
she grateful for what he'd tried to do for her?

He trailed a fingertip along the softness of her cheek.
Did she seem to lean into his touch? Her eyes went warm.
Her mouth parted. Suddenly he couldn't help himself. He
had to kiss her. Before he could think of all the reasons
against it, he brushed his mouth over hers.

She tasted sweeter than he'd remembered. Felt softer. He
wanted more, but he heard her sharply drawn breath and
stopped himself. She stared up at him, surprise warring with
need in the depths of her gaze.

"Jake," she whispered, "we can't do this."

"I know." He found himself nuzzling her ear.

"We'll only regret it."

"I know." But his hand traced the column of her neck, her lovely throat. "We couldn't make it work before."

"Right." She drew an uneven breath as his tongue traced a path along her earlobe. "You know what you're doing doesn't make a bit of sense."

"Yeah," he said against her ear. "But right now if I told you to shut up and kiss me, you would do it."

"Not because you order me to," she had to emphasize. She'd do it because she had no choice.

She turned her head and found his mouth. The kiss was possessive and powerful, swamping her senses. She sagged against him, weak-kneed. The hunger would come. First she wanted to savor. His hands, strong, firm on her shoulder and back, holding her so tightly against him. His mouth, insistent, knowing exactly how to please her. Oh, the places he could take her.

His kiss was as breath-stealing as a ride on a roller coaster. As dizzying as dangling over a cliff. Sinful. Wonderful. Heaven, and she wanted to stay forever in the circle of his strong arms, wanted to feel the heat of him surround her.

She felt alive, very much a woman and very much desired. His hand moved lower, to the curve of her hip, drawing her closer still to the brink of danger. Yet she couldn't pull away, didn't want to. His other hand wound through her hair, tilting her head back so he could deepen the kiss.

Jake touched his tongue to her bottom lip, pleased when her mouth opened and she moaned softly. It had always been this way between them. The heat. The need. The give-and-take.

And right now he was taking, he thought. Katie gave herself so generously, holding nothing back. Her grip on his shoulders was fierce, as if she had to cling to him for support. Did she have any idea what that did to him? And those little throaty moans. And the way her tongue sparred with his.

He could feel the curve of her small breasts pressed against his chest. Feel her hip next to his, their thighs touching. Her breathing was rapid and shallow, like his. All he could think about was how much she wanted him and he wanted her.

The ring of the phone startled them both. She gasped, as if the full importance of what they'd done had just slammed into her. As the phone rang a second time, she started to pull away. But Jake wouldn't let her.

"Mary will get it," he told her. "Stay here for just a minute longer."

Kaitlyn didn't protest, though she knew she should. This need to have him hold her and kiss her had started when he'd pulled her onto his lap this morning. She'd wanted it to happen then, wanted it still. But it couldn't be. She sighed. There were things she had to explain to him.

"Jake, leaving you was the hardest thing I've ever done. You have to know that." Leaving had torn her apart, and it had taken a long time to put the pieces back together. She couldn't go through this a second time and survive.

"It was the hardest thing I've ever gone through, too."

She heard the sincerity in his voice and felt it tug at her heart. "Then you have to understand that we can't let this happen."

He didn't answer for a long moment. Finally he said, "You're right, I know...."

"But?" she asked at his hesitation.

He gave her a wry smile. "I wish there were some way we could make it work."

Nothing would make her happier, Kaitlyn thought, but she knew it could never be.

Chapter 6

So here comes the third degree—at last, Kaitlyn thought. But this time it was not coming from Jake. Rather, it was about him, and Shelly was asking the questions. Kaitlyn had actually expected it much sooner. She and Shelly had been shopping for nearly four hours, after all. But Shelly had had wedding details on her mind. Now that the invitations were ordered and the wedding dress was being altered to fit, the future bride was free to turn her attention to her friend.

"So how did you and Jake meet? Back then, I mean," she queried as they got into her Mustang.

"You don't really want to know."

"Of course I do."

Kaitlyn took a moment to buckle her seat belt before answering. "It's truly boring stuff."

"Liar. Now, quit stalling and give me the facts. I've been very patient." Shelly gave her a firm look before turning to back the car out of the space.

"It was late one night and I wanted chocolate milk,"

Kaitlyn began. "I—stupidly, according to Jake—walked into this convenience store."

"Why 'stupidly'?"

"Because I walked into a robbery-in-progress. Jake thought I should have known there'd been a rash of robberies in that area. I shouldn't have been out alone that late. I should have known the place had been hit half a dozen times in the three months prior to that, and that the owner started keeping a gun under the counter."

"How were you supposed to have known all that?" Shelly cried.

Kaitlyn shrugged. "I should have been more aware of the things going on around me, I suppose. However, Jake went a little too far with his tirade and it didn't take me long to get fed up with it."

She smiled to herself, remembering that night and Jake's fury at the thought she might have been hurt. He hadn't even known her then, but he'd been overly concerned with her welfare nonetheless.

"I calmly opened the carton of milk," she continued, "took a swallow, then poured the rest on him."

Shelly gaped in shock, then she laughed. "You didn't! What did he do?"

"Took down my license number when I drove off, looked me up on the computer and showed up on my doorstep the next day."

"With flowers and candy?"

"With a dry-cleaning bill. He'd had his shirt and jeans cleaned and pressed and he wanted me to pay for it."

"I don't believe you. He had his jeans pressed?"

Kaitlyn nodded. "Jake believes in looking your best no matter what the situation, no matter the type of clothes. Scruffy is not his style." She'd always liked that about him, she thought.

"Come to think of it," Shelly said, "it's not your style, either." She made a left turn out of Oak Park Mall and headed south on Quivera. "So what was the problem between you two?"

"I suppose we were both a little immature and both very headstrong," Kaitlyn said on a sigh. And they'd both needed very different things from a relationship. Still did. That was the part they would never be able to reconcile. She would have to work to remember that the next time he tried to kiss her.

It couldn't happen again—though she knew that would be much easier said than done. She could still recall the feel of his mouth on hers. The coffee taste of him. How her willpower turned to mush in his embrace. What was she going to do about that?

She sighed once more.

"Then is being together again going to cause problems for you guys?" Shelly asked.

How like Shelly to be concerned about their feelings. Kaitlyn touched her friend's arm. "We seem to be managing fairly well. But if things get difficult, Jake and I will deal with it. We've already agreed we won't do anything to spoil the wedding."

"Thanks," Shelly said with relief. "Rob really wants Jake for best man and I really want you for maid of honor." She made a right turn onto 119th Street. "You know, I've never understood what you have against marriage. Was your eight months with Jake so bad?"

"My time with him did convince me I was better off on my own, but Jake isn't responsible for the way I feel about marriage. I'd decided it wasn't for me long before he came along. I just don't want to be…married."

In most of the relationships she saw, either one person was stronger, dominant, and the other person surrendered, or both were strong and they clashed continually. In her mother's case, it had been the former and it had cost her everything. Kaitlyn had tried the latter with Jake and that didn't work for her, either. She didn't want to be in that situation of having to do battle with a strong-willed man and she couldn't tolerate living with a weak male.

Growing up, she had decided she would prefer living alone. She'd had enough of answering to another person, especially someone as demanding and critical as her father. Jake's overprotectiveness had only strengthened her conviction that she couldn't risk losing herself, couldn't risk ending up broken, devastated emotionally, helpless, unable to cope, a shell of the woman she could have been. Like her mother.

"Still," Shelly continued, "I've always liked the thought of having a best friend, a soul mate, to share my life with. I think Jake is ready to settle down and start a family."

Kaitlyn heard the note of concern in her friend's words and thought again that Shelly was well suited for a career in the public defender's office. "Don't worry. If that's what he wants, he'll find someone to make it happen. Jake has a way of getting what he wants."

"I suppose you're right." Shelly brightened as she turned into Kaitlyn's driveway and spotted her intended helping Jake with the wiring of a floodlight over the garage.

The two men had taken off their suit jackets and ties and were working in their shirtsleeves. From high on the ladder, Jake looked down at her, his gaze filled with heat. Kaitlyn knew he was recalling what had transpired in her office and that he wanted a repeat performance as much as she. But hadn't they agreed it couldn't happen again?

Jake put the screwdriver in his back pocket, climbed down the ladder, then walked over to Kaitlyn. "How'd the shopping go?" he asked, his gaze locked with hers.

"Great." Her mouth felt dry. The early-evening temperature seemed to rise several degrees.

"We got a lot accomplished," Shelly said, watching Jake with undisguised curiosity. "Wait until you see Kaitlyn's dress."

"Umm," was all Jake said in reply, his concentration on

Kaitlyn. The man had no right to look at her as if he could devour her, she thought.

Rob laughed. "I think Jake wants to be alone with his lady."

Kaitlyn frowned. Since when had she become Jake's "lady"?

Rob didn't notice her change of expression. He dropped an arm over Shelly's slender shoulders. "I know I certainly want you all to myself."

Shelly didn't waste any time. She gave Rob a peck, tossed her friends a wave, then got in behind the wheel and was backing out of the driveway in record time. Rob followed close behind her as she drove down the street.

For just one moment, Kaitlyn longed for what her friend shared with Rob. But soul mates were a rare commodity and she didn't think she dared surrender herself so completely to another person, especially one as strong willed as Jake.

Kaitlyn looked up at Jake. The heat was still there in his eyes, a heat she had to turn her back on. The risks of getting involved with him again were simply too great. "Where's your crew?" she asked, walking into the open garage.

"Finished and out of here," Jake said. "They did their final tests on the system shortly after you and Shelly left to go shopping."

Then there would be no reason for him to spend the night again. Good thing, she thought. Tonight she would have a hard time getting to sleep if he was close by. That kiss had brought back memories of other nights with him. Nights she wondered if she would ever forget.

She went into the house, pausing in the laundry room to kick off her sandals. The aroma of something spicy greeted her. She walked over to the oven and peeked inside at the Monterey Jack cheese covering the bubbly enchilada sauce. On the countertop were bowls of chopped lettuce and tomato, grated cheddar cheese and corn chips. She opened the lid to the saucepan on the stove and sampled the Mexican rice.

"I put my ladder in the garage for now," Jake said, walking into the kitchen as if he belonged there. How natural it seemed to see him here in her house. "I may need to adjust the angle of one of the floodlights later."

Kaitlyn paused, her fork poised over the rice. "Lights? Plural?"

"One for the front, the side and the rear of the condo," he told her.

"You'll have this place lit up so bright my neighbors will complain to the homeowners' association," she grumbled.

"Trust me." Jake gently tweaked the end of her nose, instantly regretting the small contact. While he'd shopped for groceries and as he'd worked on installing those lights, his thoughts had been on Kaitlyn. That kiss had been fairly tame compared with some of their more passionate ones of the past, but it had been enough to start him thinking of things he shouldn't. Such as how she'd practically melted against him. How wonderful her soft curves would feel under his hands. How good it would be to have her in his bed.

He wasn't likely to forget that kiss anytime soon. And while he longed to act on the wants and needs it had stirred, he knew that would only spell disaster for them both.

"Hungry?" he asked, seeing her dip her fork into the rice again.

She only shrugged, but Jake knew his rice dish had tempted her taste buds. Katie rarely sampled. She rarely cared whether she ate.

"Hand me a couple of hot pads and two plates," he told her, pulling the chicken enchiladas out of the oven once she'd complied.

He put one enchilada on a plate, added a generous helping of rice, put together the lettuce, tomato and cheese for a small salad, then handed her the plate. He fixed one for himself, got the sour cream out of the fridge, then joined her at the table. She'd already dug into the enchilada, he noted, pleased.

"These are fantastic," she said. "Where'd you get them?"

He pretended to be offended by the question. "I made them. I'm a first-rate cook, if I do say so myself."

"You cook? I'll believe that when I see it."

She was eating with unusual enthusiasm for her, he thought. As if she was thoroughly enjoying the food. He smiled to himself. He'd debated quite a while about whether to fix dinner for her. The scene was very domestic, especially after the kiss. She'd been distant and quiet afterward and perhaps that was for the best, since there couldn't be anything romantic or sexual between them.

Then he'd thought of Katie. She would most likely refuse to go out to dinner with him, and if he didn't have dinner ready, he figured she wouldn't eat at all. Although whether she ate shouldn't have mattered so much to him, he'd found he couldn't turn off his concern.

"So, what was Rob doing helping you with the lights?" she asked.

Jake watched her pop another forkful in her mouth. No way would he risk ruining her rare appetite with the news Rob had given him. She would have to deal with that reality soon enough. After this morning's incident, he wanted her to have a brief reprieve from worry and fear.

"You don't want to hear about my cooking chronicles?" he inquired. "I'm wounded."

She eyed him suspiciously for a long moment, as if debating whether to allow him to change the subject. Finally she nodded. "All right. Tell me about your cooking."

For the next twenty minutes he kept her smiling and laughing at stories of his early mistakes in the cooking classes he'd taken, the ensuing disastrous dishes and the more outrageous pickup lines some of the women students had tried on him. At one point he cut another enchilada in half and slid the portion onto her plate along with another serving of rice. He was pleasantly surprised when she polished that off, too, then even picked at the cheese topping on the remaining food. He pushed the serving dish toward her, but she shook her head.

"Why the urge to learn to cook?" she queried. "When we lived together, sandwiches and frozen or prepackaged dinners were the extent of your kitchen skills."

He gave her a wry smile. "I did it to meet single women. Then when the first teacher told me I was a lost cause in the kitchen, it became a matter of pride. And," he added slowly, "it filled the evenings after you left."

Her gaze was warm and sympathetic. "I know what you mean. I took so many classes that last year in college that I was swimming in homework. Then when I graduated, I went to work for a travel agency and learned everything I could about running my own business."

As if to change the subject, she got up and began clearing the table. Jake grabbed a couple of dishes, intending to help her.

"I'll take care of this part," she insisted. "It's the least I can do after you went to all this trouble."

"That's all right. I don't mind giving you a hand."

He set the two dishes on the countertop, then put the lid on the sour cream container and placed it in the refrigerator. When he turned around, he caught the annoyance in her gaze.

"What?" he asked, recalling that this was how the majority of their fights had started. They'd just shared an enjoyable meal and he didn't want to end it with a fight. But running from one wasn't his way any more than it was hers.

She glared at him. "I'm trying to do a little something to reciprocate for the wonderful meal and for everything else you've done today, but you just can't let me."

"I'm only giving you a hand. What's the big deal? Why is it always so difficult for you to accept my help?"

"Because your help soon turns into taking over whatever I'm doing." She let out an angry breath. "Jake, I don't want to spoil the evening with a fight."

"Neither do I, honey, but I need to understand what's going on here."

She looked up from loading the dishwasher and studied him. "I suppose that in my mind your taking over is more of a criticism, proof that you think I'm not capable of handling this. I feel like a little girl all over again with my father correcting, disapproving of the way I do things."

"Katie," he said softly, "you've been living on your own since you went away to college. Don't you think that after nine years you should have that monkey off your back?"

"You didn't live every day of your life being criticized for everything, and no matter how hard you tried, nothing you did was ever good enough. You don't get a chance to develop any self-esteem. No matter what Mom and I were doing, he would take over and show us the proper way to do it, then end up telling us how inept we were." She sighed. "Sometimes I don't think about it. Other times, it comes back and hits me so hard I feel just like that little girl again."

Jake nodded, understanding at last why she'd resisted his assistance so vehemently, realizing that he'd inadvertently treated her as her overbearing father had. He hadn't been trying to crush her self-esteem as the colonel had, but he had brought back those unpleasant memories. He had to make her see that his only intention had been to help her.

"I didn't mean to be so pushy. It's just that I've always been one to pitch in and help," he explained. "Mom was working a part-time job in addition to teaching. Most nights she came home totally exhausted. The girls were little, so I would take over the housework for her."

It was Kaitlyn's turn to nod her understanding. "So, think maybe you could sit down and have a beer while I finish this?"

He thought about it for a brief moment, then shook his head. "But I think I could carry the stuff from the table to the counter and let you do the rest."

She smiled at him. "All right. I'll accept that much. Then you can tell me what Rob wanted. Now that dinner's over and there's no chance of ruining my appetite, you don't have to 'protect' me any longer."

She *had* seen through his ploy, Jake realized, but surprisingly she hadn't objected. As if she'd needed the brief reprieve. Even now he hated having to tell her. Wished she would turn it all over to him to deal with. But that wasn't her way, and the truth was she needed to be fully aware of what was going on. He couldn't protect her alone. She had to be looking out for herself as much as he was.

"I gave Rob Fallon's driver's license number," Jake told her.

"And?" Kaitlyn prompted, glancing up as she loaded the pans and baking dish into dishwasher. She wasn't going to like what Jake had to tell her, but she couldn't continue to bury her head in the sand as she'd been doing.

"He's running it through the computers to see what other states Fallon might have lived in."

"They can do that?" she asked.

Jake nodded. "When you apply for a new driver's license, they make a note of the information from the old license. They can cross-reference it to see if you're wanted in other states."

"Do you think Fallon might be wanted somewhere else?"

"It's a possibility. We'll know in a week or so."

"But that's not all Rob came over to tell you, is it?" she asserted.

"The local computer check on Fallon came back. He was

arrested thirteen months ago...for beating up his ex-girlfriend. She'd left him several months before that and he'd been harassing her since then.''

"Harassing?''

"Following her wherever she went,'' Jake explained. "Letters, phone calls at all hours, standing on her front lawn and yelling obscenities at her.''

Kaitlyn shuddered. "Why did she leave him?''

"The report says he was extremely possessive and got violent a couple of times. Broke some guy's jaw because he saw the guy talking to her and she'd laughed at something he said. He did some time for that, too, but not much. He was supposed to be seeing a shrink for counseling as part of his release conditions. Rob's going to check into that.''

Kaitlyn closed the dishwasher, then wiped her hands on a towel Jake handed her. "Did he lose interest in this other girlfriend when she had him thrown in jail?''

"Near as Rob can tell so far, it appears she left her furniture behind, packed what she could in the back of her car and left.''

"Just vanished?'' Kaitlyn asked, a cold, sick feeling in the pit of her stomach. "What about her family and friends?''

"Her parents and her friends told the police she was desperate to get away from Fallon. Rob's going to question them some more and talk to the officers who were on the case at the time.''

"Question them? Why?''

"To make sure she did leave and that she wasn't possibly murdered,'' he told her quietly.

Murdered? Fighting off a shiver, Kaitlyn set the towel on the counter and looked out the window. She had a business to run. Had her mother in an apartment nearby. She couldn't just pack up and disappear without a trace to escape this man's unwanted attention.

What if the situation became as bad as the one Jake had described? What if the man had latched onto her as he had his ex-girlfriend? What would she do? She had to fight down the panic. This was all much too frightening to deal with.

Maybe it wouldn't come to this extreme. Maybe the man had made some strides in his counseling sessions. It provided precious little hope, but it was something to cling to.

She turned to Jake, noting his jaw was clenched. She sensed he hated this situation even more than she and wondered at that. She laid her hand on his forearm, drawing strength from the power she felt.

"These cases really bother you, don't they?" she asked.

"Yeah," he said grimly. "Come on, I'll show you how your system works."

She followed as he walked over to a keypad by the door leading to the garage. One day, she thought, she would ask him to tell her why the case was so difficult for him, ask him what put the silent fury in his eyes and the grim lines around his mouth.

She listened carefully as he explained how to arm and disarm the system, what to do if she didn't get the code punched in quickly enough, how to respond to the person on the phone if there was an emergency, how and when to push the panic button. It was comforting to learn all the details he'd taken care of. By the time he'd covered everything, she was sure she would feel quite safe in her house.

"Now, if anyone ever accosts you outside and forces you inside," he continued, "you let the alarm go off. Fiddle with the keypad, punch in numbers at random, act like you can't remember your code. Anything—just make sure you let the system go off. When the office calls you, give them the code but add an 'R' on the end."

"'R'?"

"For respond. If they get the 'R,' they'll hang up, call

the police, then alert one of my crews and have them out here as fast as possible.''

Kaitlyn nodded, very aware of how close he was standing. She could inhale the tangy scent of his aftershave, feel the warmth of him. This was the only man who could make her want to lean on someone—on him. She would never understand that. But to lean was to make herself vulnerable and she'd vowed long ago to never again be in that position.

She turned when the doorbell rang. ''Expecting someone?'' she asked.

Jake shook his head, following several steps behind her as she walked through the living room. When she opened the front door, he stood a few feet back, ready for possible trouble. He saw the two uniformed officers on the front stoop and figured they represented trouble of an unexpected kind.

Katie glanced back at him, laughing. ''Did you set off the alarm or something?''

''They're not here because of the alarm,'' he said, very seriously. Whatever their reason for being there, Jake had an uneasy feeling he wasn't going to like it.

''Ma'am,'' the dark-haired one said. ''May we come in?''

Kaitlyn looked to Jake, a concerned frown creasing her forehead. He nodded once. She opened the door and stepped back to let the two in. They glanced around the room, then their gazes locked on Jake.

''Sir,'' the dark-haired one said, ''are you Jacob Riley, Riley Security Services?''

''Yes,'' Jake said, putting his arm around Katie's slender shoulders. She'd been inching closer and closer to him since the two officers had stepped inside. ''What can I do for you, Officer Williams?'' he asked, reading the man's name tag above his badge.

''We need you to come down to the station with us.''

"Why?" Katie demanded, her arm going around Jake's back, holding him tightly. She was trembling.

"We have a warrant for Mr. Riley's arrest on assault charges," Williams said in what was supposed to be a calming tone.

The man could have saved his voice. Katie was not in the mood to be calmed. "Assault?" she cried out. "But who—"

"Fallon," Jake told her.

"But he's the one doing the stalking. How could he press charges against..."

"Katie," Jake said, gently unwrapping her arm from around his waist, "I'll get this sorted out—"

Her mouth opened in protest, but no sound came out. Her eyes were filled with panic.

"It's going to be all right," he reassured her. "I'll be back in a couple of hours. I want you to call my service and tell them to send Dallas and Dev over here, stat. Got that? They'll stay with you—"

"I'm coming with you," she insisted.

He ignored that. "When I leave, you set the alarm, then call and get Dallas and Dev over here. My gun is on the countertop in the kitchen. You know how to use it," he said quietly so the uniforms wouldn't overhear, aware her father had made sure she knew how to handle a weapon. "Just don't shoot my key people, okay?" he joked.

She wasn't in the mood for humor, either. "Jake..."

"Are you clear on those instructions?" he asked softly.

"Yes, sir," she said, miffed. But he knew she was upset with the situation, as well as with him. He could see the concern in her eyes, especially when the other officer proceeded to handcuff him. She drew in a sharp breath as the first cuff clicked around his wrist.

"Do as I told you, Katie," he commanded, needing to be completely certain she would follow his instructions to the letter.

She swallowed hard, then nodded slowly.

He leaned over and dropped a light kiss on her forehead. "I'll be back in a couple of hours."

Watching him being taken away was the most difficult thing Kaitlyn had ever done. She was too worried to stand still, angry enough to smash something. Craig Fallon had some nerve to press charges against Jake!

She shut the door and quickly set the alarm system, then grabbed the cordless phone, watching the police car drive off with Jake in the back seat as she dialed his service. In less than twenty minutes Jake's people were parking their cars in her driveway. Kaitlyn was surprised at how relieved she was to see the two. She had her shoes on and her purse slung over her shoulder when she opened the door for them.

"Whoa, Red," Steele said, catching her by the elbow and firmly guiding her back into the living room. Dev closed the door and threw the dead bolt. "Where do you think you're going?"

"To see Jake. Surely we can bail him out—"

"The company lawyer is on his way to do that right now, so why don't you just sit down and—"

"You go right ahead and make yourself comfortable," she retorted, glaring at the hulk standing in her path. No way was she going to sit and wait for the very slow wheels of justice to release Jake. "I'll see you when I get back."

The man didn't move, didn't even flinch as she gave him her most potent glower. He was nearly as tall as Jake and every bit as broad shouldered. Getting past him was going to be tricky. She feinted to the left, then rushed to the right. The move nearly worked, but the man's reflexes were too damn good. He was back blocking her way before she could take a second step.

"You're pretty good, Red," he said, "but Jake pays me the big bucks to be better. Now, why don't you just—"

"Why don't you—"

The woman standing with her back against the door let

out an earsplitting shrill whistle. "Enough. Why don't we just take her where she wants to go?"

"Because I think this case is personal with Jake," Steele said over his shoulder. "He won't appreciate us dragging her down to the station."

"Come on," Dev insisted. "It's the Overland Park station, not some inner-city precinct. The scum's not as low class as they are downtown."

"Jake still won't like it," Steele maintained firmly.

"Jake gets a little carried away with this protection stuff sometimes," Dev said. "It's not going to traumatize her to see the inside of a police station. The alternative is for you to tie her to a chair until he gets back and I guarantee he won't like that one bit."

Steele waggled his sandy eyebrows. "Tie her to a chair. I love it when you talk kinky stuff."

"Quit clowning and give me your car keys," Dev snapped in mock annoyance. "I'll get her in the Camaro while you set the system."

Keys in hand, she took a fast look outside, then led Kaitlyn over to the yellow '68 Camaro, letting her into the back seat. She got in on the passenger side, passing the keys to Steele as he climbed in behind the wheel. Kaitlyn noted the way the two worked together and understood why Jake had paired them up.

The friendly sniping between them, though, could not keep her mind off Jake, as they most likely intended. What were the police doing to him? she wondered as Steele drove quickly and efficiently through the streets of Overland Park. Kaitlyn knew he wouldn't be in any danger, but he was bound to be worried about her and frustrated as hell. Jake didn't handle frustration well, she mused as Steele pulled up to the building and parked his car.

The three of them walked inside and waited in the clean and brightly lit station room while a flurry of activity went on around them.

"Jake can take care of himself," Dev told her quietly at one point.

Kaitlyn nodded, relaxing a little, but still unable to sit in a chair as the other two were doing. Jake would be able to hold his own with the cops or with whatever criminal element the wealthy suburb station had in custody. But she wished she could see him, reassure him and herself that everything was going to be all right. For now, all she could do was pace the small waiting area.

It was more than two hours later when she saw him walking toward her. Relief flooded through her, almost making her knees buckle.

"Thank God," she heard Steele grumble. "I couldn't have stood another five minutes of watching her pace. All that nervous energy makes me nervous."

Jake spotted her and scowled, then aimed the glare at his two employees.

"I gave them no choice but to bring me here," Kaitlyn quickly told him, noting that his clothes were rumpled and his hair had been finger-combed repeatedly. This was one of those rare times his infinite patience failed him.

"You should have stayed home," he growled.

"You're going through this because of me, Jake Riley," she snapped. "I was worried. I was not going to sit at home." She paused for a breath. "Tell me what's going on."

"I've got a court date in three weeks," he said, putting an arm around her shoulders and leading her to the door. Dallas and Dev followed. Jake waited until they were situated in the back of Dallas's Camaro. "Meanwhile, Rob is getting me mug shots of Fallon from the time he was arrested. First thing Monday morning, we'll get that restraining order, then we'll take the photos to the security staff in your office building. If Fallon shows up on the premises, he'll be arrested."

In the back seat of the car, Kaitlyn felt the anger radi-

ating from him. She was sure it was because he'd under-
estimated Fallon's craftiness. Neither one of them had expected him to file charges against Jake.

She slid her hand in his. He looked at her in surprise,
then his hand closed around hers, his fingers gripping hers
tightly until Steele pulled into the driveway of her condo.
Once Jake had thanked his two agents sincerely, he ushered
Kaitlyn into the house.

"You reset the alarm," he told her. "I want you to get
into the habit of doing it each time."

He was very serious, almost as if he were afraid that she
would overlook some detail. But this went deeper than the
current situation warranted, she sensed. She reset the system as he'd told her, then went to stand beside him.

"You're upset," she said, "and I think it goes beyond
what we've been through tonight."

"I was worried, leaving you alone."

"But there's more to it, isn't there?" she wanted to
know, reading the anguish in his eyes.

He went to the refrigerator and pulled out a beer, twisted
off the cap, then took a long swallow from the bottle. It
required a supreme amount of effort, but Kaitlyn waited.
Finally, when he'd accepted that she would not be side-
tracked, he answered her.

"I nearly lost someone once," he said. "To a stalker. I
figured the guy was a harmless loony and I seriously un-
derestimated him."

Jake took another long drink from the bottle, needing to
rinse out the bad taste in his mouth that came with just
remembering that night.

"You miscalculated," Katie said, trying to ease the pain
and guilt that would always tear through him at the memory.

"This wasn't a matter of choosing the wrong tie or putting an important paper in the wrong folder. But that's the

way I treated it. I should have known better. In my business mistakes can cost lives and this one nearly did.''

"But, Jake—"

"Katie, it was Candy who almost died."

He saw her eyes widen first in shock, then in realization of what he was going through. He'd always been close to his sister Beth, but Candy was the youngest, the one he'd spent the most time looking after. It was Candy he'd talked to about Katie's leaving. Candy had confided in him, looked up to him, depended on him, put all her faith and trust in him, and when she'd most needed him, he'd let her down.

Katie laid a hand on his forearm. "But she's okay, isn't she?"

"Little thanks to me," he said bitterly. "The guy will get tired of hanging around, I told her. I said he wasn't all there mentally, but he wasn't dangerous. I was wrong on all counts."

Her hand was still there, warm, comforting. A lifeline he longed to latch onto. But this demon would not be banished. She gazed up at him, her eyes filled with compassion and caring, and he vowed to himself that he would protect her.

"Katie, I need to stay here tonight. With you. I need to know you're safe."

Though he hadn't phrased it as a question, Kaitlyn knew he was asking her to put aside her need to be self-sufficient. For him. And this once, she wanted to do it—but deep down she knew she wouldn't be helping him. He needed to conquer this particular fear, and as difficult as it was to refuse his request, this time she had to. For his own good.

"No, Jake," she said quietly.

His jaw clenched. His eyes went hard and cold.

"Jake, you have to be able to let go a little," she said, trying to explain. "You've put in a first-rate security system. I'll have almost instant assistance if I need it. You can even have your security car patrol the neighborhood and I won't complain.''

"Cars," he corrected. "I have more than one car a night on patrol."

She let that soak in a moment. "Someday you'll have to tell me just how big a company Riley Security Services is."

"Let me stay tonight and I'll tell you all about it."

He touched his fingertip to her cheek, the brush of his skin sending her nerve endings skittering. She leaned closer, reading the silent plea in his dark eyes.

"You have to walk away," she told him, the words very hard to get out. "You have to be able to say this is where your responsibility ends."

"Throwing me out will not make that happen."

Jake would still worry about her. Nothing would change that, except being with her. She wouldn't allow that, though. He understood why she wouldn't let him stay, but he didn't like it one damn bit. He downed the rest of the beer in one swallow, then threw the empty bottle into the trash. It landed with a loud and satisfying thunk. He grabbed his gun off the counter, checked the weapon, then held it out to her. She didn't reach for it, just stared at it.

"I want you to take it," he growled. "Keep it by your nightstand. I want to know you have a way of protecting yourself if you need it."

Still she hesitated. "It's been a long time since I handled a weapon," she said.

Jake took her hand and laid the gun in it, making her feel the weight of it. She would remember how to use it in a pinch. It would all come back to her instinctively.

"Keep it by your nightstand," he repeated. "At least do this much for me."

"Jake, I need you to understand why—"

"I understand, all right," he told her sharply. "Your

motives are noble, but I notice you're getting what you want.''

Kaitlyn raised her chin and narrowed her eyes. He'd hit a nerve and he knew it. He was angry and lashing out. She took the gun, stood in silence as he snatched his jacket off the back of a kitchen chair. Jaw clenched painfully, he disarmed the system to walk out, not even tossing the customary order to rearm it over his shoulder.

Chapter 7

He was wrong, Kaitlyn thought as he stalked across the driveway to his Town Car. She hadn't gotten what she'd wanted. She wanted him to understand. But his need to protect her at all costs had gotten in the way of that.

Jake's problem, she decided as she locked doors, turned off lights and reset the security system, was that too few people stood up to him. It was a very rare occasion when he didn't get his way and he didn't know how to deal with matters when that happened.

He had no idea how badly she'd wanted to give in, and if her situation had been the only concern, she would have. But Jake needed to put the past mistake behind him, much as she needed to kick the monkey off her back, as he'd pointed out.

She put the gun on the nightstand, then noticed the card lying there. She picked it up. It was Jake's card. On the back he'd written his home phone number. Kaitlyn smiled to herself, thinking of how he must have put it there earlier in the day. For her. So she would feel safer in the house alone.

A case of overprotectiveness or extreme thoughtfulness? she asked herself, kicking off her shoes. She voted for the latter. Should she have let him stay? she wondered, recalling the anguish in his gaze as he'd spoken of the incident with his sister. At long last she could understand why he felt it was better to do too much rather than too little, especially with those closest to him.

Kaitlyn remembered how he'd been with his family those few months she'd lived with him. He'd saved every penny he could to pay off the mortgage on his mother's house and had insisted she quit her second job. He'd moonlighted, taking a job—as most cops did—with a security firm. That's when he'd begun talking of going into business for himself.

His sister Beth had celebrated her second wedding anniversary soon after Kaitlyn and Jake first met. Kaitlyn recalled that when his brother-in-law mentioned wanting to go into the remodeling business for himself, Jake had passed out business cards to everyone he came into contact with. He'd helped Mark scout out an office location, had gone to the bank with him and had co-signed for a business loan. He'd never appeared on their doorstep empty-handed. Some delicious something from the bakery, baby food, diapers, toys—he'd brought them all at one time or another.

Then there was Candice. Jake's dad had died before Candy's first birthday, so Jake had looked after her almost from the very start. During Kaitlyn's months with Jake, Candy had come over to the apartment nearly every day to share all the little details of her life with him. She would chatter on and he would listen, occasionally worry, always advise. Then she would turn to Kaitlyn and question her about college. Candy had been a year behind Kaitlyn and a business major, also, and she'd had many questions about which classes to take and which professors to avoid.

Those evenings his sister had come over had meant a lot to Jake. The bond between the two was very special. So it was no surprise that a miscalculation on his part bringing harm to her stayed with him still. He had to come to terms with that, forgive himself for it. Kaitlyn had meant to help him along that road, but perhaps she'd only alienated him.

Something she hadn't wanted. Seeing him in handcuffs tonight, she'd realized how much he'd done to help her feel safe. The card on the nightstand was proof that he hadn't originally intended to spend the night. Only when he feared the stakes had been raised did he ask. And he'd asked, not demanded.

The big question in her mind as she got into bed that night was why this mattered so much to her. Why should she care that he make peace with himself—that this particular demon stop tearing him up inside? Why did she hate that she'd hurt him?

And why was she afraid the answers might change her life forever?

The phone rang just before five o'clock in the morning. In bed and still awake, Jake grabbed for it and had it off the hook before it could ring a second time.

"Katie?" he asked, expecting, fearing, the worst.

"Jane," the female voice on the other end corrected. "From the monitor room. You said you wanted to be notified if we got a tripped alarm at the address on 120th Terrace. We got one two minutes ago. We've dispatched a team."

Katie's address, he realized, snapping on the light. If Jane had sent a car, that meant Katie hadn't answered her phone. "I'm on my way."

"ETA for the security team is three minutes. Police should be right behind them."

He would beat them both, Jake vowed, yanking on his clothes and shoes and grabbing a weapon. Pushed by fear, he raced out of the apartment building and to his car, sped down I-35 to 119th Street, left into Hollowbrook, and pulled up to her condo a minute behind the security team. Inside, the alarm was screaming. Outside, the nearby neighbors were turning on lights to see what the commotion was about. None of the floodlights he'd installed had been tripped.

He rushed over to Max Slater and indicated the right side of the corner condo. Max nodded, then started around that side.

"Stay here," Jake told the other man, pointing to the garage and then to the front door.

Drawing his gun, Jake made his way around the condo, visually checking the living room and kitchen windows for signs of entry. Nothing. Around back he glanced at the bedroom windows. Nothing appeared to be disturbed there, either. No lights were on inside. Katie was in there. Alone? Or was Fallon there? She could be hurt, or at the least had to be frightened out of her mind.

He pulled out his key ring and found the extra copy he'd made of the key to her front door. He motioned for Max to watch the sliding glass door, then went around the front. With the second man at his back, he let himself into her house. The alarm continued its deafening blare. Jake shut it off.

The silence was worse, he thought, motioning for the other man to take the kitchen, while he would take the master bedroom. Nothing was out of place in the living room, so he made his way down the darkened hallway. Her bedroom door was open. He inched inside. The bed was empty, the covers rumpled and thrown back. Nothing out of place here, either.

Except that Katie wasn't where she should have been. He checked the closet and the master bath. Nothing and no one. The spare bedroom she used as an office was undisturbed, as well.

He told Max to wait in the kitchen for the police, sent the other man to check the laundry room and garage while he checked the basement. She wasn't in the rec room. He searched the storage area and still came up empty.

"Where the hell is she?" he growled, coming back up the stairs.

"Sir, her car's not in the garage," Martin said.

Jake frowned. Fear gripped his gut tighter. Fallon had taken her somewhere. How the hell would Jake find her? She could be anywhere. Fallon could be doing anything to her. And Jake couldn't stop it.

He should never have left her alone. Should have insisted on twenty-four-hour protection regardless of her wishes. He'd failed her. He couldn't just stand there, he decided, anger at himself mixing with the adrenaline. He had to do something.

"Slater is talking to the police," Martin said.

Jake nodded. Where could she be? The travel agency was closed on Sunday, so she wouldn't have gone in to work. She wouldn't have gone anywhere at five in the morning. She had to be in trouble. Serious trouble, and he was to blame.

He pulled out his cell phone and paged Rob. While he waited for Rob to phone back, he started switching on lights.

"Look through the whole place," he growled at Martin. "Check for signs of a struggle, a fight, a scuffle—anything. I want some answers."

Jake took the windows, starting in the bedroom, examining each for signs of forced entry. Then he checked the garage doors and the sliding glass that opened onto the backyard patio. Not a single sensor seemed to have been disturbed. Frantic, he stood in the middle of the kitchen, trying desperately to figure out how to find her.

When Rob called, Jake quickly related the situation, then asked Rob to put out an APB for Kaitlyn and her car.

"I'm going over to Fallon's address," he told Rob.

"Damn it, Jake, you just got out of jail for assaulting him. You go over there and roust him, you'll end up back behind bars and it'll take more than me and your high-priced attorney to get you out."

"I have to find her," Jake snapped, already heading for the door.

"Anything could have happened. She could have gone out for breakfast for all you know. You said there were no signs of forced entry."

And Katie wouldn't have let Fallon inside, he was sure. But to leave the house at this hour—

"Just meet me at Fallon's house," Jake barked at his friend. "If I get there first, I'm going in without you." He shut off the phone and shoved it into his pocket.

"Sir," Martin said, coming up to him. "There's no sign of her purse."

"Purse?" Jake echoed. "It's not here? You're sure?"

"I've searched everywhere. Her briefcase is in the other bedroom, but there's nothing that looks like a purse."

Did that mean she'd left on her own? Surely Fallon wouldn't have bothered with her purse. But where the hell would she have gone? And why hadn't she disarmed the system first?

Could Fallon have come up with something to lure her out of the house? A very real possibility. Jake didn't waste time wondering how Fallon had done it. He sprinted to his car. He pulled up at Fallon's town house behind Rob and a squad car. The two uniformed officers reached Rob first.

"Take the back," he told them, then glanced at Jake. "You stay here."

"Like hell," Jake snarled. He didn't see Katie's Honda, but that didn't mean she wasn't there, terrified or hurt.

Rob seemed about to protest, but took one look at Jake's determined expression and reconsidered. "All right. We'll take the front. You stay behind me, though."

As much as he hated taking orders under these circumstances, Jake stood behind Rob on the doorstep. He pounded on the door and rang the bell once, then again.

"Break it in," Jake ground out as Rob reached to knock a third time.

Finally a light came on inside. One in the upstairs, then in the living room and on the front porch. The door opened a crack. Fallon peered out. Jake clenched his jaw to keep from losing control. He slid one hand around his back, ready to draw his gun instantly.

"Police," Rob said, showing his badge. "Are you Craig Fallon?"

"Yeah," Fallon said, his voice sounding thick with sleep.

Jake knew it had to be a ruse. Katie had to be there. He wasn't wasting time standing on the porch when she might need him. He pushed by Rob and into the house, ignoring Fallon's sputtering protests.

"What's he doing here?" Fallon shouted as Jake raced up the stairs. "I don't want him in here. Do you hear? I don't want him in my house."

Jake tore through the bedroom and bathroom, not finding Katie or any sign of her. He rushed into the spare bedroom. Katie wasn't there, either.

"What the hell is he doing?" he heard Fallon demand as he came down the stairs. "I'm going to press charges again. I'm phoning my lawyer right now."

"Just shut up," Rob ordered, catching his arm when he started toward the phone. "You're not calling anyone."

Jake searched the downstairs and the basement. Katie was nowhere. Racing back upstairs, he grabbed Fallon by the T-shirt front and pulled him up until they were nose to nose. Fallon's pretty face contorted with rage.

"Go ahead," he taunted. "Hit me and you'll spend more than a couple of hours in jail."

"What have you done with her?" Jake growled, ignoring

the man's words. He had to find Katie. That was his only concern. "Where is she?"

Fallon laughed until Jake tightened his hold on his shirt. "I don't know where she is," he snarled. "But she obviously isn't clearing her agenda with you, is she?"

Rob grabbed Jake's arm before he could smash in Fallon's face. "Let him go, Jake. Let him go," he repeated when Jake didn't comply. "This isn't going to accomplish anything."

"Other than to get you arrested again," Fallon said.

Reluctantly Jake released the other man and let Rob usher him out the door.

"I'll see you in jail again, Riley," Fallon shouted after them. "I'll see you in jail." He slammed his front door shut and switched off the light.

"Go back to whatever you were doing," Rob told the two uniforms. "I'll handle the paperwork in the morning."

They nodded and walked away, obviously grateful they didn't have to file a report.

"We've got to find her," Jake insisted to his friend. He didn't know what to make of the desperation he heard in his own voice.

"Jake, she could be anywhere. Overland Park, Kansas, covers a big area, damn it. We could search for days and not find her if we don't know where to look. For all we know she drove across State Line Road and into Kansas City, Missouri. That covers even more territory."

"Fallon knows something. I know he does."

"Fallon was asleep when we got here. I'd bet money on that. Because you're a friend, I got Wilson to put out an APB on her. That's all we can do for now. Go home. Fallon hasn't done anything to her."

Jake's jaw clenched. He knew Rob was right. But no way was he going home. Not until he knew what had happened to Katie. If she needed him, he would be there. He only hoped he wasn't too late.

* * *

Kaitlyn paced a small spot in the emergency room waiting area. Sharing the room with her were a middle-aged couple, two elderly ladies and a mother with a crying toddler holding his ear. Several times she tried to sit as patiently as they all were, but she never lasted long.

She looked to the treatment area. What were they doing with her mother now? How much longer could it be before the doctor came out and told her what was wrong? All she knew was that her mother was in serious trouble. She'd phoned Kaitlyn, her speech terribly slurred. The panic in her voice had warned Kaitlyn this was caused by more than a few drinks. She'd called 911, had pulled on a pair of jeans and a shirt, then rushed over there, arriving as the paramedics were unloading their equipment.

She'd let them into the small apartment. There they'd found her mother unconscious on the sofa—not a liquor bottle in sight. Only a glass with a small amount of water in the bottom and an empty pill bottle, which one of the paramedics pocketed.

Had she had a heart attack? The paramedics couldn't tell Kaitlyn anything. She'd followed them to the hospital. They'd rushed the stretcher back into the treatment rooms and the nurses had immediately begun work on their patient, telling Kaitlyn the doctor would talk to her as soon as he knew something.

She glanced at the clock on the wall. That had been over an hour ago. She'd signed forms, given them her mother's insurance information, then had waited. And paced.

"Miss Adams."

Finally, Kaitlyn thought, whirling on her heel to see the nurse standing in the doorway. The woman led her back to a room filled with an enormous number of machines. Her mother lay on a gurney, still unconscious, her small body hooked up to several of those machines, one of them a ventilator.

Kaitlyn's footsteps faltered. She swallowed in fear. The doctor, balding already, though he was only in his thirties, finished writing in the chart, handed it to the nurse, then came to stand by Kaitlyn at the foot of the bed.

"Your mother tried to kill herself," he said gently.

Kaitlyn opened her mouth in protest, but no sound came out. She couldn't believe what she was being told. And yet she could. "The pills?" she finally managed to say when she found her voice.

"Xanax," the doctor said. "Prescribed for anxiety attacks. Do you know how many were in the bottle?"

Kaitlyn shook her head.

"Have you noticed that she was unusually depressed?" the doctor asked.

"She's been fighting depression off and on for several years. But I hadn't noticed that she was getting worse."

Of course her mother would have tried to hide it from her for as long as possible. She never wanted to be any trouble to anyone, especially her daughter. That was her way. Kaitlyn had always thought of her as a quiet little mouse, hiding in the corner until the cat was gone.

"We've pumped her stomach and she may need to have kidney dialysis to help remove all the medication from her system. The next twenty-four hours will be critical. We'll put her in intensive care and she'll be closely monitored around the clock." The doctor touched Kaitlyn's shoulder. "I'm afraid I can't tell you how this will progress. You'll just have to wait and see how she responds."

So Kaitlyn followed as two nurse's aides wheeled the gurney up to the intensive care unit. Once her mother was in the room and the ICU nurses had her hooked up to their monitors, they allowed Kaitlyn a few minutes beside her mother's bed.

She touched her mother's frail hand, the one without the IV tube, and stroked her thinning gray-red hair. She didn't know whether her mother could hear her, but she talked to her nonetheless.

"Everything's going to be fine, Mom," she said, as much to convince herself as to offer comfort. "They're taking good care of you, and when you get out, we're going to see that you get better. All you have to do is come back to me."

Then she stood there, listening to the rhythmic noise of the breathing machine until the nurses gently shooed her out to the waiting area.

There were two other families keeping vigil in the small room, so Kaitlyn couldn't pace. She found a corner chair and tried to read a magazine, but the words blurred as she fought back tears. Instead she stared at the pages and reminisced about the happy times she and her mother had shared. She'd understood how difficult it was for Kaitlyn to deal with her father, understood how hard Kaitlyn had tried to please him and how devastated she'd been when she continually failed. Sometimes she'd even nurtured her daughter's developing rebellious streak.

Kaitlyn remembered how, when it was just the two of them, her mother had laughed and sung. Those times they would have such fun. Then shortly before her father was due home, her mother would become withdrawn and nervous. That's when she would dig out the liquor bottle she'd hidden. Kaitlyn would find that her own stomach would knot in dread.

Life was so difficult for her mother. Kaitlyn had thought that the divorce would make things easier for her, but it hadn't. All the little things about living on her own seemed to overwhelm her and even Kaitlyn's help wasn't enough. She'd lost that ability to laugh and sing and it seemed nothing would bring it back. Her father had a lot to answer for, Kaitlyn thought for what had to be the thousandth time that day.

By seven o'clock that evening, one family had left the

ICU waiting room to go to the floor with their loved one. Two more smaller families came to take their places. Still there was no change in her mother's condition.

"She could be like this for several hours," the nurse told her. "Why don't you go home and get something to eat and rest? We'll notify you immediately if there's any change and you can call us at any time if you're worried."

In the end Kaitlyn decided she would go home for a short while. There'd been one enchilada and some rice left over from the dinner Jake had made last night and she was hungry just thinking about it. Then she needed to phone Mary to fill her in on what was happening, let her know that she might not be in the office much the next few days.

She pulled into her garage several minutes later, fatigued and drained, afraid that even if her mother came through this, she would try suicide again, and possibly succeed. Kaitlyn had to help her find the joy in life she'd lost so many years ago.

With a heavy sigh, Kaitlyn went into the house, set her purse on the countertop and opened the fridge. She'd just taken the enchilada out when the alarm system let out an earsplitting wail. Hands over her ears, she rushed to punch in her code. The screeching stopped and she let out a weary breath. She was so exhausted she hadn't even thought about safety gadgets.

Almost instantly the phone rang. Knowing it was Jake's office calling to make certain she was all right, she dug in a drawer for the card with her response code. She picked up the phone and read the number to the woman on the other end.

"Mr. Riley has been notified and is on his way," the woman said.

"Mr. Riley?" Kaitlyn repeated. "Why? I forgot to punch in the code, that's all."

"He's asked to be notified whenever the system is activated," the woman replied, then hung up.

Kaitlyn ran a hand across her forehead. She wasn't up for company, wasn't sure this was such a good time to deal with Jake—a man who could make her want to forget all her hard-learned lessons about relationships. Now more than ever, seeing what a relationship had cost her mother, Kaitlyn needed to stick to her resolve not to tie her fate to that of another person.

She put the leftovers in a glass dish, laid it in the microwave, then set the timer just as the doorbell rang. Wiping her hands on a towel, she walked over to open the door.

The sight that greeted her made her take a step backward. Jake. Unshaven. His hair finger-combed and falling across his forehead. His clothes badly wrinkled. His eyes blazing fury. She took another step back, realized what she'd done, then stood her ground.

"Where have you been all day?" he growled, pulling the door out of her hand and shutting it firmly.

He looked dangerous to the core. She had to resist the urge to run from him. The microwave chimed. She turned on her heel and walked to the kitchen without answering him.

"I asked you a question," he said, storming into the kitchen after her.

"Jake, I'm extremely tired, physically and mentally. I don't want to get into a fight with you because I came in and forgot to punch in my code."

"That was tonight. Just now. What about when you left right before five o'clock this morning?"

He knew what time she'd left? Frowning, she took the steaming dish out of the microwave, then slowly turned to face him. "What do you mean?" she asked, fearing she knew the answer.

He leaned on the countertop, one hand on either side of her, pinning her to that spot. He towered over her, dark and menacing. Anger poured from him.

"I have been worried since five this morning, wondering

where you were, what made you leave this house...."
When the intensity in his eyes made her look away, he
caught her chin and forced her to meet his gaze. "Whether
Fallon had hurt you."

"Fallon?" She blinked under the deepening scrutiny of
his gaze.

"When the alarm went off this morning and I couldn't
find you, I went over to his house."

"Jake!" she cried out, remembering he'd been ordered
to stay away from the other man as part of his release
conditions. "Why? You could have been arrested again."

"I had to find you. To make sure you were all right. And
I couldn't sit around waiting. I had to do something. I've
been checking every place I thought you might be. I even
got Rob to put out an APB on you."

He'd been through hell and back. She could see it in his
eyes, in everything about him. He'd done it for her, to make
certain she was safe. And he'd gone through it all for nothing, anticipating a catastrophe as usual, never thinking there
might be a perfectly logical, and non-life-threatening, ex-
planation for her forgetting to disarm the system before
leaving the house.

She wanted to hug him for caring and rake him over the
coals for going overboard with the worrying. She laid her
palm along the side of his roughened jaw.

"Jake, I'm so sorry," she said sincerely. "Sorry you had
to go through all this. I should have had someone else put
in the alarm system."

His eyes narrowed. "What are you talking about? This
isn't a case of a faulty system."

"I didn't mean to imply that it was. It's just that I know
how you are and I know how I am. I should have figured
that something was bound to happen sooner or later to
make me forget the alarm and I should have known that
you would overreact when it did."

He leaned an inch closer. "Overreact?"

"I was perfectly safe. But you didn't know where I was, so you let it eat you up inside all day." She sighed. "Look at you, Jake," she said gently. "You're a basket case. And it's totally uncalled for."

"I care—"

"I know, but it's not your place to. For all you know, my boyfriend could have come into town this morning and I was so excited at the prospect of seeing him again I forgot the procedure for leaving home."

His frown changed to a full scowl. "You're not seeing anyone. You would have mentioned it, because you're so ethical in everything. And...I asked Shelly."

She shook her head. "The point to all this is that you have to set limits. I did not hire you as my bodyguard."

"Katie—"

"This was not your responsibility." She punched him in the chest with her index finger, touched at his concern and exasperated with it, as well. "Your job was to install the system, and once that was done, your job was over."

"So when that alarm went off this morning, I should have ignored it?"

"You should have let your people handle it. Without you. They would have assumed, and rightly so, that I left the house in such a hurry I forgot about the procedure."

"And when they reported it to me, as they're supposed to do with incidents like this? What should I have done then? I can't turn off my caring just like that." He snapped his fingers.

"You're not supposed to care, Jake. Our relationship is a businessman-client one. No more."

She was serious, Jake realized, running a hand over the back of his neck. He'd just spent fourteen of the worst hours of his life and she was telling him he had no right to the feelings that had torn him up inside. It just didn't work that way with him. Never had. Never would. Maybe it was time to stop trying to talk to her and show her what he felt, instead.

He pulled her into his arms and lowered his mouth to hers. She stiffened. Her mouth opened on a protest, but he merely took full advantage of her surprise to slide his tongue inside. He sampled her sweetness, savoring the tastes and textures, assuring himself that she was alive and whole. He shouldn't be handling things this way, but right now it was the only way he could let her know just what her absence had meant to him.

He'd thought he had lost her, but pressing her body to his, he realized he was the one who was lost. She was telling him he shouldn't care, but it was far too late for that. He wanted her. Needed her. The feeling went all the way to his soul and there wasn't a damned thing either one of them could do about it.

The kiss was rough and in it Kaitlyn could feel his desperation. In a very short time her resistance slipped away. As his hand wound through the strands of her hair, angling her head so he could deepen the kiss, she gave up the struggle. She tasted all the anguish he'd endured today and she couldn't deny him. Couldn't deny herself.

She wanted this. Had longed to feel his arms around her all through this long and difficult day, though she'd refused to admit it even to herself. Her breath snagged when he caressed her nape. His other hand slid lower to crush her hip to his and her heartbeat quickened. The soft voice of reason was drowned out by the strength of desire, the need to give comfort, to experience all his passion.

Her breasts were pressed against his hard chest. His breath was warm, his arms around her were strong and his mouth had gentled. She moaned softly and his embrace tightened. She ran her hand through his thick hair, loving the feel of it.

She sagged against him, let him press her body to the length of his. His hand traveled so slowly to the base of her spine. His hardness pushed against her and she felt a low, burning need flare to life within her. She'd wanted him before, but never like this. His heat enveloped her. He cupped her breast in his large hand and the sensations ricocheted through her. Her head spun; her heart raced frantically.

She remembered this all so well and yet she might have been experiencing it for the first time, the sensations were so sharp. But how often had she been in this position before? She'd paid a very dear price for giving in to the longings he could bring to life so easily.

She could never resist his passion, withstand her own need for him. And he knew that. Was he using it against her?

She made herself think of her mother lying, desolate and possibly dying, in that hospital bed, then she imagined herself in that very position. She pushed at Jake's hard, unyielding chest with all her strength. He finally allowed her to break the kiss.

His breathing was ragged. His eyes as he looked down at her were still dark with the strength of his desire for her.

"Now tell me that you don't care that I went through hell today," he demanded with a growl. "Tell me that it doesn't matter to you."

"It matters," she said. "But I will not let you manipulate me this way again."

Jake scowled. "This wasn't manipulation—"

"Wasn't it?" she countered. "This was the one area in which you could get me under your thumb and you still can. You can make me needy, clingy, mindless to the point that I'll let you do my thinking for me."

"That's not…." What could he say to make her understand? "I wanted you to know how I feel, to make you understand why it tore me up to think you might be in danger."

"And I do," she said quietly. "But next you're going

to ask me to check with you whenever I want to leave the house. To let you know every move I make.''

He didn't answer. But he didn't have to. She was on target and she knew it.

"Katie, I…" He needed to know she was all right, safe, unharmed, every minute of the day. She needed room to breathe, to be free from restraints. There was no compromise. But there was passion and caring and he couldn't ignore either.

The ring of the telephone interrupted him, but it didn't matter. He couldn't find the words he needed to say. He stepped aside and allowed her to get the phone.

"Hello," she said, her voice surprisingly shaky when it had been so strong and confident only a moment ago.

Jake frowned. She listened to the voice on the other end of the line and he saw the color drain slowly from her face. Fallon? he wondered, half-ready to grab the phone out of her hand, but her grip on it was white-knuckled.

"Yes, do what you have to do," she said. "I'm on my way back there right now."

She hung up the phone, took a glance around the kitchen, spotted her purse and snatched it up. Thankfully she didn't make him ask the questions that were spinning through his mind.

"That's the hospital," she told him, pausing to look at him as she headed for the garage. "My mother. They've called a code blue on her."

Chapter 8

Jake couldn't miss the sadness and worry in her face and longed to go with her. To be there for her. But she would turn him down, he knew, so he didn't ask. He just let her go.

Once he'd heard her pull out of the garage, he leaned back against the counter and replayed their conversation in his mind. Her message had been loud and clear. They didn't have a relationship. She was the client and he was providing a service. That was all, according to her words.

But her response to his kiss told another story. She wanted him, needed him, as much as he wanted and needed her. Physically. Emotionally, though she refused to get involved, refused to let him in. Or rather, she refused to admit that she still had feelings for him.

She cared, all right. Last night when those cops had arrested him, she'd been concerned for him, not for herself and what Fallon could have done to her. Then Jake had told her about Candy and she'd felt the pain he went through each time he thought about his part in that incident. She'd tried to do what she could to ease that pain. For him.

He hadn't been very appreciative at the time, but lying awake in bed last night, he'd thought about her actions and her motives. Regardless of what she said about their relationship being business only, she still had feelings for him.

And he still cared for her. Cared that she was in some hospital, worried whether her mother would pull through, and she was going through it alone. He couldn't bear that.

He remembered how close she and her mother were, how much Kaitlyn had worried about her. He could picture Katie, pacing relentlessly, biting her bottom lip the way she did when she was very upset. He thought about the food on the counter behind him and knew she hadn't eaten all day. She needed someone to take care of her.

He pushed away from the counter. To hell with where she said his responsibilities began and ended. He couldn't take this wondering what she was going through. Couldn't stand knowing she was alone. His actions would undoubtedly earn him another lecture, but he couldn't turn off his concern.

He picked up the phone and dialed a friend at the ambulance company. "Mick, you got a call, probably from Overland Park, just before 5 a.m. A woman in her fifties, Gloria Adams. I don't know the address...."

It took a few moments for Mick to check the records and find the information. "Here she is. Apparent attempted suicide."

Suicide? Katie had to be frantic with worry. No wonder she hadn't given the alarm a thought.

"Where did you transport to?" he asked his friend.

"Shawnee Mission Hospital."

Jake took a deep breath, thought once more about doing this Katie's way, then decided he couldn't. If she were going to the movies or out to dinner with a friend, that would be one thing. But sitting in a hospital, not knowing if a

loved one would make it through the night, that was another. He'd been through that. It was something she
shouldn't go through alone.

Kaitlyn stood beside her mother's bed, fighting back her
tears. The doctor said they'd stabilized her mother's heartbeat. The machine mounted over the bed beeped a steady,
even rhythm. But they'd been very emphatic that the patient
wasn't out of the woods yet.

Gloria Adams was extremely pale. Her thin body was
full of tubes and needles, fluids going in and out. She'd
undergone the kidney dialysis, then her blood pressure had
dropped dramatically and they'd almost lost her. Could lose
her still.

"Hey, Mom," she said softly as she held the older woman's hand. "You've got to pull through this. There's so
much I want to do with you. Remember you're going to
Hawaii with me in the fall? We've already made the res-
ervations and everything. You wanted a real muumuu and
a lei with real flowers. We were going to sit on the beach
and watch the sunset from a boat."

Of course there was no response. Not even the flutter of
an eyelid. Kaitlyn sighed deeply, then tried again. She had
no idea how long the nurses had let her stay there, talking
soft words of encouragement to her mother, but when they
finally came in to take vital signs and draw blood, her legs
ached from standing in one place.

"Why don't you get something from one of the vending
machines?" one of the nurses suggested. "We'll call you
if there's any change at all."

With a slight nod and one last glance at her mother,
Kaitlyn walked out of the room. Would she ever hear her
mother's voice again? Ever hear her laugh, see her smile
even a little? Her mother had gone through a lot in her
fifty-two years, but she'd never been able to hold it together
for long.

Kaitlyn pushed through the door of the ICU and walked across the hall to the waiting room. She had the place to herself at the moment, except for one large-framed man standing with his back to her. There was something very familiar about the width of his shoulders, his height, the dark brown of his uncombed hair. Then he turned and her breath caught.

It was all she could do to keep from going to him, keep from rushing into his arms. She made herself stand her ground, knowing she had to. The risks of leading with her emotions were too great, the stakes too high.

But how she wanted to feel his arms around her, holding her, comforting her, reassuring her. How she wanted to lean into his strength. She knew she had to be strong.

She should be angry with him for being here. Yet when she looked at his unshaven face and saw the concern there, all she could summon was gratitude. Fatigue lined the corners of his wonderful mouth and dark eyes. His wrinkled suit slacks and shirt were the same ones he'd put on Saturday morning.

She shook her head. "You should be home catching up on all the sleep you've missed," she said quietly.

"I wouldn't be able to sleep, knowing you were up here, worried about your mother."

She crossed over to where he stood, took his hand in hers and tugged until he sat in the chair next to her. "Jake, we can't go through this a second time. We still wouldn't be able to make it work. You know that."

He nodded. "I told myself that same thing on the way over here. I'm just borrowing trouble. But, Katie, I can't deal with that now. Later, when your mother's doing better... We'll sort all this out then."

She sat back in the chair and sighed heavily. "I'm not sure she wants to make it."

Jake covered both her hands with his and squeezed gently. She looked up at him, tears filling her eyes.

"Thank you for coming," she whispered as one tear trickled down her cheek.

He wrapped his arm around her shoulders and pulled her close, letting her cry against his shirtfront. Later she would be strong, would call up her resolve and would walk away from this temptation and danger he represented. But for now, it felt so good to be held by him. She needed his support, the comfort he offered so generously. She needed a shoulder to cry on and his was wide enough and strong enough to handle all her troubles.

So she wouldn't think about the future right now. She would simply take what he gave her, what she needed. When her sobs abated, he pulled out a handkerchief and gave it to her. Other family members in the waiting room, needing to do something to help their loved ones, tried over and over to press them to eat or drink. Once Jake would have done the same with her. This time, though, he just held her, as if sensing that was what she most needed.

"I should send you home," she said sometime before dawn. "You haven't had any sleep in so long."

"Do you want me to leave?" he asked, his chin on the top of her head as she leaned against his chest.

She sighed, knowing the wise thing to say, then just said what she wanted to. "No. I don't want you to go."

She felt him let out the breath he'd been holding and his arms tightened around her. She'd been like this for hours, taking strength and comfort from him. Later she would have to deal with some serious fallout, but each time that thought crept into her mind, she shoved it aside.

"Miss Adams," a woman called from the doorway.

Kaitlyn raised her head and braced herself, expecting the worst. Then she noted the nurse smiled slightly.

"Your mother is awake," she said. "Would you like to see her?"

Kaitlyn looked to Jake, her heart pounding furiously. Af-

SILHOUETTE®

AN IMPORTANT MESSAGE FROM THE EDITORS OF SILHOUETTE®

Dear Reader,

Because you've chosen to read one of our fine romance novels, we'd like to say "thank you"! And, as a **special** way to thank you, we've selected <u>four more</u> of the <u>books</u> you love so well, **and** a Cuddly Teddy Bear to send you absolutely *FREE!*

Please enjoy them with our compliments...

Leslie Wainger

Senior Editor,
Silhouette Intimate Moments

P.S. And because <u>we value our</u> customers, we've attached something extra inside ...

EDITOR'S
FREE
GIFT
SEAL
THANK YOU

PEEL OFF SEAL AND PLACE INSIDE

HOW TO VALIDATE YOUR
EDITOR'S FREE GIFT
"THANK YOU"

1. Peel off gift seal from front cover. Place it in space provided at right. This automatically entitles you to receive four free books and a Cuddly Teddy Bear.

2. Send back this card and you'll get brand-new Silhouette Intimate Moments® novels. These books have a cover price of $3.99 each, but they are yours to keep absolutely free.

3. There's no catch. You're under no obligation to buy anything. We charge nothing — ZERO — for your first shipment. And you don't have to make any minimum number of purchases — not even one!

4. The fact is thousands of readers enjoy receiving books by mail from the Silhouette Reader Service™ months before they're available in stores. They like the convenience of home delivery and they love our discount prices!

5. We hope that after receiving your free books you'll want to remain a subscriber. But the choice is yours — to continue or cancel, anytime at all! So why not take us up on our invitation, with no risk of any kind. You'll be glad you did!

6. Don't forget to detach your FREE BOOKMARK. And remember...just for validating your Editor's Free Gift Offer, we'll send you FIVE MORE gifts, *ABSOLUTELY FREE!*

© 1991 HARLEQUIN ENTERPRISES LTD.

ter the hours of worry she could hardly believe her ears. Jake gave her a nudge to her feet.

"Go ahead," he told her. "I'll be here when you get back."

Kaitlyn realized she didn't want to leave him behind. He'd been with her through the worst. She wanted him by her side for this, too. She grasped his hand. "Come with me."

Surprised and pleased, Jake got up and followed her into the intensive care unit. He hadn't expected her to accept his comfort, to let him stay with her, but she had. He hadn't expected her to cry, to let him hold her. He didn't think she would even lean on him. It felt so wonderful, so perfect. The day of reckoning would come soon enough, but for now he wouldn't think of that.

The nurse led them back to a corner room, peeked inside to let the patient know she had visitors, then quietly left the three of them alone. Kaitlyn's mother lay on the bed, eyes closed, her mouth drawn in a tight, thin line.

"Mom," Katie said softly as she leaned over the bed.

"You should have left me," Gloria Adams whispered, her voice hoarse from the recently removed breathing tube. "You shouldn't have brought me here."

"But, Mom," Katie said, a note of desperation in her voice. "You called me. You didn't really want to do this.... It's the depression...."

Her mother didn't answer. Katie sighed and turned to Jake. He gave her a nod of encouragement.

"Mom," she said. "Jake is here with me. You remember Jake?"

Slowly Mrs. Adams opened her eyes and looked at her daughter. Katie inclined her head toward Jake, standing at the foot of the bed. He walked over to stand beside Katie so her mother could see him. She stared at him for a long moment, then turned back to her daughter.

"Jake Riley?"

Kaitlyn nodded. "Remember Shelly?" she asked her mother, trying very hard to sound cheerful and upbeat. "Turns out her fiancé and Jake are good friends. Jake's going to be the best man at the wedding."

"I always thought you two would be married," she said, her voice slightly sad.

"No," Katie said gently, "but I think we might manage being friends." She glanced at Jake for confirmation.

"Definitely." He smiled at her, thinking that wasn't enough, but it would be a start. "When you get out of here," he told Mrs. Adams, "I'll cook you and Katie the best meal you've ever had."

Katie squeezed his hand in silent thanks. "If the last meal he cooked for me is anything to go by, we're in for a real treat, Mom."

Katie did most of the talking, working hard to cheer her mother up and give her something, anything, to look forward to. Jake listened, added encouragement whenever he could. Then soon the nurse came in and suggested they let the patient rest.

"You and Jake look as if you've been up for days," Mrs. Adams told them. "Have you been here with Kaitlyn all this time?" she asked Jake.

He was about to shake his head, but Katie answered for him. "He's been here ever since he found out," she said. "He was worried about you."

Her mother nodded slightly. "If anything, he was more worried about you, dear," she told her daughter, then turned to him. "Maybe you'll come back. And maybe you'll look after my Kaitlyn...."

Katie gave her a wry smile. "That's Jake's specialty." She leaned down and kissed her mother's cheek. "We'll see you later today."

She took Jake's arm and together they walked back out of ICU. In the hall, she paused to take her first really deep breath.

"She's going to be all right," she said, as if still trying to convince herself of that.

"They'll treat the depression," Jake said, steering her toward the elevators. "The medication will help stabilize her and the doctors will watch her. And you'll be there to keep an eye on her."

"Hmm." She tightened her grip on his arm. "Thank you for going in the room with me. She really brightened when she heard you were there. You always had a way with her. Always made her smile."

"I could help you keep an eye on her," he offered as they walked across the hospital lobby.

Outside, the sun was coming up over the horizon. It had been a little more than twenty-four hours since the call that Katie's alarm had gone off. A very strenuous day for them both, and now in a couple of hours they would both have to head for the office. He would have to see what he could arrange on that restraining order, but decided not to mention it to her until necessary.

"I would appreciate your help with Mother," she told him, then fell silent as they walked across the parking lot and over to her car. Once she'd unlocked the door and had gotten in behind the wheel, she looked up at him. "I meant what I said about us being friends. I think we might be able to handle that."

"Meaning that anything more is out of the question?"

She nodded. "I can't give you anything more, Jake. It's just too big a risk for me. I don't want either one of us to get hurt."

And she was sure that would happen. He could hear it in her voice. Perhaps she was right. They'd tried it once, and when it fell apart, it had taken them both a long time to pick up the pieces. He was probably foolish to think they had a better chance the second time around.

"I'll follow you home," he said, closing her door and waiting for her to lock it.

Kaitlyn wanted to tell him no, but decided he wouldn't listen. He had to know she made it home all right. Tomorrow she would start insisting they put their relationship into perspective, a perspective that was best for them both. She would start bringing her feelings in line, corralling them, giving them boundaries.

Tonight—and this morning—it had felt good to lean on him, to have him by her side. But now it was time for her to stand on her own again, she decided as she pulled into her driveway. She paused a moment to let the garage door raise all the way, waved goodbye to Jake, then drove inside.

Her car phone rang as the door was on its way down. "Don't forget the alarm," Jake told her.

With a laugh she thanked him and hung up.

In the laundry room, she kicked off her running shoes and dropped her purse on the dryer. She could grab a couple of hours of sleep before going into the office, maybe three if she went in a little late.

Deciding that was what she would do, she walked into the bedroom, unsnapped her jeans, then sat on the edge of the bed to push them off the rest of the way. Just as she kicked them off, the phone rang. She smiled to herself, wondering what she was going to do about Jake and his protectiveness.

"Hello, Jake. What did I forget?" she asked.

The voice that answered was not Jake's.

"So Riley knows you're home, does he?" Craig Fallon snarled. "He was real hot and bothered when he couldn't find you. Did he tell you that?"

Kaitlyn felt her stomach knot. She thought of Jake, worried about her, confronting Fallon. Thought of the man smirking at Jake's concern. It made her blood boil.

"What do you want?" she demanded.

"To tell you to stay away from him. You're mine once we're married. And I don't want Riley in the way. Got it?"

She slammed the receiver down in its cradle, staring at

the phone in repulsion. Hers. The man felt she belonged to him. Thought she would marry him, and nothing anyone said could make him see reason. Somehow, though, she would have to make him understand she wanted nothing to do with him. But how?

She debated calling Jake, then decided she couldn't. For her own well-being she had to learn to handle this on her own. She stretched out on the bed, but as soon as she pulled up the sheet to cover her, the phone rang again. There was a chance it might be Jake, she reasoned, and he would be worried if she didn't answer.

She picked up the receiver and said a quiet, "Hello."

"It won't do you any good to hang up on me," Fallon said. "I'm not going away."

"Why me?" Kaitlyn asked in exasperation. "You don't even know me and I don't want anything to do with you. Why don't you find someone else?"

"Because I've wanted you from the first time I saw that beautiful red hair of yours—"

Kaitlyn hung up again, unable to stomach hearing any more. She finally had her answer to why he'd latched onto her, but it didn't do a thing for her peace of mind. Or for her peace in general. The phone rang again. This time she let the answering machine pick up the call. Fallon apparently didn't appreciate that. He called back over and over again. After more than a half hour of that, Kaitlyn decided to forget sleep, and shower and dress for the office, instead.

Once he finished helping Rob move many of his things into Shelly's house, Jake opened a bottle of beer and carried it out onto the deck in time to see Kaitlyn walking around the back of the house. She was dressed for the warm weather—a pair of navy shorts that showed off her long legs and hugged her slender hips, and a blue knit T-shirt that clung to her curves. She'd pulled her hair up. A big, white clip held it in place.

His first thought was that she appeared fatigued. Her eyes were tired and her shoulders seemed to slump slightly. It had been four days since he'd sat with her in that hospital waiting room. Monday morning they'd finally gotten the restraining order and he'd taken Fallon's mug photos to the security man in her office building. Since then Jake had given her space, figuring he needed some time and distance to evaluate where his feelings for her were leading him.

In the end he decided he'd better slow himself down. He wanted her. He doubted that would ever change. However, she was determined to limit him to friendship. He had to face the fact that she might never offer him more, and that even if she did, they still needed very different things from a relationship.

So, he hadn't called her, had only checked on her through third parties—Shelly, Mary, her mother. He'd paid the price in worry and frustration. Seeing her now he was ready to change his mind about giving her—and himself—this space. He wanted to go to her, hug her fiercely, but he forced himself to lean casually against the deck railing and remain there as she walked up the three wood stairs.

She greeted Rob and Shelly, then smiled at Jake. "How are you, Jake?"

"I'm fine," he said, longing to wrap an arm around her and tug her to his side, but knowing he couldn't give in to that longing. "It'll be a while before I recover from moving Rob's piano over here, though."

"Don't wimp out on me," Rob said. "This weekend you promised to help me dig that hole for the basketball goal."

Jake groaned. "You know, I think I promised Katie I would help her paint this weekend," he said with a wink to her.

"Won't work," Shelly said. "I already know she's going to San Francisco tonight and won't be back until Sunday evening."

"San Francisco?" Jake asked, glancing sharply at her.

He wasn't sure traveling was such a good idea under her current circumstances. He had no facts or stats to back him up, just a gut feeling that he didn't want her halfway across the country.

Katie nodded. "I've had this trip planned for a month now. Going to check out the changes the airline has made, check out the hotel. Going to get away by myself for a couple of days."

"What about your mom?" Jake asked.

Katie stared at him, eyes narrowed slightly. "She says she'll feel guilty if I stay because of her, then in the same breath she says that you will be there to look after her while I'm gone."

Jake cleared his throat, unsure how to take that pointed look she gave him. "You said you would appreciate it if I helped look after her."

"That was before I knew she was your number one fan," she replied around a quiet laugh. She turned to their friends. "When I go up to the hospital, Mom spends most of the time singing his praises." She mimicked her mother's soft, wistful voice. "'Jake was here again,' she says. *Again.* 'Oh, and he talked that awful Hilda into letting him take me for a walk outside. He's so charming and such a nice man—'"

"So I've got charm," Jake said. "Nothing wrong with that."

"Well, you've got it in spades." Kaitlyn looped her arm through his. "Mom loves the flowers you sent. The ones I brought her, she gave to the woman in the next bed. Yours she puts on the bed tray so she can see them all the time."

"What can I say? The lady has taste," Jake said proudly, pleased that Katie seemed to appreciate his efforts to help her mother.

"Watch out," Shelly said, grinning, "it sounds as if she'll have you two married by Halloween." With that she took Rob's arm and tugged him toward the sliding glass doors that opened into the kitchen. "Time to put the chicken breasts on the grill."

Married? Jake thought as the two walked inside. Damn, but he liked the sound of that. It wasn't very likely, though.

Katie's eyes had filled with momentary panic at the mere mention of it. Friendship was all she wanted to give him. So the smart man wouldn't hold out hope for any more than that, wouldn't plot how to go about changing her mind. The smart man would go about business as usual. He wondered just how smart he was.

He moved to stand in front of her and leaned forward, arms on either side of her as he rested them on the deck railing behind her.

"What are you doing?" she asked in surprise.

He thought he heard her breath snag a little.

"Saying a proper hello," he answered, flashing her a rakish grin. She smelled so good.

"Improper," she scolded, her voice definitely shaky. "We're friends, that's all. Remember?"

"I didn't agree to that. Not completely."

"Jake—"

"Relax, Katie," he said, leaning close to her ear, trying hard to resist the temptation to nuzzle. "My only intention is to say that you look tired and ask what's going on."

"Then why are you…"

"I figured that when I'm this close, it makes you nervous—too nervous to evade answering me."

Nervous was right, Kaitlyn thought. Nervous and downright jittery. She could feel his breath, warm against the side of her face. The woodsy scent of his aftershave was hypnotic. Her pulse was thrumming. She wanted to lean closer still, to wrap her arms around him. Hot as the August evening was, she still wanted to feel his heat. His nearness short-circuited her thinking, made her forget her priorities.

"So, what's kept you from sleeping, Katie?" he persisted, his voice too close, too seductive.

Kaitlyn struggled to think. "Phone," she finally managed to blurt out. She pulled a card out of her pocket and handed it to him, pointing to the number she'd written on the back. "That's my new phone number. It's unlisted, so don't lose it."

He scowled at her for a long moment as her words sank in. "Fallon's been calling you?"

She shuddered, recalling the number of calls he'd made in the past few nights. "Starts about ten minutes after I get home and keeps going until I leave for work in the morning."

Jake slammed the heel of his hand against the railing. Kaitlyn jumped. "Damn it, Katie. Why didn't you tell me about this?"

"Tell you I was getting annoying phone calls?" she snapped back at him. "What could you have done to stop it? Nothing, except tell me to change my number. So I handled it myself. That's what's bothering you, isn't it? You always hated it when I handled things on my own."

His jaw clenched. "It has nothing to do with who handled what. I'm upset—"

"So am I now," she muttered.

"Because you didn't ask for my advice. You ask your accountant for financial advice, don't you?"

She nodded.

"Then why is it so difficult for you to ask for mine. I'm an expert in this field—"

"That's what you keep telling me," she noted sharply, then softened slightly. "Jake, I didn't want you to worry."

"I'm the one in the protection business, not you."

"Yes, but when you worry, you usually hover," she insisted. "I...I didn't want to deal with that."

He looked to the heavens in what was probably a silent plea for patience with her and her reasoning. Seeing him upset was becoming more and more difficult for her to take. What was happening with her?

"All right," she said. "Pretend I'm asking you now. What would you advise?"

That you move in with me, that you let me deal with this situation, that you turn it all over to me and let me take care of you. That's what he wanted. But Jake knew he would have to settle for a whole lot less.

"That we put the son of a b—" He cut himself short, breathed deeply to get hold of his temper and his concern for her safety. Things with Fallon would only escalate from here, he was certain. "That we call the police and have the bastard arrested."

"Arrested? For phoning me?" She frowned.

"The restraining order," he said with strained patience. "It says he can't try to contact you or harass you in any way. Phone included." He took another deep breath and cast her a sympathetic look. "I'm not surprised you don't remember. We were both zombies that day we went to court. It's my job to take care of those details for you."

Kaitlyn didn't like the sound of that. He was taking over, or would if she let him. "Your job," she said, "was to install—"

"My job is whatever I make it," he declared. "As your 'friend' my main concern is getting this jerk out of your life."

"Then call someone and have him picked up," she said, aware her voice was rising sharply.

She'd had a very rough few days between worry about her mother and then the phone calls, and being without Jake. She'd needed to handle matters on her own, to take charge. Now here he was, angry because she didn't ask for his advice.

She'd leaned so heavily on him at the hospital. She found herself wanting to lean more, but she knew how disastrous that could be. So she had to pull back. He had no idea how very difficult that had been for her, and how frightening it had been to find herself becoming dependent.

"I would have him arrested," Jake rasped. "But we have to have proof. If you had asked me, which you didn't, I would have told you to keep your old number and let the answering machine take his calls—"

"I did. He filled up the tape each night." She had wondered if the man ever slept.

Jake's eyes narrowed. "Tell me you didn't erase the tapes each night."

"I didn't know I should keep them." She certainly hadn't wanted to hear the chilling, angry things Craig Fallon had spouted, let alone preserve them. She just wanted him gone.

"Because you never asked anyone." He slammed his hand on the railing once more. "Damn it, Katie…"

"Don't swear at me, Jake Riley." She put both palms against his solid chest and pushed until he backed up a step. With that tiny bit of room, she shoved past him and rushed into the house.

"Drinks are in the fridge," Shelly said over her shoulder as Kaitlyn entered the kitchen, then she went back to instructing Rob on how often to baste the chicken breasts.

It was obvious Shelly and Rob didn't need her help, but Kaitlyn didn't want to go back outside. She needed to do something—she was too agitated to stand still. She reached into the fridge, pulled out a wine cooler, twisted off the cap and had managed a swallow, when Jake stormed into the house. He spotted her in the doorway to the living room and turned his menacing gaze her way.

"I swore at the situation," he said with controlled fury. "Not at you."

"I distinctly heard my name," she challenged, fighting down the memories of the distant past. She had to remind herself she was no longer a little girl in her father's house. She straightened and gave Jake her most determined look.

"I took charge of my life," she said with all the firmness she could muster in the face of his fury. Why did his anger with her always upset her so much? "Maybe I didn't do exactly what you would have done, but you have no right to be angry with me because I didn't come running to you."

"Lovers' quarrel?" Shelly asked from the counter by the sink.

Jake and Kaitlyn whirled to see their friends watching them with avid curiosity. "No," they both said simultaneously.

Shelly and Rob exchanged glances, then began gathering up the bowls and plates from the counter. "We'll just get the chicken started," Shelly said, shooing Rob out onto the deck.

Jake waited until the door shut behind them, then set his beer bottle on the table. He had to resist the urge to shake Katie. His temper was getting the best of him and that would do no good with her. He ran his hand across the back of his neck and counted to twenty.

"I'm angry because you won't come to me when the problem falls into my area of expertise," he said, striving for calm.

"You can tell yourself that," she insisted, "but you're furious because I didn't come cowering to you, period. I didn't let you take care of me."

"All right," he barked, acknowledging to himself, and to her, the truth of what she'd said. "All right. I admit you're right, but in return I want you to admit that this situation is getting serious. Was he hostile on the phone, verbally abusive—"

"Livid over the restraining order? Fighting mad over your interference? He was all that and more," she said quietly.

Jake nodded once, grateful that she was cooling down enough to listen to what he had to say. "You have to work with me on this, Katie. I've nearly gone crazy this week, afraid something would happen once they served that restraining order.''

''It started before then,'' she told him. ''At first he mainly wanted to gloat that you didn't know where I was that day, and to tell me...'' Her voice caught. She took a deep breath and continued. ''Tell me that I 'belong' to him.''

Jake felt every muscle in his body tense. Why did she *have* to go through this on her own? he wanted to demand, but he bit his tongue. She was talking to him and he wouldn't risk having her withdraw now.

''Okay,'' he said, ''you cut off one avenue for him to vent on you. He may start phoning at the office.''

''He's tried that a couple of times already, but Mary recognizes his voice now and she doesn't let him through.''

''Then he's going to switch tactics. He may start following you.''

She stiffened, eyeing him as if trying to decide what his motives were.

''I'm not saying that to scare you,'' he said carefully. ''But I should have talked to you earlier about the various situations that are bound to come up and the best ways to handle them. I should have told you to save the answering machine tapes, for instance. Should have explained that we—you—could have had him arrested.''

''Why didn't you?'' she asked, still wary.

''I wanted to spare you for a while. You had your mother in the hospital, had been worried whether she would make it. I wanted to give you a break. And...I'd hoped we had established a working relationship. That you would call if something happened. I was counting on that.''

''Really?'' she asked, considering his words. Had he truly refrained from checking up on her despite his worry over her safety? Had he really been that considerate of her feelings and needs? And had he waited, giving her a chance to make the first move? But when she hadn't followed his "plan," he'd been very upset with her—and probably with himself for doing it her way in the first place. Would he try to accommodate her again, or would he revert to his past methods?

"When you get back from San Francisco, we need to talk about the situation," he said. "What could happen, how to handle various incidents. You should let someone know where you'll be at all times. Then if you don't show up when you're supposed to, we can start looking for you immediately. You shouldn't go anywhere alone. If he follows you, accosts you, you want witnesses. And having someone with you may give you some degree of protection. You—"

Kaitlyn raised her hand to halt him. "Enough. I don't like this. Not one bit."

His expression hardened. "Like it or not, your life changed the moment Craig Fallon walked in. You have no choice but to adjust."

Chapter 9

Your life changed the moment Craig Fallon walked in.

Jake's words echoed in her ears as she drove to the airport later that evening. She'd been fairly quiet during dinner and every so often she'd caught Shelly's worried gaze on her. She'd wished there'd been some way to ease her friend's mind, but Kaitlyn had been too upset to find one.

She was upset still. At first she'd wanted to disregard Jake's words as another of his ploys to scare her into submission; however, that didn't last long. His reasons weren't the issue. The truth was she would have to make these changes, no matter how much she disliked doing so. She would have to be aware, alert, on her guard. All the time.

Sighing, she checked the cars behind her. Traffic on the stretch of I-29 going through the northern part of Kansas City was heavy as usual. In the coming twilight, she made note of the cars around her, then let her foot off the accelerator. Frustrated drivers immediately switched lanes and sped past her, one or two pausing to flash her a dirty look.

When she could see no one behind her, she let out the

breath she'd been holding. Relieved, she brought the car back up to speed, but still kept an eye on the cars that came up in her rearview mirror. If Jake was right, which she feared he was, she couldn't afford to relax too much.

She took the airport exit and followed the road around to Terminal B. She parked in the long-term parking, then grabbed her carry-on bag out of the trunk and walked the distance to the terminal. The automatic doors opened with a quiet whoosh, then closed behind her.

With a sense of anticipation she hadn't felt in a long time, she walked up to the monitors to check the gate assignment for her flight. It would be so good to get away for a couple of days, to wander around on her own, to luxuriate in a hotel for a night and not worry about phone calls awakening her.

She found her gate number, then checked the overhead signs. Her gate was to the left. Heading in that direction, she glanced over the few passengers standing in line at the ticket counter. Since her flight was the only one scheduled for this airline at this time of night, these people would be on board with her.

Her gaze slid past the two businessmen, past the two middle-aged women, and stopped on the man at the counter. Normally she wouldn't have paid him a second glance, but something made her look closer. Blond hair, a little under six feet tall, medium build. He had his back to her, but Kaitlyn knew him instantly. Craig Fallon.

It couldn't be him. She was upset over her conversation with Jake and her imagination was running wild. But he turned his head slightly and she knew it was him. She spun on her heel and all but ran for the door.

Outside the terminal she raced back to her car. Hands shaking uncontrollably, she fumbled in her purse for her keys. Twice she dropped them and had to fish for them on the ground. Finally she got the key in the lock and the door open. She threw her bag in the back seat, then got in behind the wheel, quickly locking the doors.

Still trembling, she worked the key into the ignition. Her heart beat furiously. Her stomach knotted. Nausea swept over her. She had to force herself to breathe deeply—she couldn't be sick now.

Fallon had followed her to the airport. The thought raced through her mind again and again as she backed out of the parking space. And after she'd been so careful to make sure she wasn't being followed. But, no. He was already there buying his ticket when she walked in. He had to have been there before her.

How had he known? How in hell had he known she would be there? No way would she believe his being there was a coincidence.

What was she going to do? Where could she go? Where would she be safe from him?

No one was behind her car as she paid for her parking and raced out of the lot. No one was behind her as she pulled into the light evening traffic. Once out on the interstate, she floored the accelerator and sped away from the few cars around her. No one seemed concerned about her moves.

She wouldn't have long, though. Craig Fallon would soon realize she wasn't getting on that plane. He would figure she'd spotted him first and had run. He would pursue.

What would have happened had she not seen him? If she'd gotten on that plane and not been able to get off? Horrible visions filled her mind. Nausea washed over her again. She didn't have time for it. Not now. She had to think. Quickly.

Where could she go? Whom could she turn to?

Jake. She was dialing his cellular number on her car phone as she took the exit onto I-635 South. He would protect her. Take care of her. Tell her what she should do. He would keep her safe.

But as he answered with a warm hello, she faltered. Uncertainty shoved aside the fear and panic. Did she want to do this? Place her existence in Jake's hands? She could trust him with her safety, she knew. But she was apt to become very dependent on him. Would she lose herself in the process?

Did she have a choice? The alternative was to live in constant fear. Perhaps chance getting killed. She needed Jake. Desperately.

"Hello," he repeated sharply when she still hadn't answered him.

"J-Jake...I..." She couldn't get out the words.

"Katie?" She heard the growing alarm in his voice. "Katie, what is it? What's wrong?"

"He...I...he... Oh, God, Jake." Her voice broke on a tiny sob of hysteria. She was losing control, she knew.

"Katie, take a deep breath," he commanded. "Deep."

She had to fight for air. After three tries, she managed one semicalming breath. "It's Fallon, Jake. He was there. At the airport."

Jake was absolutely silent for several racing heartbeats. Kaitlyn nearly panicked.

"Where?" he finally demanded.

"At the ticket counter. I saw him there. I...saw him there." The gravity of the situation hit her again, knocking the air out of her lungs.

"Where are you?" Jake asked.

"On 635." She struggled to read the overhead sign ahead. "Coming up on the Parkville exit."

"I'm on 635 South. I was headed home, but I'm turning around right now. I'm going to meet you, probably just before the ramp to I-70. On the left is a wide place where you can pull off. I'll be there."

"Okay," she said with a touch of relief.

"Is he behind you?" Jake asked.

She glanced in the rearview mirror. There were two sets

of headlights in the growing darkness, but both were a ways behind her. "I don't think so. I don't think he knows I saw him. He had his back to me."

"That's good," he said. "Katie, I need to call for backup."

Kaitlyn felt the panic rise again. She didn't want him to hang up on her. As long as she could hear his voice, she felt somewhat safe. It was a false sense of security, since he was miles away, but she clung to it anyway.

"Backup? Why—"

"Someone to drive your car back to your condo. You're coming to my apartment where I can keep you safe," he said emphatically.

His apartment. Panic of another kind welled up inside her. Staying with Jake wasn't wise. But she had no other choice. Once Fallon realized she was not getting on that plane, he would come looking for her. Only Jake could hide her, protect her from the madman stalking her.

"It'll only take a minute, Katie," Jake crooned soothingly, breaking into her disturbing thoughts. "Just one minute, then I'll call you right back. I promise."

Reluctantly she agreed, and just as reluctantly, Jake pushed the End button. He couldn't stand not knowing what was happening to her. He quickly phoned Dallas Steele and arranged for him to meet at the rendezvous, then punched in Katie's car-phone number. She answered on a half ring, her voice as shaky as it had been when she'd first called him.

"Where are you now?" he asked. If he could keep her thoughts on her driving, she would stay calmer. He needed her calm and able to think.

"Just crossing the Missouri River," she said. "I'm on the Kansas side now."

"Good. I'm on 635." He was making great time, thankfully weaving through the Friday-night traffic with amazing ease. But he couldn't get there fast enough to suit him. Katie was in peril. He had to reach her.

What if Fallon *was* behind her and she didn't know it? What if Jake couldn't make it in time? He would never be able to live with himself if something happened to her. He would get to her, and once he had her safe, he was calling all the shots. He would protect her. Guard her every minute. Once she was over her initial fear, she might balk at the restrictions he'd have to place on her, but he would be firm. He couldn't take any chances. Fallon had turned violent once before. Jake couldn't risk her getting hurt.

Still talking to her on the phone, he came up on the area between the north and south lanes and quickly pulled over. Katie was passing Parallel Parkway, approaching State Avenue. She would be there soon.

"Look on your left," he told her. "I'm sitting with my hazard flashers on."

"I see you," she said, sounding breathless with relief.

"Pull over in front of me." He wanted to be able to see her very clearly, to make sure that if Fallon was behind her, Jake would be between her and him.

She eased onto the shoulder, slowing the Honda. Gradually she came to a stop. Jake was beside her before she put the car in Park. As soon as she unlocked the door, he opened it. She flew into his arms, shaking violently.

Kaitlyn buried her face in his shirtfront. It seemed it had taken so long to get to him, but at last he was here with her. He smelled of soap and cologne. Safety. His strong arms wrapped around her. Cradling. Protecting. She closed her eyes and sagged against him. She couldn't stop shaking.

He reached into the back seat for her carry-on bag, locked her car, then led her over to his. "Dallas is coming for your car," he told her once they were inside. "He'll drive it back to your place and park it in the garage. If anything happens at your house tonight, he'll respond."

Kaitlyn nodded. "What about his car?" she asked.

"He'll have someone with him to drive it."

That someone turned out to be Dev. The two arrived in a matter of seconds. Jake gave them Katie's key ring, showed them the key for her house and told them the code he'd programmed into her security system, then the pair were gone.

As Jake sped off, leaving the other two behind, Kaitlyn sank against the leather upholstery and rubbed her arms. She was colder than she ever remembered being. Her stomach was tied in a painful knot.

"How did he know I would be at the airport? How did he know I would be on *that* flight?" she asked.

"He must have followed—"

She shook her head. "He was there before me, standing at the ticket counter. He had to have been there for a while. But how did he know which airline and which flight?"

"There are lots of ways he could have found out," Jake said. "He could have overheard you talking to someone. He could have gotten into your office when you were out and Mary had her back turned. Maybe you had the flight information written on a piece of paper and he went through your trash to find it—"

"Then I'll have to watch everything I say and do." She gave a bitter laugh. "I'll even have to watch what I'm throwing away."

Jake reached over and took her hand in his. He was warm, strong, solid. Kaitlyn wanted to hold on and never let go. She didn't want to think any more about what had happened tonight, about what worse things could have happened if she hadn't seen Fallon first, about all the changes she would have to make, starting now. She couldn't deal with it all at once. So she concentrated on the feel of Jake's hand around hers. For a few minutes she tried to dwell on feeling safe, shoving aside thoughts of the price she would have to pay. Right now she was sheltered.

She took a deep breath and focused on stopping the shivers coursing through her. Jake turned off the car's air conditioner and let the heat of the night seep in. Gradually it drove away the chill of fear. But her stomach remained knotted.

Very soon they were pulling up to a three-story brick building. Jake parked in a single-car garage in the back, then led her into the building and over to the elevator. He inserted a key, then pushed the button for the third floor.

"I keep the whole third floor for myself," he told Kaitlyn. "Security purposes."

"You own this building?"

He smiled proudly and draped an arm around her shoulders. She leaned into him, his hard muscles pressing against her side. Nothing could harm her here. She closed her eyes and tried to will the lingering nausea away, but without success. It stayed with her as he led her down a short hallway and into his apartment. He set her carry-on bag on the floor by the sofa, then offered her a quick tour.

The rooms were large, the colors masculine, the furniture big—except in the one guest bedroom, which definitely showed a woman's touch in decorating.

"Candy travels a lot on business," Jake explained. "Anytime she's in town, she stays here."

"She doesn't live in Kansas City now?"

"Too many bad memories," Jake said quietly.

He took Kaitlyn into the master bedroom—the biggest room in the apartment. A king-size bed dominated one wall. Along the others were a sizable dresser and a large armoire. The carpet was deep navy and the comforter on the bed was a navy-and-burgundy print.

Kaitlyn had only a moment to admire it all before her stomach lurched in a final warning. She raced for the master bathroom and dropped to her knees in front of the commode.

Jake watched, helpless. Her hair had come loose from the clip and all he could do was hold the strands back and croon to her until the vomiting subsided. When she sat back on her heels, he reached for a washcloth and dampened it with cool water. Her hands shook as she took it from him.

"I'm sorry...I..." She laid the cloth on the side of the whirlpool tub, then let him help her to her feet.

Arm tightly around her shoulders, Jake walked her over to the bed, pulled back the comforter and sheet, then settled her against the pillows, taking off her shoes and covering her legs. She was still incredibly pale. He went to get her bag and a heating pad. He set the bag on the foot of the bed, then reached to plug in the heating pad.

Telling her to change out of her shorts and T-shirt, he walked out of the room, returning a few minutes later with a small glass of club soda and some crackers. Sitting up in bed, she took a sip of the soda, then handed the glass back to him.

"I didn't think big, strong guys needed heating pads," she quipped as he laid it over her stomach.

"We come home with a few aches and pains," he said. "After that piano of Rob's, you may have to share it with me."

The smile she gave him was shaky around the edges.

"How are you doing?" he asked.

She looked up at him and he saw the fear still in her eyes. He stroked the side of her face, noting how cold her skin felt under his fingers.

"It'll be all right," he told her softly. "You're safe here. I'll see to that."

"I know." She closed her eyes and leaned into his touch. She was still shivering.

"Come on. Get under the covers," he told her.

"Jake, this is your—"

"It's big enough for the both of us," he insisted. "And I won't let you argue me out of this."

She nodded and slowly complied. Jake was grateful she

didn't fight him. As upset as she was, she was likely to have a nightmare and he wanted to be close by.

"I'll leave the door open," he said, tucking the covers over her shoulder. "Call if you need anything."

"I will."

He kissed her forehead, wishing he could make her fears disappear. "Get some sleep. You'll feel better in the morning."

It was dark. Totally black between the flashes of lightning. Kaitlyn couldn't see. Didn't know where she was. Walls were on both sides. She had to feel her way down the endless corridor. The walls were narrowing. Someone was breathing behind her. Chasing her. He was getting closer. She could feel the hot breath on her back.

She had to run, but she kept stumbling over the uneven floor. The corridor would go straight for a while, then turn suddenly. Each time it took her precious seconds to get oriented. Lightning flashed in the distance. Thunder rumbled behind her. Or was it footsteps?

She had to get away, but she couldn't run fast enough. No matter how fast she went, he was right behind her, breathing down her neck. She had to find someone. Had to get help. Her legs ached unbearably. Her lungs were on fire. She couldn't draw in air. But he was gaining on her. She couldn't stop.

She didn't know whom she was running from, but she knew whom she was running to—

"Jake," she shouted, finally forcing the words out of her constricted throat. "Jake."

She struggled to pull free of whatever was wrapped around her. A blanket. Tight around her.

From somewhere his voice called to her. "Katie. Katie, I've got you," he soothed. "It's okay. You were dreaming. It's over now."

Dreaming. A nightmare. It was over and Jake was there

with her. She quit struggling and let him unwind the blankets she'd managed to tangle herself in. Very quickly she was free and his arms were around her, holding her, protecting her. Driving away the demons.

"I was running," she said, breathless. "I couldn't get away from him. He just kept coming."

Jake's arms tightened around her. He propped the pillows against the headboard and switched on the light, as if knowing it would be a long while before she could sleep again, then pulled her to his side, tucking the sheet around her shoulders. Thunder rumbled in the distance. Kaitlyn buried her face in his chest and pressed her body closer to his.

"It's just a summer thunderstorm," he said softly against her hair.

"There was thunder. In my nightmare."

"It's all right now," he murmured. "You're safe here."

But was she? Kaitlyn wondered, her head on his bare chest. The scent of him, the enticing feel of his hair under her cheek and palm, the warmth of his skin, the hard plane of his torso—all of it called up memories. Making love, lying like this afterward, cradled in his arms, often making love again. The danger was every bit as serious as the one that had sent her to him. But she didn't know what to do.

"How's your stomach?" he asked, his voice husky.

"About the same." She sighed, knowing she should move to the guest room bed. Knowing, too, that she wouldn't go anywhere.

She needed to be near him, despite the way he brought her senses alive. She needed to feel his arms around her, to feel his powerful body next to hers. Beneath the fear she felt was that aching awareness of him. He wore only a pair of briefs. That virility tugged at her senses, called to the woman in her. Desire teased at the fringes of her mind, too strong to ignore, but what she needed now was his strength, his ability to keep her safe from harm.

"Jake," she said in a whisper, "I'm scared. What's going to happen now?"

Jake gave her shoulders a reassuring squeeze, knowing what she most needed now was assurance that she could get through this. Fallon was truly stalking her and she couldn't hide from that reality any longer. She was frightened and Jake knew how she hated feeling vulnerable.

"Tomorrow we'll talk about it," he told her, not wanting to upset her further tonight. "In the morning, I'll tell you all the possible situations you could be confronted with and all the procedures I want you to follow."

Head against his chest, she nodded. Thunder boomed through the room, making her jump.

"The storm is getting closer," he said against her flower-scented hair. "It'll pass over soon."

She burrowed closer still. There was no space between their bodies. She was pressed to the length of him, all softness and gently rounded curves. Jake wanted her so badly he hurt. Too clearly he could remember letting his hands explore her beautiful contours, could recall the feel of her breasts in his palms, the softness of her skin. He longed to explore her all over again, to tug the cotton sleep shirt from her body and make love to her. But that's not what she needed. She needed to be held.

"I'll take good care of you, Katie," he crooned, rubbing her back with the palm of his hand, feeling her tensed and knotted muscles. "Just leave everything up to me."

She nodded again and sighed quietly as he kneaded her shoulders, working some of the tension out. If he didn't get her to relax, he knew, she was apt to end up with one of her killer headaches.

"Come on," he said softly. "Lie down on your stomach and let me do this properly."

After a moment, she complied. He understood her hesitation. Many times he'd given her a massage as a prelude to lovemaking. He would work away the tension of the day, the tension she tended to hold on to, then kiss her soft skin until he created a tension of another kind. That had never taken long, but often he had deliberately prolonged the sweet torture until both of them were mindless with need.

He groaned silently as he worked his way to her shoulder blades. His thoughts were going to land him in an icy cold shower.

Katie opened her eyes, angled her head so she could see him, and as he looked into her eyes, he realized she was remembering, too. And wanting. He could take her. It would be so easy and so very wonderful. But it would also be wrong. She was defenseless right now. Vulnerable. He couldn't take advantage of her this way and be able to live with himself. He placed a tender kiss on her forehead.

"Close your eyes," he said in a hoarse whisper. "Go to sleep. Let me take care of everything."

With a quiet sigh, she closed her eyes and very soon was sleeping again, her breathing deep and even. Jake watched her for a long while. For the first time, Katie was placing her fate in his hands, allowing him to take care of her. This is what he'd needed from her. What he'd wanted those brief months they'd lived together.

He wouldn't let anything happen to her, he vowed as he felt her snuggle against him. He reached to switch off the light, then pulled the sheet over her shoulders. He wouldn't fail her. Whatever it took, he would keep her safe.

Slowly Kaitlyn realized she was holding Jake's pillow instead of Jake. She experienced a moment of panic before she remembered she was in his bed, in his apartment. He'd held her most of the night, letting her know she was safe, chasing away her fears. But now it was morning. Time to find out what the future had in store for her.

With her stomach knotting already, she went to the bedroom door and opened it. The smell of coffee and the sound of male voices greeted her. Jake had company. Kaitlyn spotted the plaid robe he'd laid out on the foot of the bed, slipped into it, then walked down the hallway, through the living room and into the kitchen.

Jake stood at the stove, his jeans and black knit shirt hugging his long, muscled frame. The momentary heat in his gaze made her breath snag. She smiled at him and he gave her a warm smile in return, then inclined his head toward the table.

Dallas Steele sat sprawled in one wooden chair, his feet on the rungs of another. He raised his coffee mug in salute.

"Hey there, Red. How are you doing this morning?" he asked brightly.

She frowned at him in semiannoyance. "Hasn't anyone ever told you it's rude to wake up so cheerful?"

He chuckled. "Haven't been to bed yet."

She tensed, certain Craig Fallon was the reason. "What happened?" she asked him.

He looked to Jake for permission before he answered her. Jake considered it for a moment, then nodded. "She needs to know," he said.

"Fallon showed up at your house at least twice," Steele said. "Or rather, he got close enough to the place to set off the alarm twice. Once about midnight, then again about four o'clock."

Kaitlyn sank into a chair at the other end of the table. Fallon had been at her house, probably had lurked in the shadows for some time, waiting for her to come home. She could only guess what he'd planned to do when she showed up. It wasn't a pleasant thought. A chill climbed her spine.

"Did he try to break in?" she asked.

"The first time he may have been trying just to see if you were there," Steele told her. "Neighbors said he was pounding on the front door, yelling your name. They said he quit and ran off just before we got there."

"We?" Kaitlyn asked, giving Jake a small smile when he set a glass of chocolate milk in front of her.

"I'm not the only one the service calls when the alarm goes off," Steele explained. "They notify the patrol unit in the area and the police. We generally all show up within minutes of one another."

Jake, his back to them as he stirred something in a pan on the stove, turned toward her. "We particularly want the police to respond to each incident in these cases."

"Stalking cases, you mean," she muttered, staring into the glass in front of her.

"The police will file a report," he continued. "We want everything documented. Each and every single time he tries anything."

"I got that message loud and clear at Shelly's yesterday," she told him fervently. She wanted him to know she would not repeat the mistake she'd made with the answering machine tapes. "But don't the police get tired of being called in and having to file reports?"

"That's their job," Jake insisted.

"And," Steele added, "they understand the situation and the need to have the documentation. Most of the time they're as frustrated as you are because the guy usually takes off just before they show up on the scene."

Meaning it would be difficult to actually catch him in the act of harassing her. "But they can pick him up, can't they?" she asked with a touch of alarm. "For violating the restraining order?"

"They have to find him first." Steele stretched his long arms and legs. "We spent a lot of hours trying to track him down last night. Rob was even waking up the guy's neighbors, asking if any of them knew where he hangs out."

"Rob Donovan?" Kaitlyn asked. "You got him out... Jake, you can't be dragging him away from Shelly every time—"

Jake placed the spoon on the counter, then turned off the stove and reached for three bowls. "Katie," he said patiently, "Rob wants to be in on this. All the way. And Shelly goes along with him on this."

"But—"

"They're your friends," he went on. "They want to be there for you, want to help in any way they can."

"But…" She couldn't disrupt her friends' lives, couldn't impose; more important, she couldn't expose them to danger of any kind. What if one of them were hurt because of her "problem" with Fallon? She would never be able to forgive herself.

Jake placed the bowls of oatmeal and a basket of croissants on the table, then sat down next to her. "Katie," he said in a tone that didn't allow for disagreement, "you can't hold on to your independence here. I know you prefer doing things on your own, but from now on, you're going to need help. As much as you can get."

In other words, Kaitlyn thought, it would take all of them to keep her safe. Gone would be the peaceful, relatively carefree life she'd known for the past few years. But not only would she worry about herself, she would have to worry about her friends, as well.

With an inward sigh, she picked up her spoon and sampled some of the oatmeal flavored with brown sugar. It was delicious, but her stomach protested. She set her spoon in the bowl, noting Jake's scowl as she did so.

"You can do better than that, Red," Steele coaxed. "Jake's oatmeal is great. The only oatmeal I'll eat."

"He says that as if he doesn't care for oatmeal," Jake said, "but don't let him fool you. He's never met a food he didn't like."

"I've never disliked anything you've ever made, that's for sure," Steele quipped. "Now, Red's cooking may be another thing entirely. The only thing I saw in her house was peanut butter and a freezer full of these chicken-and-rice entrées. You must really like rice."

"We never had rice when I was growing up because my father hated it," she said with a tiny smile. "I've developed quite a taste for it, though." She pinned Steele with a steady glower. "So, tell me why you were snooping through my freezer."

"Just checking things out," he said, raising a hand in a gesture of surrender. "Making sure everything would be all right for the weekend, so you wouldn't have to come home to spoiled food. Where do you think that chocolate milk you're not drinking came from?"

Arching an eyebrow at him, she took a swallow from the glass. "From my refrigerator? How...thoughtful of you."

"Yeah, well, before you start feeling too generous toward me," he said, "the last time I phoned to report your alarm went off, Jake told me that if there was a carton in your fridge, I should bring it over this morning."

Lying beside Jake, she must have slept through the ringing of the phone. She glanced at him, thinking again how thoughtful he was, about how safe he made her feel. When she laid her hand over his, he turned his hand palm upward and wrapped his fingers around hers. He squeezed gently.

"Try to eat," he said softly.

She would need her strength for the ordeal to come, he was telling her, though he didn't say the words. He would worry about her if she didn't eat, and this time she hated to have him upset.

Nodding, she picked up her spoon and managed a couple of bites before Steele's cellular phone rang. He pulled it out of his jeans, exchanged a few words with the person on the other end of the line, then replaced the phone in his pocket.

"Looks like our man was back," he told Jake. "Martin says he broke out some windows in the rear of the house."

Her bedroom windows, Kaitlyn thought, setting down her spoon and pushing away her bowl. She saw Jake frown at her again, but she couldn't manage to swallow another bite around the lump in her throat.

"Go put your clothes on," he finally told her. "We'll go over there and see what kind of damage he's done."

Chapter 10

With a shudder, Kaitlyn closed the book she reading on stalking crimes and got to her feet. Dallas Steele slept on Jake's couch, stretched out on his back and snoring softly. Back at her condo new unbreakable windows had been installed, the broken glass cleaned up, and Jake was now overseeing placement of the security sensors.

Before leaving, Jake had given her this book and one other on the patterns of stalkers. The picture of what she had to look forward to was pretty bleak. Boiled down to basics, a stalker was irrational, obsessive and absolutely relentless. Many turned violent at some point. Craig Fallon had resorted to violence with his former girlfriend, and he'd obviously lost control last night at Kaitlyn's house.

What if she'd been there—alone? she asked herself as she paced the carpet in front of Jake's balcony doors. What if she'd had to deal with Fallon pounding on her front door and yelling for her to let him in, breaking out her bedroom windows? She could imagine the horror of waiting long, agonizing minutes for help to come, wondering who would get to her first.

She shivered despite the heat of the sunlight that streamed in through the sliding glass doors. Suddenly she needed to be outside. Wanted to feel the full warmth of the sun on her skin and breathe the air. She reached to push the glass panel aside, but a voice from the couch stopped her.

"Jeez, Red," Steele said, sitting up to cast her a frown of mild annoyance, "don't touch the door. The pacing was bad enough—"

"You were snoring," she said, straightening and glaring back at him. "You could not have known I was pacing."

"Lucky guess," he said with a maddening grin. "Now, about the balcony door..."

"Yes, about the door. How did you know I was planning to go outside?" she demanded.

"Rule number one—Always sleep with one eye open when you're baby-sitting," he said, stretching, then getting to his feet.

"Baby-sitting," she muttered in irritation. The least the man could do was refer to his being assigned to guard her as something other than baby-sitting.

"Jake would have been real upset when the service phoned to tell him there was an alarm at his apartment," he continued as if she hadn't spoken.

"You guys and your gadgets and gizmos," she mumbled, rolling her eyes heavenward. The need to be outside was so strong she hadn't given a thought to the alarm system, hadn't given a thought to how frantic Jake would be if he envisioned something happening to her. She would have to be more cautious in the future, she told herself.

"In time you'll learn to love them as much as Jake and I do," Steele said, coming to stand beside her.

"Appreciate them, maybe," she corrected, staring at the book in her hands. If the text was anything to go by, there could be many times when she would be very grateful to have the system at her house. Not a comforting thought.

"Not exactly pleasant reading," he said sympathetically. Seeing her gaze longingly at the balcony, he ran a hand over his stubble-covered jaw. "All right," he said, "let me turn off the alarm, then we can sit outside."

"We?" she asked, not certain she wanted company. The book had her spirits even lower than they'd been when she'd looked at her shattered bedroom windows earlier today. At the moment, she didn't feel up to making small talk.

"Jake wouldn't like the idea of my letting you sit out there alone," Steele explained. "It's my only offer. Take it or leave it."

Now she couldn't even sit on a balcony by herself, she thought morosely. Her chest tightened. She felt as if the apartment walls were closing in on her.

"All right," she said wearily. "*We'll* sit outside."

With a small nod and a big yawn, Steele walked over to the keypad and punched in the code. As soon as she spotted the green light on the pad, she opened the glass door and stepped out onto the carpeted balcony.

Breathing deeply, she turned her face to the sun, leaning against the railing that overlooked the south section of the parking lot. The heat was wonderful. The fresh air, hot and humid from last night's brief thunderstorm, blew across her cheeks and neck. Free. She felt free, as if a burden had been lifted temporarily. For a moment she forgot her fears, forgot Fallon existed. For a moment she could pretend...

Then Steele walked onto the balcony and she remembered why they were both there. He eased his tall frame into a plastic chair, slouched down in it, then stretched his legs out in front of him.

"So, what is it you like about being outdoors?" he asked her. "The heat, the sun?"

"The fresh air. I get antsy being inside all day. I like to feel the wind on my face."

"It's the sun for me. I hate those long stretches of cloudy days in the spring, the fall and winter. Give me the summer and the sunshine twelve months out of the year."

Kaitlyn could have guessed as much by merely looking at his bronzed skin and the blond streaks in his light brown hair.

"Don't care for those windy days we get, either," he went on to say. "Interferes with my golf game."

"Golf?" Kaitlyn asked, stretching out in the chaise longue across from him, leaving the book she didn't want to finish in her lap.

"Sure. Jake and I have closed a lot of important business deals on the golf course."

"I just figured you for something more...physical," she said, taking in his muscled biceps.

"Basketball. My second love." He laced his fingers behind his head and leaned back in his chair. "Jake's first love. He plays golf only as a necessity. That's why he loses his shirt every time we play."

"You bet on the game?"

"We're men," he replied, as if that explained everything—and it nearly did. "We bet on our scores for each hole, how long our drives will be, whether we can make a putt, how many tries it'll take Jake to get out of a sand trap. Hell, I've made a fortune betting on how bad his slice will be."

Didn't sound very sporting, Kaitlyn thought, but she could tell by the humor in his voice that it was all done in fun.

"I can look at the way he stands and how high his shoulder is and tell you how bad the ball will slice, what direction it'll take and damn near where it will land," he said, shaking his head. "I can even tell you how far he'll throw the club after the ball hits the ground."

Kaitlyn found herself laughing as he continued with tales of various incidents on the golf course. She smiled as he told of Jake's prowess on the basketball court—and the betting that went on there, also. She was pleased to learn that Jake usually managed to win back what he lost at golf.

Before she knew it, she'd been in the sunshine for over thirty minutes and Jake was walking in the apartment door. Steele, she realized with a touch of gratitude, had entertained her—deliberately working to take her mind off her worries and fears. Perhaps she would be nicer to the man in the future.

"Out here, Boss," he called to Jake.

Pocketing his keys, Jake stepped onto the balcony. He looked so tempting in those jeans and the black knit shirt, she thought as he took the chair beside her and reached for her hand. A small touch, holding her hand, she mused, but it made her want more—to have his arms around her again, to lie next to him and feel safe and sheltered, to give herself to him.

She was quickly losing her resolve to stand on her own. And after reading most of this book of Jake's, she was even more afraid of Fallon, more afraid of being on her own. How she would be able to remedy any of it, she didn't know.

"Everything all right at my house?" she asked him.

He nodded, then squeezed her hand. "Thought we'd have some sesame chicken and wild rice for dinner."

She gave him a small smile. She still didn't have much of an appetite, but she would try her best to do justice to his cooking.

"Sounds great to me," Steele put in, getting to his feet. "I'm going to grab a couple more hours of sleep before dinner."

"Did you invite him?" Kaitlyn asked Jake teasingly.

"I don't stand on formality," Steele told her. "Especially not when Jake is cooking. He can't golf worth a damn, but he can snooker me in basketball and he can cook. And I've got dibs on anything you leave on your plate,'' he finished with a wink at her, then sauntered back to the couch to catch another nap.

Kaitlyn managed to hide her smile until his back was turned, but just barely.

''Does he get under your skin?'' Jake asked quietly.

She shrugged. ''It's that damned cocky attitude of his. But now that I've spent some time with him, he seems to be growing on me.''

Jake smiled at her. ''Good, because he's my first choice to stay with you if I can't be here.''

Kaitlyn nodded her understanding, then inclined her head toward the book in her lap. ''Will things get as bad as this book indicates?''

''It's very possible,'' Jake told her reluctantly.

The conversation had just begun and she was already biting her lower lip. He didn't like that. Wished there were something he could do to change this whole situation. But all he could do was protect her, take care of her.

She opened the book to a page with the corner bent, then read a passage. '' 'This crime—unpredictable and long-term in nature—is one of the most life-altering and emotionally scarring ordeals a person can go through.' I think I'm finding that out already.''

''We'll get you through this, Katie,'' he said sympathetically.

She flipped to another page. '' 'Events may taper off for a short time, then start up weeks later.' ''

''Katie, we'll take all the precautions—''

''Precautions,'' she said, finding another page. ''This one advises taking precautions, then hoping you can outlast him. *Outlast* him, Jake.'' Her voice rose slightly.

''Yes, but—'' Panic was setting in, he realized. Fear of what she might have to face. She was finally absorbing the horrible realities of the situation and it was scaring her through and through.

"How do I outlast someone who creates his own version of reality and acts accordingly? How do I deal with someone who is not rational?"

"You don't," Jake said firmly in an effort to calm her as much as possible when nothing she said could be refuted. "You put yourself out of his reach. Eventually he is likely to become interested in someone else."

"Eventually can be a really long time."

"It could also be much shorter than that," he told her. "Meanwhile, our primary goal is to prevent encounters between you and him. That's one of the reasons I brought you here last night instead of taking you home."

Another was that she'd needed a break—time to think about her situation without fear of what Fallon might do to her. And Jake had needed to be with her, looking after her. He hadn't wanted her to be alone.

"So, are you saying I can never go home?" she demanded.

"Of course you can—"

"How, though?" She slammed the book shut and handed it to him. "I'm scared to death at the thought of what he might do. How am I supposed to handle being alone in my own house?"

"You're not alone in this," he told her emphatically. "We can arrange for someone to stay with you. And you can stay here as long as you want to."

He wanted her to stay, he realized. He could take care of her here, make certain she ate and slept, that she was free of worry, that no harm came to her. There were too many variables when she was away from him, too many chances she might get hurt. When she was with him, he could protect her.

And when she was with him, he felt whole, he decided.

As if she was the element that had been missing in his life lately.

"I can stay here and you'll take care of me?" she asked, testing the idea and his response to it.

"As long as you need," he said, hoping the idea would appeal to her as much as it did to him. Last night, holding her, comforting her, had felt very good. He didn't want their time together to end. Not yet. Maybe not ever.

But when he glanced at her, for the first time he could remember he couldn't read her expression. She'd become quiet, had averted her gaze. It felt as though she was withdrawing from him. He frowned, not liking the thought of that one bit.

"Katie, there are ways in which you can take control of this situation."

She shot him a skeptical look.

"You start by making yourself inaccessible. Mary's already helping you with that. She doesn't leave you alone in the office and she doesn't put through his calls. You simply do that on a larger scale."

"Larger scale," she repeated flatly.

"Yes. When you want to go to the grocery store, the post office, the dry cleaner's, say, you give me a call and I'll go with you. When you want to go shopping with Shelly, or you want to have lunch with her, have her pick you up rather than meeting her."

"What about delivering tickets? I can't discontinue the service to my clients."

He rubbed his forehead. "I think you should hire an older retired person or a young college student to do that, someone who wants just a few hours a week. Or use an overnight delivery service."

What about making calls to drum up business? she wanted to ask. A part-time person couldn't do that. But neither could she—not without great personal risk.

Her freedom to come and go at will would be curtailed

completely. She would have to alter the way she lived entirely. Impose on her friends. Give up her privacy. Her independence. Let her business suffer.

"Then you start documenting every single thing the way we discussed," Jake continued. "Mary should write down each time he phones you at the office. You let your answering machine at home screen all your calls so you'll have him on tape when he gets your new number and starts calling again."

When he gets her new number? Kaitlyn found herself clenching her teeth. She couldn't even answer her phone at home. Jake wouldn't bring up the possibility of Fallon's getting her unlisted number unless he thought it was likely to happen.

"You keep a copy of these records in your safe-deposit box," Jake said.

Meaning it was also likely that Fallon might get his hands on or destroy the originals? She didn't want to know the answer to that, not right now.

"Who should I have accompany me to the bank to put those records in the lockbox?" she bit out instead, fury and frustration getting the better of her.

"I'll be glad to drive you. I'd like to have copies of everything for my files, too. It's good to have the backup documentation."

"I suppose I should ask the bank to put me on the list for a bigger box," she said angrily. "It sounds as if I'll need it."

Jake's mouth tightened in a thin line. "Katie, you have every right to be upset about the situation, but understand this. In these situations we have to change the one person who can be reasoned with. Nothing any of us say to Fallon will make him act rationally. So *you* change the way *you* do things to protect yourself."

There was no alternative to that, she realized unhappily, unless she chose to disappear, as Fallon's ex-girlfriend had done. To do so effectively she would have to give up her dream of running her own travel agency, become an unknown face in a sea of nameless office workers. Move her mother to another hospital, and with her current fragile state of mind, that was not something Kaitlyn wanted to consider.

And what about Jake? How would she feel about leaving him?

"The main thing," Jake stressed, "is to avoid dealing with Fallon alone. There is safety in numbers. If you're always with someone, he may become discouraged and latch onto someone else."

How likely is that? she wanted to demand, but she already knew the answer. Knew that she would have no choice but to go along with all the courses of action Jake had laid out. Knew that her life would not be her own for a very long time, if ever.

Jake would look after her, keep her safe. She trusted him completely. She could depend on him. That's not what she wanted for herself, to be dependent on anyone, but it appeared she had no other options. She was scared to go home and even more panicked at the thought of staying in his apartment.

"I didn't get enough sleep last night," she said, standing. "If you don't mind, I'm going to lie down before dinner." She handed him the book, then went down the hall to the guest bedroom.

She wasn't asleep when Jake went to call her for dinner, and she hadn't slept the two hours she'd been in the room, he could tell. She was too tense, too distant. She'd lain in there, mulling over what she'd read and what they'd discussed on the balcony, and none of it was sitting well.

As he and Dallas dug in to the chicken breasts, wild rice and fresh asparagus, she picked at her food, putting something in her mouth only when she caught Jake's gaze on her. He glanced at his friend and the two of them launched into a lively discussion of the KC Royals. When baseball didn't draw her out, they turned to the Chiefs' preseason football games, then to movies, the economy, the upcoming presidential elections. Their efforts were futile. Nothing they talked about drew her out of her melancholy.

"Jeez, Red, Jake and I could save our breath," Dallas finally said, helping himself to half of the untouched chicken breast on her plate and a couple of asparagus spears.

She blinked at him as if it took a moment or two for her to catch his meaning. She'd been that lost in her own unpleasant thoughts. Jake wanted to pull her into his arms, but was afraid that would be the wrong move this time. She wasn't reaching out to him as she had last night. In fact, the opposite was the case this evening. Perhaps she just needed a little time to herself. He'd given her a lot of serious stuff to think about.

"At least finish off your rice," Dallas urged. "I know Jake made it especially for you. I'm a potato man myself."

Jake glanced at her and caught the hint of a smile of apology she gave him, then watched as she managed a few bites of the rice. She wasn't enjoying the food, though, not the way she had with the Mexican rice and enchiladas. He would give her time, he figured—wouldn't push. In a day or two she would see that things would not be as bleak as she must be imagining.

In the meantime, he decided later as they sat in front of the television, not really watching the romantic comedy that was playing, it was tearing him apart to see her anguish. From time to time he looked over to catch her biting her lower lip, her gaze unfocused as she stared into the distance. When he spoke to her, she gave him her attention, but would give little response to his small talk.

Things would look better to her after a good night's sleep, he finally decided, switching off the TV after the nightly news was over. He tried to coax her into sleeping in his bed again, promising to behave himself, if that's what she wanted. She wanted to be alone.

Jake wasn't certain that was such a good idea. She needed sleep, not more long hours of chasing her gloomy and frightening thoughts around in circles. But when she insisted she would be all right—and as close as the next room if he was concerned about her—he reluctantly let her go, then lay in bed, worried that she was fretting about the future rather than sleeping.

He managed to doze off for a few minutes, then was awakened by the ringing of the telephone. Groggily he fumbled for the receiver.

"Riley," he mumbled into it.

"We have a silent alarm at your garage," the woman on the other end said. "Do you want the police to respond?"

"Let me check it out first," he told her. "Send a patrol unit and I'll call the police if I need them."

He hung up, then found his jeans folded on a chair and stepped into them. Katie was opening his door as he pulled on his shoes. She didn't look as though she'd been asleep. Her eyes were clear and alert, and worried.

"My house again?" she asked, her voice trembling.

He shook his head as he reached behind him to position his revolver at the small of his back. About then the wail of a car alarm traveled up to the apartment.

"My garage," he said, grabbing for a shirt and yanking it over his head. "That's my car alarm."

He rushed past her and headed for the apartment door. Hurriedly he disarmed the security system, then showed Kaitlyn how to arm it again after he left.

"Stay inside," he ordered, planting a light kiss on her forehead. "I'll be back in a few minutes."

He took the stairs, catching up with his maintenance man and the building security guard in the parking lot. Eddie had his nightstick in one hand, flashlight in the other. Frank had brought a hammer. Carefully and quickly, the three made for the garage. As they approached the open overhead door, Eddie aimed the flashlight beam inside. Jake pulled out his keys and shut off the screaming alarm.

The patrol unit arrived a moment or two after that and Max Slater got out. By then the other three had determined that there was no one inside the garage. Jake switched on the lights and walked over to his car. The windshield had been shattered and the tiny fragments of glass were everywhere—inside and outside the vehicle. There were deep dents in nearly every piece of sheet metal. The intruder had used silver paint to spray obscenities and the words *she's mine* on the sides and trunk.

"Fallon," Jake muttered along with a few choice curses.

"That the perp's name?" Max asked, shining a light on the driver's door.

"Yeah," Jake said. "Think he left any prints?"

Slater shook his head. "Didn't have to touch the car to do any of this." He got down on the ground to look under the car, then got up and glanced around the garage. "Took his paint cans with him. Looks like he may have used one of your golf clubs on the windshield and the body," he said, peering into the car to see a club lying on the front seat. "Might—*might*—get prints off the grip, but I wouldn't count on it."

Jake nodded. "Get some Polaroids of this. I'll have Eddie call the police and get a report filed on it."

While the security guard went inside to use the phone in his office, Jake borrowed Max's cell phone and called Katie. He could picture her in the apartment, pacing and worrying, waiting for some word from him. When she answered on the first ring, he knew that was exactly what she'd been doing.

"I'll be here a few minutes more," he told her.

"Did someone try to steal your car?" she asked, still sounding shaky.

Jake wished he could lie to her, tell her anything but the truth, but he couldn't do that to her. She needed to be fully aware of what Fallon was doing. She had to be on her guard.

"Someone vandalized it," Jake said, seeing her silhouette at the balcony doors. She held the phone in one hand and had the other arm wrapped tightly around her waist.

"Fallon," she said tonelessly, the emptiness and distance back in her voice.

"Yeah," he said tightly, wishing he could have caught the bastard and given him what he deserved for putting Katie through this. "Looks like it. I'm waiting for the police. As soon as they finish, I'll be up. Why don't you go back to bed?"

She gave a hollow laugh. "As if I would be able to sleep."

Letting out a weary breath, he went back to Max. The man was an artist with a camera, Jake thought, examining the photos laid out on the trunk of the car.

"Got several to give to the cops," Max said, shooting another angle of the words painted on the passenger side. "There should be plenty left over for you." He straightened, and closed up the camera. "Who's the 'she' in 'she's mine'?"

"Kaitlyn Adams," Jake said, selecting several of the photos he wanted to keep. In the morning he would put them in a safe place. "Soon as we finish here, I want you to come up and meet her. I want her to know your face."

Max nodded, then inclined his head toward the squad car coming around the side of the building. They gave the officers a rundown on the situation, answered their questions, told them who they suspected had done this, then waited as the cops gathered what evidence they wanted.

"We'll have to take the golf club," one of the men told Jake. "We'll check it for possible prints and hold it for evidence, then we'll get it back to you."

He shrugged. "Keep the damn thing."

The officers left, Eddie and Frank went to find something they could use to secure the garage door, then Jake led Max up to the apartment. Kaitlyn was standing a few feet from the door when they walked in. She'd been pacing, Jake figured.

"This is Max Slater," he told her. "Study his face, because he's one of the people who will be looking out for you. He probably won't be in uniform the next time you see him. He's just picking up the slack on patrols for a while."

Kaitlyn nodded. This would be another of the new faces in her life, she thought, studying the man as she'd been told. He was as tall as Jake, his hair not quite as dark and his features rougher than Jake's. There was a sadness, a painfulness, in his whiskey brown eyes that told her the man was going through his own personal torment. Kaitlyn doubted his troubles would have a happy ending.

Rob showed up a few minutes later. She sat on the couch beside Jake while the three men discussed details of the incident, but she wasn't listening to the conversation. Her thoughts were on Fallon and the fact that he'd known how to find Jake's car, Jake's apartment. He'd known she was there and he was warning Jake off.

Relentless. Obsessive. The words from the book. They described Fallon perfectly. He was destructive and would undoubtedly become violent. It was just a matter of time.

What was she going to do? How long could she go on dealing with this, living in fear? How would she survive? How would her mother handle this? Kaitlyn couldn't expose her to the danger and the fear, yet there was no way to keep her sheltered once she got out of the hospital. She would find out and would be frightened for her daughter.

No matter where Kaitlyn went or what she did, the man would somehow find her as he'd found her here. She would never be free of him and the threat he represented. Never be completely safe. And there was very little she could do about it.

"By the way," Rob said, getting to his feet, "I spoke to Fallon's shrink. Seems the bastard took a swing at the good doctor during their last session. He was supposed to make an appointment with another of the doctors in the clinic, but he never did. We may be able to pick him up for parole violation."

"That'll carry more of a penalty," Jake murmured.

Rob nodded. "The doc also said that in his opinion Fallon is brilliant and unbalanced."

A dangerous combination, Kaitlyn thought, hugging her arms to her chest.

"And we finally located the former girlfriend's parents," Rob continued. "They haven't heard from their daughter since the day before she disappeared. Three months ago, they hired a private investigator to look for her. He hasn't found a trace of her yet."

"The parents don't think she disappeared on her own?" Jake asked, frowning.

Rob shook his head. "They say she was terrified the last time they talked to her. Said she told them Fallon was going to kill her if she didn't get away from him." He glanced at Kaitlyn. "Interesting coincidence—seems she has red hair, too."

Kaitlyn got to her feet, unable to listen to any more.

"Going back to bed?" Jake asked her.

"Yes," she replied flatly. "Until he makes his next move."

Jake watched her walk away, not liking the slump of her shoulders or the lifelessness in her voice.

Thirteen days later Jake knew something had to change. Kaitlyn had become completely withdrawn. He was certain she wasn't sleeping at night and she definitely wasn't eating much at all. She went to work each day, but there was no enjoyment in it, or in anything else. The only time she forced herself out of her melancholy was when he took her to the hospital to visit her mother. Gloria Adams was improving slowly and Kaitlyn didn't want to impede her progress, but as soon as they got in the elevator to leave, Katie went back into her shell.

Jake didn't know how much more of this he could take. She had no animation, no pleasure, no real interest in anything. He'd taken her out to dinner several times, only to have her leave her food virtually untouched. Last weekend he'd invited Rob and Shelly to go to the movies with them, hoping the company would stimulate Katie, but while she was there physically, mentally she was in her own unhappy and fear-filled world.

She couldn't go on this way, he thought, walking into her office building shortly after three o'clock. Mary had called him to say that Kaitlyn had a headache and should go home. When he entered the office, Mary pointed to the other room.

"I got her to put her head down on the desk," she said.

A sure sign Katie's headache had gotten the best of her, Jake knew. He'd seen her plow on with headaches that would incapacitate most people, but eventually she came to the point where she'd pushed herself too far.

This was one of those times, he realized angrily as she raised her head. Her eyes were clouded with pain. Her face was drained of color. Every muscle in her face and neck was drawn tight in an effort to fight off the pain.

"How long have you had this one?" he demanded.

"It started last night."

Why hadn't she said something before it had gotten this bad?

"Come on," he said, gently rolling her chair away from the desk. "I'm taking you back to the apartment."

She didn't protest his making her leave early, as she would have in the past. But lately she hadn't protested anything he insisted she do. He'd once thought he could do without that stubbornness of hers, but now that it was gone, he longed to have it back. A little of it, at least. He was losing the essence of Katie and he didn't like it one bit.

He got her into the apartment and took her down the hall to his bedroom. After sitting her on the edge of his bed, he went to fill the whirlpool tub. A long, hot soak would start the relaxation process, he hoped. He found a prescription bottle in her purse, gave her two of the pain tablets, then ordered her into the tub for at least twenty minutes—an order she obeyed without even a hint of objection.

She who had never taken orders from him in the past was now letting him tell her what to do. Once, he'd thought that was what he wanted and needed from her, but now he knew that wasn't the case. He couldn't stand seeing her beaten down like this.

When she came out of the bathroom, he had the bed turned down. The pain pills were slowly kicking in, he thought as she eased under the sheet and light blanket. He began to gently massage her back and shoulders, easily finding the knots of tension, listening to her soft sighs whenever he hit exactly the right spots. Very soon she was asleep.

He found a container of chicken soup in his freezer— he'd made a batch for his mom to help her get over a summer cold and had put the extra away for an emergency. He sat the container on the counter to thaw, hoping he would be able to convince Katie to eat some later.

Meanwhile, he needed to plan his strategy. The Katie he'd known was gone and it was up to him to bring her back. How to get her past the fear was his main concern. She'd yielded to her fears and was paralyzed. He would have to give her a gentle push out of that paralysis.

But doing so would cost him dearly. The way she was now—very manageable—he could easily protect her. She didn't balk at his restrictions, didn't object to having someone with her at all times. If she regained a measure of her independence, that could change, thus making his job more difficult. More nerve-racking. Did he want to put himself in the position of having to worry about her?

At nine o'clock he heated a bowl of the soup and warmed half of a croissant, then took a tray to Katie, along with two more of the pain pills. He knew from experience she needed to completely relax to get over the headache. Still groggy from the first pills and still in some pain, she wasn't real enthusiastic about the food, but Jake managed to get most of it down her. Then he gave her the medication.

"Will you stay with me?" she asked as he picked up the tray.

"I'll turn out the lights and be right back."

In the kitchen he placed the dishes in the sink, then called the service and told them to make their reports to Dallas and Max that night. Fallon had pulled one of his stunts every night and the telephone had gotten Katie out of bed each time. Tonight Jake wanted her to sleep soundly and without interruption.

Katie was still awake, waiting for him, when he got into the bed. She tucked herself against his side and sighed. Then to his surprise, she began to run her fingers through the hair on his chest, brushing her palms over his nipples. The exquisite torture made him throb, but he couldn't summon the will to stop her—even when her hand moved lower and lower. Only when she reached the waistband of his briefs did he catch her hand.

"Make love to me, Jake," she said.

He closed his eyes and groaned inwardly. What he wouldn't give to do exactly that, but she was doped up on pills and still in pain and still afraid. Her defenses were down. It would feel so good to have her under him, to explore her body with his hands and mouth, to feel her come alive for him. When that happened, though, he

wanted her fully aware, a willing participant, no baggage
between them, no resentment afterward.

He kissed her hand, laid it firmly on his chest, then pulled
her closer to nuzzle her ear. She moaned sleepily. She
would be out like a light soon. He would cuddle her until
then.

"Tell me that again when you're not medicated," he
whispered to her. "I'll take you up on it then."

She pressed a kiss to his shoulder, then fell asleep. Jake
lay awake for a long time, trying to decide which he needed
more—to have her depending on him, yet withdrawn and
afraid, or to have her back, spirit and spunk and all the
stubbornness and independence that were her.

Either way, he was afraid he would lose.

Chapter 11

Jake's decision was made the next morning when she sat at the table, picking at her breakfast. He couldn't stand the distance in her manner, the fear in her eyes, any longer. He yanked the plate off the table, pleased to see the look of shock cross her lovely face. So there was life behind that empty expression.

"Headache gone?" he asked brusquely after he'd scraped her breakfast into the sink.

"Yes," she said, still registering surprise. "Thank you for taking care of me last night."

He breathed deeply and steeled himself to do what he had to do. "I'm glad I could help, but now it's time you started taking care of yourself."

More surprise, then full-fledged alarm flickered across her face. "What do you mean?" she asked hesitantly.

He had to turn away from the silent plea in her gaze, then he walked out of the kitchen and into the living room. "Come on," he said over his shoulder. "You need to get packed."

Kaitlyn felt her heart catch. Her breath lodged in her lungs. Packed? Surely she hadn't heard him right. He hadn't said... He didn't mean... But when she raced into the guest room, he had her suitcase open on the bed.

He'd said she could stay as long as she needed, and she needed to still. Fallon had broken out windows on the first floor of Jake's building, had vandalized cars in the parking lot, had spray-painted his warnings and obscenities on the building—all without ever being caught. The police could never find him.

Fallon was toying with her, terrorizing her. He hadn't shown up at her office during the day, as if he somehow knew the security staff had orders to call the police if they saw him. But if she went back to her house, he would transfer his attentions there. She would be an easy mark. Jake had to realize that.

He pulled several hangers out of the closet, dresses, skirts, blouses. "You want to fold them, or shall I?"

She looked at the determination in his gaze and felt her stomach knot painfully. "You can't throw me out," she said past the lump in her throat.

"It's time you went home, Katie," Jake said, softening at the panic in her eyes. He wanted to pull her into his arms and promise to protect and take care of her forever, but he knew he would end up with only the shell of the woman she was. He couldn't bear that.

"Home to what?" she demanded. "Having my alarm go off every night? Jake, I can't do this."

"You can. You have to—"

"Why? Am I in the way here? Encroaching on your love life, perhaps?"

He dropped the clothes on the bed, then stormed over to her, grabbing her by the shoulders and hauling her up against him. "The only love life I want is with you," he growled.

Kaitlyn went very still as he lowered his mouth to hers.

For all his anger and determination, the kiss was surprisingly gentle and tender. This was the man who had cared for her last night and for the past two weeks. He caressed and coaxed, tempted and teased. One hand on her nape, the other arm around her back, he held her against the hard length of him. His tongue brushed her lower lip. She opened her mouth to his gentle exploration.

But behind the tenderness was all the passion she craved. An ache deep within her flared to life. She wound her arms around his neck, threaded her fingers through his thick hair, traced his lip with her tongue. He groaned, a deep, primal sound that only fed the fires he ignited. Then his hands were around her waist and he was holding her away from him. His breathing was as ragged as hers.

"I want *you*, Katie. The real you," he added, peering down into her puzzled expression. "The past two weeks you've been just going through the motions. Not sleeping, not eating. You've been withdrawing further and further—"

"And throwing me out there as an easy target for Fallon will solve that?" she cried. How could he not understand? Where was the sympathy and compassion she'd come to expect from him?

"Never, ever, will I allow you to be an easy target," Jake said. "You will have protection at all times. It'll just be handled differently."

She pulled out of his light grasp, knowing this was a battle she would not win. She pointed to the doorway. "Get out so I can dress and pack the rest of my things," she said.

He opened his mouth as if to say something, decided against it, then walked out, closing the door behind him.

Jake turned his attention to his driving. Katie sat ramrod stiff beside him in the Caprice he'd borrowed from the agency's fleet until his own car was out of the shop. Anger still radiated from her. As much as he hated having her upset, though, he knew this was a sign of progress. Anything was better than the nothingness she'd been experiencing.

"Anger can be a good thing in this case," he said, noting she didn't comment as he drove south past 119th Street instead of turning onto it. "It can be empowering. You can use it to assert yourself in this situation."

No response. He kept trying, hoping she was listening. "The thing is to hold on to it, but not let it get the better of you to the point where you take unnecessary or dangerous risks."

Kaitlyn sighed. Wasn't going home a dangerous risk? Apparently Jake didn't see it that way. Nothing she'd said had deterred his determination to get her out of his apartment.

"You don't want it to create a false sense of security," he continued.

"Pardon me," she said, unable to hold her tongue any longer, "but as I see it, I have no sense of security at all."

He gave her a sympathetic smile. "That's what we're going to get you now."

She shot him a quick glare, then turned back to her window and the scenery passing by. At 167th Street, just when she was beginning to wonder if he was taking her out of the city, he made a left turn onto a gravel drive. Once the dust settled she saw the old house with the wide front porch. A man in his early forties came down the steps to greet them. He and Jake shook hands vigorously.

Once Jake had introduced the man as Barry Jackson, the three of them walked around the side of the house. Barry opened the fence gate, then led them inside. Kaitlyn followed hesitantly. From somewhere not too far away, she heard a large dog barking.

Once Jake closed the gate, a Doberman came running at a gallop. Kaitlyn stopped dead in her tracks as the dog, its head reaching nearly to her waist, came up to observe the strangers. It nudged her hand. She reached for Jake's arm and held on tight. Chuckling, he pulled her against his side.

"This is Star," he said as the dog sat at her feet.

Looking at the dog planted firmly beside her, Kaitlyn suddenly realized what was happening here. "Jake, what am I going to do with a dog?" she wailed.

"Sleep at night," he said insistently. "Go for walks or a jog around the neighborhood. Take her with you when you run short errands. She's a guard dog."

Kaitlyn was beginning to see the possibilities, but she still had her doubts about the value of a dog, even one as big and intimidating as this one. Then Barry returned, a padded sleeve in his hands.

"Star, guard," he told the animal firmly, then donned the protective covering for his arm. When he made a slight move toward Kaitlyn, the dog stepped in front of her, bared its teeth and growled deep in its throat. When he advanced another step, the dog's growling became more fierce. When he still didn't stop, the dog lunged for his extended arm and sank its teeth in, holding on until he gave the release command.

"Impressive," Kaitlyn said in awe. She would never have guessed the docile-looking animal could have turned so violent so quickly. For several minutes, Barry worked with her, teaching her the various commands to use with the dog and the procedures she had to follow. Then he pulled a leash out of his back pocket, fastened it to the dog's collar and handed the end to Kaitlyn. Still a bit uncertain about her new responsibilities, she started toward the gate. The dog, getting the idea she was going somewhere, ran ahead, yanking roughly on Kaitlyn's arm.

Jake reached to grab the leash. "Star, heel," he commanded. The dog instantly came to a halt, standing obediently at Kaitlyn's left side. Jake let go of the leash.

"You're the boss here," he told her, chuckling. "You like giving orders, right?"

"Just to you," she murmured.

"Well, you can practice on Star."

With the dog panting happily in the back seat, he drove to a pet store. Once they got out of the car, he made Kaitlyn manage the dog as they shopped for everything the animal would need. By the time they got back to her condo, Kaitlyn was feeling more comfortable about having charge of the dog, but not about being alone. Jake was going to leave her by herself soon, she knew. She wanted to put off that moment for as long as she could.

"Groceries," she said, glancing inside the refrigerator. "I need groceries, maybe something for dinner," she added hopefully.

When Jake saw her bite her bottom lip, his resolve nearly caved in. It tore him up inside to think about leaving her on her own, but he knew his job now was to help her face her fears, not shelter her from them. She had to stand on her own to feel whole. Otherwise he would lose her entirely.

"Let Star explore the backyard," he said. "I'll take you out to lunch and to the grocery store."

She relaxed a little as they ate lunch, then shopped for groceries, but Jake sensed she was still on edge, thinking about the time she would be alone in the house. He wanted to tell her he would take her back to his apartment, that he would take care of her. But that was not what she needed most. She needed him to watch over her, not take over completely.

He'd handled many stalking cases, protected many clients as they went through their daily routines. He knew what he had to do with Katie—keep her safe from a distance, help her regain a measure of her independence. And not fail her.

He wasn't happy about what he had to do, but it was the

right thing, he knew. As they shopped, she made an effort to break out of the melancholy she'd been in the past two weeks. Later, while playing with the dog after the steak dinner he made, she even laughed. Quite a change. Once the playing was over and the dinner dishes were loaded in the dishwasher, though, she grew nervous and quiet.

He leaned against the cabinets and drew her into the circle of his arms. When he felt her trembling slightly, he ran his hand up and down her back. "I'm not leaving you completely alone," he told her.

"I know," she replied. "I'll have the dog here with me."

He slid his hand under her hair to stroke her nape, remembering the past and how she'd resisted his protection then. Now she was finally leaning on him and he had to push her away for her own good. He would give her back her independence, then he would have to learn to live with the worry that came with it.

"You'll have me, too, honey," he said.

She raised her head from his chest, a small frown creasing her brow. "What do you mean?"

"Max is on duty tonight. He and I will be in a patrol car parked where we can keep an eye on the house."

She laid her hand along his roughened jaw. "So you aren't deserting me totally," she said quietly.

"Katie—" He caught her hand, realizing she felt as if he were abandoning her. He had to make her see that would never happen. "You know me better than that. Don't you?"

"Yes, I do."

"But you were beginning to have doubts?" He wound a hand through her soft hair, toying with the strands, wondering what the future would hold for them, wondering if there would be a future for them together.

"I wasn't so much doubting you as surprised at what you were doing," she said. "This isn't like you."

He exhaled slowly. "You couldn't go on the way you were going. Something had to give."

"So you decided to try the tough-love approach?"

It was apt to be as tough on him as it was on her—if not tougher. Ironic how things had turned out, he thought, smiling.

"Is something funny?" she asked, gazing up at him.

"I was remembering how you used to view my protectiveness as smothering," he told her.

Fear had an interesting way of changing a person's perspective, Kaitlyn mused. It had her becoming clingy, becoming everything she didn't want to be. And instead of rejoicing at his good fortune, Jake was pushing her to stand on her own, to face her fears.

Was it fear that made her want him? Made her lean against his solid chest and absorb the feel of his hands on her back and in her hair? Made her want to keep him by her side? Or was she just wanting him as she always had in the past, without reason or logic?

"I appreciate your looking out for me," she told Jake. "But are you sure you want to be in a cramped car all night? Wouldn't you be more comfortable—" she breathed deeply "—with me?"

He raised her chin, his dark eyes searching her face for a long moment. "The next time you make that offer, honey," he said solemnly, "I'll take you up on it. But I want you to be very sure before we take that step again."

She knew he was right; there would be no going back once they gave in to desire. Making love would change things between them irrevocably. They would undoubtedly move in together and it wouldn't take long before Jake was asserting his "rights" as man of the house. That's when their troubles had begun the first time around.

Could they work it out this time? she wondered as she let him out of the condo and closed the door behind him. Through the window she watched him cross the street and get into a car with the Riley Security Services logo on the door. The car was parked on the street in plain view of anyone and everyone, and Kaitlyn knew the car would be there all night. Fallon would be a fool to try anything.

She closed the curtain, then reset the security system, looking at the keypad and smiling to herself. She'd always hated the things, but the current situation had changed her mind on that. And on a few other things.

Seeing Jake again for the first time that day in her office, she'd thought she would be foolish to get involved with him a second time around. It might still be a mistake, but she could no longer deny that she wanted him. She could still remember the feel of his hand up and down the length of her back, in her hair, on her nape. That had always been her weak spot and Jake knew it. A touch or a kiss on that very sensitive place and she'd always melted.

Then there was the way he was putting her needs ahead of his own. Very unusual for a man whose need to protect was so strong. He'd had her where he'd always wanted her, weak, needy, clinging, depending on him for everything. He'd driven her to work each day and picked her up afterward, had even taken her to deliver tickets and run her errands. He'd comforted her after the nightmares and nursed her through the migraines.

When she'd offered to give herself to him, he'd held her, instead, as if knowing it was the fear talking and not her heart. Tonight he'd told her he wanted her, but not until she was truly sure. He wouldn't take advantage of her momentary weakness.

As she lay in bed, the dog settled on the floor beside her, she considered how quickly the fear of Fallon had taken over her life. The thought that he could find out about her plans to fly to San Francisco had made her feel vulnerable, as if he'd invaded every facet of her life. She'd been frightened to the point where she couldn't function.

The fact that she'd fallen apart so completely and so

quickly scared her through and through. If it happened
once, it could happen again. True, this situation was unusual and her reaction was typical, but it was very unsettling to discover she wasn't as strong as she'd believed.

And what about Jake? He'd practically forced her to take
back control of her life. Today it was the dog, Monday
evening she would start self-defense training with Dev and
the next evening he would take her to the shooting range
for a refresher course on the use of the gun he'd given her.
Each night she would have a car stationed outside her
condo.

All courtesy of Jake. He was giving her back her sense
of security at the expense of his peace of mind. What
should she make of that?

With a frown of concern, Kaitlyn studied Jake as he slept
on her sofa, the baseball game on the TV, the remote control and his cellular phone lying on the floor within his
reach. In the week since he'd brought her back here, his
evening naps on the couch were becoming routine. As were
his cooking adventures in her kitchen. In these few short
days, he'd brought over so many of his pans, baking dishes
and utensils that she'd had to rearrange her cabinets and
drawers, though with the few things she had, making room
for his hadn't involved much effort.

Sighing quietly, she picked up his phone and the remote
control, then sat in the chair across from the sofa. She
switched the channel to the evening news, but didn't really
pay much attention to the day's events. She was more concerned about Jake. Two hours of sound sleep each evening
were not enough. He claimed he managed to doze a little
in the patrol car, but dozing and sleeping were two different
things.

When the sports segment of the news began, she carried
Jake's phone into her bedroom and shut the door. The man
on patrol duty—probably Max Slater—would call soon to

let Jake know he was there. Tonight, she decided, Jake would not be joining him.

"Jake needs some real rest," she told Max when he phoned.

"You're right," Max said. "The man can't function at his best the way he's going. I'll call in for someone else to stand watch with me."

She was grateful for his understanding. "Good night, Max."

"Yeah," he said as if no night was good for him. "You, too."

Pushing the End button on Jake's phone, Kaitlyn briefly wondered what demons kept Max working such long hours. She would have to ask Jake about that, she mused, but first she would do what she could to ensure he slept through the night. She found a light blanket and carefully covered him, then rechecked the door locks and the security system. Finally she switched off the television. Jake didn't rouse. Satisfied he was sleeping deeply, she whispered to the dog and led her to the bedroom. Once Star settled in to her usual place beside the bed, Kaitlyn turned off the light, then lay back, listening to Jake's soft snoring.

He was becoming a fixture in her life, she thought. The dog had quickly gotten accustomed to his being around. The neighbors they met while walking Star in the mornings greeted him by name. People in her office building frequently asked where he was if he wasn't there beside her. At the final tux fitting for the groomsmen, Rob and Shelly had both declared that Jake and Kaitlyn would soon tie the knot.

Kaitlyn cringed now, as she had then, at the thought of marriage. Spending time with Jake lately had been wonderful. She was giving more and more thought to making love with him. The frequent hugs he gave her, the way he held her hand or draped his arm around her shoulders when they walked, the long tender kisses in the mornings and the passion-filled ones at night—she liked it all.

She liked having his things around her house—his toothbrush in her bathroom, his clothes in her closet, even this T-shirt she'd swiped from him to use as a nightshirt. She liked helping him in the kitchen as he put together dinner for them, liked having him to talk to, laugh with, sit outside and watch the sunset with.

Add making love to the equation and that would be enough to make her completely happy, she decided with a yawn. Tomorrow she would tell Jake she was ready.

Then she would have to be on her guard to make sure their relationship stayed on the same track. Right now Jake was working with her to regain and maintain the independence she'd lost through fear, but once intimacy entered into the picture, that could change. This time around, though, she just might be able to deal with him.

That decided, she went to sleep, only to be awakened much later by the dog's growling. She glanced first at the clock on the nightstand—1:56—then at the dog, standing with her ears erect. When Kaitlyn laid a hand on the animal's neck, she felt the raised hairs.

What had the dog heard that Kaitlyn hadn't? Had the noise come from inside or outside the condo? Whatever it was, Star was clearly on alert. Kaitlyn's heartbeat quickened.

"Easy, girl," she cautioned, just in case Jake had awakened and was checking the house. Star didn't usually react this way to his presence, but then, he'd always left the house before Kaitlyn went to bed.

Keeping a hand on the dog's head, she got to her feet, then inched to the doorway. As she stepped into the hallway, a large shadow loomed in front of her. A strong hand clamped over her mouth. She froze, a scream trapped in her throat.

"Get back in the bedroom and stay there," Jake commanded, his voice lowered. "Take Star with you. Star, guard."

"Why?" she whispered when he took his hand away. "What's going on?"

"All the outdoor lights have come on. I'm going to check it out."

Kaitlyn opened her mouth to protest, but he didn't give her a chance.

"Get back in the bedroom and take the dog." A glimmer of light glinted off the gun in his hand as he turned away and silently made for the back door.

Her heart hammering now, Kaitlyn watched him until his shadowed form disappeared. Fallon was out there. She was sure of it. The vandalism had stopped once she'd moved back into the condo, as if his rage had cooled now that she was no longer staying with Jake. Then, tonight, the first time Jake hadn't left after the evening news, Fallon had struck again.

What was he doing out there? she wondered, backing into the bedroom, the dog following. More vandalism? When would it ever stop? Rubbing her arms against the chill she felt, she sat on the edge of the bed close to the nightstand. With the tiny bit of light from her clock radio, she could make out the shape of the 9 mm Jake had left with her.

Eyeing the weapon, she chewed her lower lip. She couldn't sit in her room, waiting. The fear was killing her— fear of what was going on, fear that Jake would be hurt. She had to do something, anything. Part of her knew she had to follow his orders, but a bigger part of her worried he might need her help.

Gripping his revolver with both hands, Jake inched toward the corner of Katie's condo. A moment ago, a dark figure—most likely Fallon—had been crouched down behind one of the forsythia bushes at the back of the house. When he'd heard Jake slide the glass patio door aside, the man had moved to the corner of the condo and around to the side.

Jake followed. He was certain Max would have seen the outdoor lights come on and expected he would be in the front of the house. Hopefully Jake would drive this midnight intruder right toward Max. They could catch Fallon in the act of violating the restraining order and have him arrested.

Jake made his way silently to the condo's corner, pausing to listen for sounds from the other side. Nothing. Keeping close to the house to minimize his shadow, he stepped around the corner. Instantly the dark-clothed figure reared up at him. Jake had only a second to react. He aimed his gun, but was already too late. The blade of a knife arced downward, slicing into his left shoulder.

Pain seared through his shoulder and down his arm. His breath rushed out of his lungs. Blood ran down his arm. He sank against the house and slid to the ground. His world went black.

Kaitlyn couldn't stand the waiting. What was going on out there? What was Jake doing now? How much danger was he in? Suddenly she wondered if Fallon was armed. Her stomach knotted. She got to her feet, desperate to know for certain that Jake was unharmed. Star stepped in front of her and wouldn't budge. The animal's attention was focused on the room's windows.

Kaitlyn listened and heard the sound, too. Footsteps. Running. Her breath caught as she heard a second set. Jake's? She sat down on the bed again, gripping the edge of the mattress with all her strength.

Then came the gunshot. The raised voices. Her chest tightened and she couldn't breathe. Unable to sit still any longer, she jumped to her feet. Jake could be hurt. He could be lying on the ground, shot, bleeding. She had to go to him. He might need her.

Grabbing for the gun, she ordered the dog to follow her

down the narrow hallway. As she stepped into the kitchen, two men came through the door—Dallas Steele and Jake.

Relief rushed through her that he was safe, then she realized he was leaning on the other man for support. Blood covered his left shoulder, ran down his arm and chest. She dropped the gun on the table, whirled a chair around and watched, shaking, as Steele eased Jake into it.

"Jake," she cried, kneeling in front of the chair. "My God. You're hurt."

"I'm all right, Katie," he said, his teeth gritted.

She refused to believe it. There was so much blood. His face was drained of color. "Fallon shot you?" she asked weakly.

"Knife wound," Steele corrected, rummaging the drawers for a clean towel. "That was my gun you heard."

"Bastard was waiting for me when I came around the corner of the house," Jake said angrily. "He knocked the gun out of my hand, then stabbed me. Dallas got there just as he took off."

She glanced at Steele. "Did you…" She halted, unable to ask if he'd shot the other man.

"I missed," Steele said with a muttered curse. "He was already headed down 120th Street when I fired at him."

"There were two police officers in pursuit," Jake managed to add. "We'll get him."

She stared at the amount of blood soaking Jake's knit shirt.

The red stain had drenched his sleeve and was spreading down his chest. So damn much blood.

He could have been killed. Kaitlyn could have lost him forever. She felt the world spin.

"Put her in a chair," he commanded someone behind her.

She hadn't seen Max Slater come into the room, but he was there now. He caught her by the upper arms and guided her into another chair.

"I'm all right, Katie," Jake repeated, his voice strained but strong.

She nodded weakly. There was so much blood and his face was lined with pain. Steele ripped away the shirt to expose a gash several inches long. The room spun again. Slater shoved her head between her knees.

"Deep breaths," Max said, his hand on the back of her head. "Deep."

Kaitlyn inhaled, held the breath for a couple of seconds, then exhaled. When she felt able to cope, she looked up. Steele had a clean kitchen towel pressed to Jake's wound and was applying pressure. Rob Donovan walked in and silently assessed the situation.

"Looks like Fallon got away," he said angrily. "We're bringing in some more units to canvass the neighborhood, though. If he's anywhere around, we'll find him." He eyed Jake's wound. "How bad is it?" he asked Steele.

Steele glanced at Kaitlyn. "Don't worry, Red. Half a dozen stitches and Jake'll be as good as new," he said brightly.

Chapter 12

A dozen and a half. That's how many stitches it actually took to close the wound. Standing beside the gurney in the emergency room, Kaitlyn counted each one and, as each one was completed, thought about how close the knife had come to Jake's heart. A few inches lower and to the right and Fallon might have killed Jake.

She had no doubt that was what the man had intended. He wanted Jake out of her life. He'd almost made that happen. Had almost taken Jake away from her forever. Jake could have died before she'd had a chance to tell him she wanted him, that she cared for him. Fallon had brought Jake into her life again and could have taken him out, as well. She shuddered.

"It's almost over," Jake said, squeezing her hand as he gazed up at her.

She nodded weakly. The ordeal wasn't over by a long shot. Fallon was still out there, waiting to strike again. Waiting for another chance to kill Jake.

Because of her. She'd called Jake in on this matter and

he'd stayed to do what he could to keep her safe. He'd thought nothing of the danger to himself tonight when he'd gone out into that yard. He'd sent her to the bedroom and commanded the dog to guard her. If she were to ask why, he would say it was his job. It was his nature, she knew. But Kaitlyn was certain his reasons went deeper.

She was frightened of where her feelings for him were carrying her, but the thought of never making love to Jake again was more frightening. As Steele drove them back to the condo, she sat next to Jake, holding his hand tightly until he wrapped his arm around her shoulders and pulled her close.

"You've been very quiet through all this," he commented, kissing the top of her head. "Are you all right?"

"I was just worried about you," she said, choking back the tears that filled her eyes at his thoughtfulness and tenderness.

She might never have experienced either again. Might never have known his wonderfully strong and gentle touch. There was so much about him that she would have missed, she thought as she led him back to the bedroom once Steele got them home. So many things they had yet to do together.

She helped Jake over to the bed, and knelt to pull off his shoes and socks, then helped him stand so she could ease his slacks down. Traces of blood stained the khaki fabric. Her breath caught again.

"Jake... I'm so sorry... I shouldn't have..."

"Katie," he said, lifting her chin until she looked into his eyes, "none of this is your fault."

"I know." She sniffed back her tears, then cupped his handsome face in her hands. "But I could have lost you."

"Ah, Katie..."

He patted the bed, and when she sat beside him, he held her as tightly as he could with only one free arm. She buried her face in the crook of his shoulder.

"I don't know what I would do without you," she whispered. Her life would be so empty.

He kissed her head. "You won't have to find out, honey. I'm here and I'm not going anywhere."

She wished she could believe that nothing would take him away from her, but she knew better. "Fallon might have other plans—"

"If he shows up before morning, the guys outside will have to take care of him. I'm too weak right now."

Kaitlyn heard the extreme weariness in his voice and remembered the nurse had given him a shot for pain before they'd left the hospital. She wriggled out of his light embrace, pulled the sheet out of his way, then eased him back onto the pillows.

"Go reset the alarm," he said on a sigh as she covered him. "Then come back and grab a couple more hours of sleep."

Kaitlyn did as she was told, but lying beside him, sleep eluded her. All the horrible possibilities kept running through her mind. She couldn't put aside the thought that Jake might have been killed, leaving her alone and very lonely.

A little before dawn, her thoughts turned to what she would do about her feelings for him. She wanted him in her life. She didn't know how things would work out for them in the long run, but she decided she would let the distant future take care of itself.

Right now she would concern herself with getting him well, healed, then with starting a relationship with him. A second time around. Right now she wouldn't worry whether they could make it work. She would take it one day at a time, dealing with whatever problems might arise, not anticipating them.

"Katie, honey, what are you doing?" Jake asked, coming slowly awake to realize she wasn't lying beside him.

She was sitting up, pillows propped against the head-

board. In the early dawn he could see she was fretting over
something and probably had been stewing about it for hours
while he slept.

"You should be sleeping," he said, reaching for her
hand and tugging until she slid down beside him. He was
beginning to feel she belonged there.

"Does your shoulder hurt?" she asked, laying her head
in the crook of his good arm.

"A little," he said, though it was beginning to throb.
But he would handle the pain for now. Knowing what had
been going through her pretty head was more important.
He nuzzled her ear, noting how wonderful she smelled, and
how much he wanted her despite his injury. "What's kept
you awake?" he asked.

"I was thinking how much I want you."

His heartbeat stumbled, then picked up an erratic rhythm
as she ran her fingers through his chest hair, slowly, over
and over, stirring his need for her. Jake considered stopping
her, but it felt so good and he'd been wanting her for so
long. Wanted her now, before anything could come between them. Still, he had to be sure of her.

"Katie," he said, his breath catching as her hand inched
a little lower. "Are you sure this is what you want? You
know there'll be no going back? No being 'just friends'?"

"So you said the last time I asked you to make love to
me." He could feel her smile against his skin. "When
you're able to handle it, I intend to seduce you. And you
won't be able to think, much less question my reasons."

He was rapidly losing all train of thought, he decided as
she continued to trace a pattern through the hair on his
abdomen, but he had to be certain there would be no regrets
on her part. "Honey, I have to know why— Why now—"

His breath snagged again as she raised up on one elbow
and kissed his chest, then nuzzled his nipple. Wave after
wave of need crashed over him, pulling him under, drown-
ing him in desire. She'd once said he could seduce her so

easily, but the reverse was just as true. One look, one tiny kiss, and it was all he could do to hold back.

"I want you, Jake," she said with emphasis. "I've wanted you since that day you walked into my office." She brought her hand up to stroke his roughened jaw. "I've wanted you because you have that effect on me. I've wanted you when I've been afraid, when I haven't been afraid, when I've been in this house alone and you've been right outside, protecting me."

"I've wanted you, too," he said softly.

"Then there's nothing more for you to analyze."

She kissed him then, her mouth gentle as her lips brushed over his. He closed his eyes, savoring the heady taste of her, the feel of her hair as it skimmed over his skin. All too soon she'd pulled away.

"I'll get you a pain pill and something to eat," she said.

He caught her arm before she could leave. "Katie, I don't want food and pills. I want you. Here and now."

Her eyes widened in surprise. "Jake, you're hurt—"

"I'm hurting, all right, but it's another part of me that's in agony. I don't want to wait any longer. It feels as if I've been waiting forever to make love with you."

The aching for her had never been more intense, Jake thought. It was as if he'd known that the times she'd asked before, a part of her had been holding back. Now that she'd made it clear how much she wanted him, he didn't want to wait another moment.

"Kiss me again, Katie," he ordered gruffly. "Kiss me like you mean it."

Kaitlyn didn't have to be told a second time. All the pent-up longing rushed to the surface. She leaned over him, looking deeply into his midnight eyes, reading the caring behind the need. That was her undoing.

Slowly she lowered her mouth to his handsome face, kissing first his forehead, then the straight line of his nose, the square angle of his strong jaw. She feathered the lightest of touches across his full lips, once, twice, a third and fourth time. When she would have continued, he wound his fingers through her hair and held her captive, his mouth only a breath away.

"No more teasing, honey," he said on a groan. "Kiss me."

"Umm," she said, running a hand through the richness of his hair. "For a man who wants something from me, you're giving quite a lot of orders."

One dark brow arched and a smile crooked one corner of his mouth upward a notch. "You want me to beg, is that it?"

Kaitlyn hadn't finished the nod before she found herself flat on her back, Jake looming over her, large and all male, looking not the least bit wounded despite the bandage on his left shoulder. She opened her mouth to remind him to be careful of his stitches, but he took it as an opportunity to plunder.

His mouth was hard, firm, as he took hers. As always, the fire sprang immediately to life. Heat coursed through her veins. She wound one arm around his waist, the other around his neck so she could continue to run her fingers through his hair. The strands slipped between her fingers, cool and thick and soft.

The kiss became more insistent, more demanding. When his tongue pressed against her lips, she let him inside, willingly giving him what he wanted. Bursts of longing shot through her with every bold stroke of his tongue. She moved beside him, trying to bring herself closer to his heat.

"That's it, honey," he said on a moan of male satisfaction. "Show me I can still make you hot."

He nudged her head until she turned to give him access to her neck. He rained warm, damp kisses on her ear, her neck, then worked his way to her collarbone. A sound, half sigh and half moan, escaped her parted lips.

"It's always been this way between us, hasn't it?" he asked against her throat.

Yes, Kaitlyn thought, he'd always been able to arouse her so easily, so instantly, but the feelings went even deeper this time. The sensations were sharper, more intense. She wanted him with an aching that was near agony. No amount of time apart or together would change that. The need would always be there, deepening, becoming stronger. It would always bind them.

"Jake, please touch me," she said, knowing his ego would get a tremendous amount of satisfaction from her plea. Another time she would have worried that he could make her weak enough to plead, but this time she gloried in what he could do to her. She'd never craved another man's touch this way.

Jake reached for the hem of the T-shirt she was wearing—his T-shirt, he noted with supreme pleasure—wincing as pain shot down his arm. He had no intention of letting it stop him, though. He'd waited five years for this moment. Five long and empty years without her. He couldn't wait any longer.

Katie, too, was determined to have the thin cotton barrier out of the way. "Let me," she said, sounding impatient with his slowness.

Carefully, so as not to bump his shoulder, she wriggled out of the shirt and tossed it to the floor. Jake gazed down at her, as always stunned by the beauty of her softly rounded breasts. The sight of her was even more mesmerizing than he'd remembered. He covered one small mound with his hand, pleased to hear her soft sigh of pleasure and feel her almost melt beneath him.

He bent his head and reverently took one nipple in his mouth, tasting the sweetness of her. God, but he'd thought he would never get this close to heaven again, never get this close to her. He'd been wanting her and now she was his. Completely. She was giving herself to him without reservation. He traced his tongue over the taut bud and she arched against him, calling out his name and clinging to him.

Kaitlyn tightened her grip around his waist, sank her fingers into his right shoulder, holding on with all her might as the sensations tore through her. Then he took the other nipple and sent another wave of desire flooding across her.

She couldn't think, couldn't worry about where she would end up once this moment was over, couldn't do more than want him. She'd craved his touch for so many long and lonely nights, longed to be in his arms, to have him touch her this way. All these years she'd been waiting just for him. Only him, she realized with a jolt.

He reached to unzip her jean shorts with deliberate slowness. Her breath snagged. Her body tensed in anticipation of his bold touch. He pushed the denim aside and let his fingertips travel over the bit of skin he'd exposed, sending tingle after tingle of pleasure skittering across her nerve endings.

Then he bent his head and kissed her stomach just above the waistband of the nylon-and-lace panties. Her grip on his shoulder tightened as she felt the brush of his tongue along her skin. She arched closer, craving more and more.

When he raised his head to look into her eyes, she smiled at him, a smile meant to welcome him home. She heard his breath, sharp and quick.

"Still have any doubts this is what I want?" she asked him, her voice sounding husky to her own ears.

He managed something between a moan and a chuckle. "My only doubt is whether I'll be able to get our clothes off before I explode. Think you might lend a hand?"

"I believe I might go you one better," she said boldly, then carefully pushed him back onto the bed.

His perplexed frown lasted only a moment, until she'd slid her jean shorts down her hips and then the nylon scrap of panty she wore. Before the fabric hit the floor, she was leaning over him, trailing a string of passion-filled kisses across his collarbone, along his chest and down his abdomen.

One finger under the waistband of his briefs, she paused. He was aroused and ready for her. She recalled other times when he'd had her mindless with need and had deliberately prolonged the sweet torture, and she decided to attempt a little torture of her own. She pulled the waistband down the slightest bit and kissed the skin she'd exposed, much as he'd done with her.

"Don't stop there," he urged her stridently when she raised her head to gaze into his eyes.

"Umm." Without removing the cotton briefs, she caressed him intimately.

He groaned, moved beneath her, then reached to push her back down onto the bed. She refused to relinquish the bit of control she had. Drinking in the rough gasp that he gave, she slowly eased the briefs down over his hips and muscular thighs, then tossed them on the floor beside her clothing.

Then she straddled his waist, leaning forward to kiss him again, intimately brushing against him as his hungry mouth ravaged hers. One hand tangled through her hair, the other cupped her breast. When his thumb and index finger toyed with the firm nipple, Kaitlyn was the one who moaned. He took the other in his mouth, letting his tongue trace a mesmerizing pattern over the taut bud until she arched closer to him.

His hardness pressed against her. She remembered how it had always been between them, remembered the feel of him inside her and recalled the wonderful things he could do to her. Suddenly she had to have him, had to feel him inside her.

She started to move off him, but he stopped her.

"I need you, Jake. Need you now."

"You can have me, Katie, honey. Right here. Right now. Like this."

Her breath caught. This was something he'd never done before, Kaitlyn thought dimly. He'd always set the pace, had always taken charge. She eyed him questioningly.

He nodded. "You do it this time. You lead."

He moved slightly, silently guiding her hips into position. Then he slid inside her. Kaitlyn gasped as he filled her, felt the world tilt and spin. She heard Jake's sharply in-drawn breath and knew that he'd felt it, too.

Slowly she moved her hips and felt Jake grip her waist. Intoxicated with this power she had over him, she set the rhythm, designing every movement to heighten the intense pleasure for both of them. She loved each of his throaty groans, loved watching his eyes darken as his need increased.

Somewhere in the deep recesses of what mind he had left, Jake knew Katie was enthralled with her newfound power and the knowledge made him even harder still. There was something very captivating about letting her take charge of their lovemaking. About letting her learn that she could set him on fire as thoroughly as he could her. He might have created a monster, but it was one he would relish submitting to again and again.

She moved above him to the rhythm she created, taking and giving pleasure—exquisite pleasure. The sensations built and grew. Jake could hardly breathe, could hardly think. He closed his eyes and savored what she was doing to him, the way she moved, the way she moaned deep in the back of her throat.

Then he had to see her. He opened his eyes to take in the sight of her above him. She was beautiful, her skin creamy and glossy with the fine sheen of perspiration. He took her lovely breasts in his hands, caressing and stroking them, feeling the nipples under his rough fingertips. She moaned again—a sound he would never get enough of.

Little by little she quickened the pace, until his thoughts scattered into a million disjointed fragments. He could only feel. Feel the exquisite pleasure rip through him time after time. They both breathed in short gasps.

Hand high on her back, he urged her to lean closer to him. Her breasts brushed his chest with every motion. Her hair fell across her lovely shoulders, a cascade of red and gold. The dawn light shimmered through the strands and over her silky skin. Her heart beat a racing staccato against his chest.

Passion consumed Kaitlyn. She was mindless with need. Ravaged with it, by it. She took him inside, deeper and deeper, pushing him faster and faster until she felt the explosion of her own climax. She cried out his name and he wrapped his arms around her, driving into her one final time.

Kaitlyn lay limp on top of him, careful to avoid hurting his wounded shoulder. She had to work to slow her rapid breathing. Her heart continued to beat frantically, and under her cheek she could feel Jake's pulse drumming wildly.

This time was even better than she'd imagined, the sensations stronger and more consuming. She wanted to experience the thrill of loving him again and again.

"Maybe we shouldn't have..." she began, seeing the lines of fatigue and pain on his face. "I mean, perhaps it was too soon. Your shoulder..."

"Is fine," he said, tugging her closer until his breath fanned her face. "You did most of the work, after all. And what a wonderful job you did."

Irrationally, she felt herself blush at his praise. "But, Jake, we could have hurt—"

He ran his hand over her shoulder and down her back, sending delicious shivers cascading along her spine. "Honey, if there'd been any danger of that, I would have told you. What is it you're really worried about?"

She raised her head to peer into his eyes. There was so

much concern there, so much tenderness. Where was that domineering brute she used to fight with so often?

"I don't know," she told him. "It's just that *this*—making love with you again—was so wonderful...."

"It was incredible. Better than ever before."

"It was," she agreed, then breathed deeply, searching for the right words. "Almost too good to be real."

"It's real, all right," Jake said, wrapping his one arm around her and holding her close to his side. "I felt you. You were hot and tight and you felt so damn good." He kissed her forehead. "You aren't trying to say you regret—"

"No, never." She raised up on one elbow and gazed down at him. "Never," she insisted, laying her hand along his roughened jaw.

Jake was relieved. "Then you're not upset?"

She smiled at him, the grin full of sexual satisfaction. "I'm very content, in fact."

"Very?" he asked, an answering grin tugging at the corners of his mouth. "Let's try for completely."

With that he eased her back onto the bed, then leaned over her. Her eyes widened as she realized his intent. Starting with her slender shoulders, he skimmed his fingertips over her skin in a pattern of tiny circles, over and over until he heard her breath snag yet again. Then he moved to her collarbone and slowly toward the hollow between her breasts. Her eyes closed as he traced the outer edge and with deliberate slowness worked his way to her nipples. She bit her bottom lip as he brushed his fingers over the sensitive peaks.

Kaitlyn struggled to breathe as the sweet torture continued, first his fingers, then his tongue. Ripples of renewed longing raced through her with each tender stroke. She wound one hand through his thick hair and held on.

"You still like that?" he asked against her breast.

"Oh, yes," she whispered.

He remembered, she thought with what little mind she had left. Five years and he hadn't forgotten that detail. Hadn't forgotten any detail of making love to her, she realized as his hand slid across her abdomen and settled between her thighs.

"Jake," she cried out as he found the warm wetness there. Her legs parted and he began to stroke her in that most intimate caress. She struggled to keep from crying out again as he gradually quickened his pace.

In a slower rhythm, he flicked his tongue over her nipple, sending another set of seductive sensations coursing through her. Her back arched and she knew he realized she was completely lost in the sensations he was creating. As she reached the highest peak, he kissed her, drinking in her sharp cry of pleasure. When she lay limp beside him, he nuzzled her neck.

"I love doing that to you," he said, his breath warm on her skin.

"Imagine how I feel." There weren't words powerful enough, emotional enough, to describe all that she felt when he touched her that magnificent way. She could still feel the pleasure he gave her, coursing through her body.

"I know exactly how you feel," he said. "It's what you do to me."

Looking into his eyes, she knew they shared the same experience, the same emotions, when they made love. She cupped his face in her hands and kissed him tenderly, then passionately as need built again. The taste of him made her crave so much more. She didn't want to wait.

"I want you again," she told him.

She caught his hip and tried to ease him between her legs. Taking his time to draw out the waiting, he slowly situated himself over her. He kissed her, letting her taste his passion and need for her. Then he pressed himself against her wetness.

Jake watched her face as he entered her again. Her eyes

darkened, nearly glazed over as all her being focused on him and how he felt inside her. Her hand tightened on his hip. Then, as she caught her breath, she moved beneath him, silently urging him to begin that primitive rhythm. He followed her lead, deciding it was very erotic giving Katie this bit of power.

Never had he felt so alive as when he made love to her. Never had his senses been so acute. When she gently nipped his chest, every nerve ending in his body sang. He could feel every satiny inch of her beneath him. Her longs legs wrapped around him, holding him her willing prisoner.

When he felt her tighten around him, he pushed her to the summit, then gently nudged her over the top. As she sighed her satisfaction, he moved within her, quickly bringing her to the top again. This time when she went over, he fell with her, floating languidly back to earth wrapped in her loving embrace.

Kaitlyn buried her face in his chest. Each time they made love would be different. It would never be mundane, even if she made love with him a million times. And right this moment, she felt as if a million times would not be near enough to satisfy her need for him.

No one could satisfy her as he did. No one could be as thoughtful, as caring and tender. She lay beneath him, absorbing the feel of his weight on her. His hair lightly tickled her skin. His warm breath fanned the side of her face and the column of her neck.

"Jake," she said softly.

He breathed deeply. "Hmm?" he managed to inquire, his voice barely strong enough to be heard.

Kaitlyn realized he was falling asleep. She'd taxed his strength, she thought guiltily, but then recalled that he'd been an active participant in their lovemaking.

"Jake, lie down here," she whispered. "You need to rest."

Reluctantly and slowly, he did as she commanded, settling beside her and reaching for the sheet, all without opening his eyes. She caught the corner of the sheet and pulled it over him.

"Do you need a pain pill?" she asked. He was clearly drifting off to slumber land, but she didn't want him to awaken in a few minutes with his shoulder in agony.

He shook his head slightly, then reached for her. "Sleep with me," he said.

Kaitlyn settled beside him, carefully shifting his arm across her ribs to a comfortable position. She closed her eyes, but soon discerned she was feeling way too much to sleep.

She and Jake had made love again. Wild, passionate, fantastic love. He'd been so wonderfully tender—as always. So hungry for her. He'd set her on fire with his need, had ignited her own with his passion. That would never change, she realized. Whenever they came together, it would be this way.

And now that she'd found this magic with him again, she would only want him more and more, would need to experience these heights, this rapture, again and again. No one else could take her to the places he could. No one else could satisfy her so completely, leave her weak, yet ready for more. With one touch, one smoldering look, he could make her want him. It was that easy. That quick. That intense.

But now it would become difficult to think with her head and not only with her heart. She hoped she would be up to the task.

Realizing how completely she'd let her heart call the shots, she felt traces of worry begin to creep in. What would the future hold for the two of them? How would they deal with each other now that they'd become lovers again? Would the past repeat itself?

Jake was strong willed and had a definite inclination to take over. He wanted a woman he could take care of. That wouldn't change. Now that he thought she was his, the tendency to dominate and overprotect might be stronger than ever. The challenge would be to maintain her own strength and independence. Could she do it?

She would have to be on her guard. Jake had warned her there would be no going back to being just friends, and in truth, she didn't want to go back.

But the past was very fresh in her mind.

Jake awoke, his shoulder throbbing. Memories of his moments of ecstasy with Kaitlyn, moments when he'd felt only her touch and the power of their passion, were clouded with the pain.

But Katie was lying beside him, curled on her side, her back against his chest. They'd made love again and it had been even better than before, she doing everything in her power to drive him wild and he returning her wondrous gift. She'd given herself to him completely, holding nothing back.

She was his now, body and soul. His to treasure and take care of. Nothing could diminish the pleasure that knowledge gave him. He loved her, he realized with certainty. The thought didn't surprise him. He knew now that all those long years apart, he'd never really stopped loving her, never stopped longing for her. And he never would.

He peeled back the sheet and eased his legs over the side of the bed, carefully, so as not to disturb Katie. She needed the sleep and he felt a surge of satisfaction to think his lovemaking had provided her this rest.

Not bothering with underwear, he went to the kitchen in search of the medication they'd given him at the hospital. He found the plastic bag on the counter and, after a brief struggle, got the pill out of the foil wrapper.

Food, he thought, swallowing the white tablet. What he really wanted was a thick steak with all the trimmings, but staring into the near-empty fridge, he decided he would have to make do with peanut butter. He'd intended a trip to the grocery store last night, but had fallen asleep.

Getting the lid off the jar was a snap compared with spreading the sticky stuff on a slice of bread, especially for a left-hander with a wounded left shoulder. The bread bunched and tore under the knife. He looked at the finished product, which amounted to several wads of peanut butter and bread, but he was just famished enough to eat them, then wash them down with a glass of milk.

Still starving, he decided to order a large pizza with everything and hoped he could last the thirty minutes until it arrived. Meanwhile, he figured he ought to put on some clothes. He shuffled back to the bedroom and tiptoed around the dog as he gathered his briefs and slacks. He went around to the other side of the bed to sit and pull on the briefs, unintentionally groaning at the added pain the movement caused.

Katie rolled over and stared at him. "Jake? What are you doing?"

"I'm on a mission for nourishment," he said, then explained about the pizza and his need to be decently clothed when the delivery person arrived.

Yawning, she scrambled across the bed to help him into his briefs. She draped his slacks over the bed, though, saying she would answer the door. Jake grabbed the pants and insisted she help him get into them.

"You will not answer the door," he maintained despite her protest. "I told Max and Dallas they didn't need to hang around after about ten o'clock this morning. It's now nearly one."

"What are you going to do?" she grumbled, easing his arm into the sling and fastening it around his neck. "Answer the door with money in one hand and a gun in the other?" He would scare the pizza delivery kid to death, she thought.

"Whatever it takes." He caught her and tugged her onto

his lap, then nuzzled her neck, inhaling the scent of her until he heard her quiet sigh. "You told me that if things got ugly, you would follow my instructions without question," he reminded her.

This was about as ugly as the situation could get, Kaitlyn thought, with Jake being stabbed frighteningly close to his heart.

"My wounded warrior," she whispered, gently kissing his ear. "You're injured, but still your first thought is protecting me."

"It always will be, Katie."

His mouth found hers, the kiss tender and full of promise. Warm and lazy, his tongue traced her lower lip until she granted him entrance. He teased and tested, tasting ever so slowly. The fire built slow, but strong, the heat coursing through her body and settling at the center of her being.

Carefully she wrapped one arm around his neck as he reached under her T-shirt to hold her breast in his hand. The warmth of his palm flowed over her skin. A wave of sensations rocketed through her as he stroked her taut nipple.

She arched closer to him, moaning for more. He drank in the sound, his mouth hungry and demanding. When his other hand slid down her back and came to rest on her hip, she felt herself melting against him.

"Katie," he said, his breathing already sounding ragged. "I want you all over again. I swear, I'll never get enough of you."

She wound her fingers through the hair on his chest, knowing she would never get her fill of him, either. He could make her weak with need so easily.

Suddenly she was a little afraid of this power he would always have over her. She swallowed past the lump in her throat.

"Your pizza," she said, carefully working out of his

embrace, snatching up her jean shorts, then pulling them on.

He didn't say anything as she helped him into his khaki slacks, but she could feel his gaze on her, searching and determined. In the kitchen she made him sit while she cleaned up the small mess he'd made with the peanut butter and milk, all the while avoiding his gaze as she wiped down the countertop and set his empty glass and dirty knife in the sink.

Her hand trembled with her nervousness. She hoped he didn't notice. She wouldn't hurt him for the world. How could she tell him that she was worried about the future, their future, together? How could she make him understand her fears? She didn't regret their lovemaking, but where did they go from here?

She didn't like uncertainty. That was it. With the two of them there were so many unknowns. No one could anticipate all the problems. This time, if it were to fall apart between them, leaving him would be much more painful than before....

"You may as well get it out in the open," Jake said, his deep voice holding a hint of resignation.

She whirled around, towel in her hand. "What do you mean?" she asked, her mind racing for a way to postpone the conversation.

"Whatever is bothering you. I'm not letting you continue to stew about it the way I used to. Let's get it out in the open and discuss it."

She could feel the first bead of perspiration pop out on her forehead. Her thoughts were still a jumble. She needed time to sort them out. How could she tell him how she felt, when she couldn't admit it to herself?

"Katie..."

He held out his arm and she slowly went to him, looking down into those dark eyes of his, reading his tenderness— and his determination.

"It's just…" she began, pausing for a deep breath. "Just that I…was wondering where we go from here."

"Where would you like to go?" he asked softly. When she didn't reply, he sighed. "Katie, you're remembering the past, aren't you?"

She nodded.

"This time is different. We're different," he insisted. "We've been able to work out all the problems we've come across."

"Because of the danger. What happens when our lives aren't in jeopardy and we have to deal with things like where we'll live, and whose furniture will go and whose will stay, and how late I work at the office in the evenings?"

Jake squeezed her hand. She needed reassurance, he realized. Reassurance that this time they could weather the storms. She needed to realize that their relationship five years ago had been rocky because it had been based on chemistry and their physical need for each other. This time his feelings went much deeper, and so, he was sure, did hers.

"Katie," he said, kissing the back of her hand, "this time *is* different. This time I know I love you."

She drew in an uneven breath and smiled down at him—a shaky smile, but it was a start. "Jake, I care for you, too.…"

She leaned down to kiss his forehead. After the unrestrained passion they'd shared earlier that morning, this little kiss and her tame declaration of "caring" were much too cool and distant.

"Why can't you say you love me?" he asked hesitantly, knowing she was holding back, knowing he couldn't let her.

"I did," she protested. "I said I cared—"

"Cared isn't the same." It was much too mild for what he felt, for what he wanted from her, for what he had to have. "I love you. I want us to be together for the rest of our lives. I want to take care of you. Katie, I want you to marry me."

Marriage? Kaitlyn's heartbeat stumbled. He was moving much too fast. "Jake, you're way ahead of me here."

"No, I'm not. Honey, if you think back to how you felt when we made love, you'll know that we're on the same page. You just aren't willing to admit it."

She let that issue slide for now. She didn't know how to respond to it. For now she would concentrate on the one that frightened her the most.

"Marriage? Jake, there are so many unknowns here. We need to take this slow—"

"We did that the last time, Katie, and in the end it was only that much easier for you to walk away. I'm not going through that again. This time I have to know that you're willing to commit to us. Completely. If you can't do that, then perhaps we should put things on hold until you can."

Kaitlyn felt the ground shift beneath her. This wasn't the direction she'd pictured their relationship taking at this point. She needed time to adjust, to get used to having him in her life again. But that wasn't what he wanted, so he was issuing an ultimatum—just how she'd feared things would go between them.

She took a step back and folded her arms across her chest. "Why marriage, Jake? Why can't we try living together for a while first?"

"It's the level of commitment—"

"No piece of paper ever kept two people together," she pointed out firmly.

He ran a weary hand across the back of his neck, reminding her that he was injured and in pain. She longed to go to him, to tell him she would do anything to make him happy. But he was demanding the one thing she wasn't sure she could give him, so she stood her ground.

"You're already thinking it's not going to work between

us," he said, pushing back his chair. "You're already prepared for us to split up. I guess that says it all."

He stood up, then walked away, down the hall to the bedroom. Kaitlyn knew he was leaving her, just when they'd begun to connect. She wanted to shout at him, demand he come back. But there was no compromise on this issue.

This was just what she'd feared would happen. Jake would make rules for her and demand she follow them. She couldn't live that way. Gone was the man who'd bargained with her on so many things. In his place was the man she couldn't deal with.

As she folded the towel she held, the doorbell rang. She grabbed her wallet off the counter and, determinedly ignoring Jake's earlier order, walked through the living room to answer the door. Through the peephole, she saw a man dressed in a knit shirt with the Pizza Store logo over the pocket, his ball cap tugged low over his forehead, his head bent as he studied the delivery ticket. Pulling out a twenty-dollar bill, she turned the knob.

The door flew open. Craig Fallon glared at her, a knife in his hands, insanity in his eyes.

Chapter 13

Kaitlyn gasped in horror. She turned to run, but Fallon caught her by the hair and jerked her against his chest. Tears of pain filled her eyes as he yanked her head back and held the knife to her throat. The cold steel stung her skin. A chill of fear rushed down her spine.

"Where is he?" Fallon demanded, his mouth against her ear. "Where is Riley?"

Jake. Fallon would kill him. Kill them both. She had to do what she could to prevent that. But what? She could barely think past the panic rushing through her.

"He's not here," she said, her voice quivering. "He had to leave."

Fallon's arm around her waist tightened, driving the air from her lungs.

"You're lying," he growled. "I've been watching the house. I know he's still here. Call him."

When she didn't comply immediately, he pressed the knife harder against her throat. Kaitlyn couldn't breathe, struggled to think past the fear consuming her. She had to warn Jake. Could he hear what was going on from the bedroom? Did he realize Fallon was here?

"Now," Fallon ordered. "Call him."

"Jake…" His name came out in a croak. Kaitlyn cleared her throat and tried again. "Jake, darling…" An endearment she never used. Would he understand that she was warning him? His cell phone was in the bedroom. Had he perhaps called for backup, already alerted the police? Would help come shortly?

Fallon tightened his arm around her waist again. "Tell him to come out here."

She swallowed carefully. What was he doing? Surely he'd heard the door crash open. He was planning something. A trap. He had to be. How could she help? If she did the wrong thing, they could both end up dead.

"Tell him," Fallon growled in her ear.

"Jake, come out here, darling."

She bit her lower lip, hoping she'd done the right thing, knowing she had no choice. Silence was her only answer. Her heart thudded against her ribs. If only she knew what Jake needed her to do.

Maybe she could still convince Fallon they were alone in the house. It might be their only chance of getting out of this alive.

"I told you he's not here," she said, her voice raised slightly. Hopefully Jake would hear her and understand what she was trying to do.

Fallon kicked at the pizza box on the floor. "He's here, all right. It's a large. You wouldn't order a large pizza for yourself."

Still holding her tightly, he shoved the door shut with one foot. Remembering her self-defense training, Kaitlyn shifted her weight hard against him, throwing him off balance. They tumbled to the floor, Fallon on his back, she on top of him. She heard his breath rush out on impact.

She rolled to her side and scrambled to her knees. Fallon

caught her ankle before she could get to her feet. She kicked at his arm, but he easily fended off the blows. He held her firmly as he got to his knees, then jerked her back against him and hauled her to her feet. Her breath caught as he raised the knife to her throat again.

"Damn you," he snarled. "You're mine and I won't let you go. Not even Riley will be able to save you this time."

Rage burned in his voice. She could feel him tremble with the force of it, felt the fear settle in the pit of her stomach. He meant to kill Jake, she was certain, and afterward he would kill her.

From the hallway, Jake watched the brief struggle between Katie and Fallon, remembering his sister and how he'd let her down. He would not fail Katie.

He had the 9 mm from her nightstand, but he couldn't get a clear shot at Fallon. The man managed to keep her in front of him, just close enough so Jake couldn't fire. There was a tiny trickle of blood where he'd nicked her skin. Jake vowed the man would pay for that.

She had to be frightened out of her mind, he knew, yet she was keeping her cool. He had to do the same, though as he saw the blood, it was harder than hell to remain calm. He wanted to kill Fallon with his bare hands. But first, he had to be sure Katie was safe.

Finally curious as to what was going on, the dog slowly walked out of the bedroom and came to stand beside Jake. Ears erect, she growled deep in her throat. He laid a hand on the animal's head to quiet her. He didn't want to startle Fallon as long as the man held a knife to Katie's throat. The dog stood still, but growled again. Jake flattened himself against the wall as Fallon whirled toward the sound.

"It's just the dog," Jake heard Katie say. Had she seen him? Did she know he was there, waiting for the right moment? Did she trust him to rescue her, take care of her?

"Put it in the basement," Fallon ordered, shoving Katie

forward slightly. "Don't try anything. Just get it out of here or I'll kill it."

Careful to keep Katie between him and the snarling animal, Fallon inched forward. Another few steps and he would have a clear view of the hallway. Jake silently eased his way back into the bedroom. Listening, he could hear Katie in a shaky voice instruct Star to go downstairs, then close the door on the dog. Sensing something was very wrong, the animal began barking and scratching at the door.

"To the bedroom," Jake heard Fallon say over the noise the dog made. "You and he spent the night there, didn't you? You were together."

Kaitlyn's stomach knotted. Jake was in the bedroom. He had to be. Fallon would find him. She had to do something. She dug in her heels, but Fallon pushed her on.

"Why the bedroom?" she asked loudly, dragging her feet as he continued to push her down the hall.

He didn't answer, just kept shoving her in that direction. Had Jake heard? She wished he could give her a sign, but she knew he couldn't. She was as afraid for him as she was for herself.

Fallon stopped in the doorway to look around the room. He pushed the door flat against the wall. Satisfied Jake wasn't behind it, he nudged Kaitlyn into the room, inching her toward the rumpled bed.

"He *was* here with you," Fallon snarled, looking at the shirt and shoes on the floor. "You bitch. I said you belong to me."

Again Kaitlyn felt him trembling with rage. He hurled her onto the bed. She twisted onto her back, to see him raise the knife above his head. She kicked at him, but he dodged her foot. She prepared to lash out again, then saw movement out of the corner of her eye—Jake, standing just inside the closet, his gun aimed at Fallon's head.

Fallon followed the direction of her gaze. Whirling

around, he grabbed her off the bed, holding the knife to her throat once more.

"Put the gun down," he ordered Jake, his voice full of malice. "Put it down or I'll cut her."

Kaitlyn could see Jake consider his options and come up empty. Reluctantly he laid the gun on the floor. Straightening, he leveled a calm gaze at her.

"You don't want to hurt her," Jake told Fallon. "You love her. It's me you want."

Fallon didn't answer. Kaitlyn felt his breaths coming in short bursts. Hatred and anger emanated from him. Jake, she realized dimly, was feeding those emotions. He wanted Fallon to lose control, wanted Fallon to attack him.

"I'm the one you want out of the way," Jake continued, taking one cautious step forward, then another.

"No, Jake," she whispered, realizing he was offering himself in her place. She thought of all that could happen to him—because of her. She'd brought him into this. He was already injured. He couldn't take on Fallon, not in his condition.

But there was unwavering determination in his eyes. He held out his arms and motioned for Fallon to make the first move. She could feel the man tense. Hear his breaths coming closer together. Then slowly he lowered the knife and loosened his hold around her middle.

He was going to attack Jake. She thought of Jake mortally wounded, dying because he wanted to save her. Giving his life for her. She couldn't bear that thought, couldn't stand by and do nothing.

Shoving fear aside, she thought again about her selfdefense classes. She rammed her elbow into Fallon's stomach. It connected with a solid thump. He doubled over. His breath rushed out.

"Katie, move," Jake commanded. "Now."

She realized Fallon had the knife raised. She twisted out of his grasp as it arced toward her. Jake lunged for the gun.

He picked it up, but Fallon was on him before he could aim it.

Jake braced as Fallon pounced on him. He had his finger on the trigger, then felt a sharp, white hot pain run up his arm. Fallon's knife had sliced his wrist. The gun fell from his hand and bounced across the carpet.

The knife was coming toward him again. Jake caught Fallon's arm and tried to wrestle the knife from Fallon's hand. More pain shot through him as he felt something in his left shoulder tear. The knife came closer to his chest. And closer. It scraped across his skin, drawing blood. Jake felt himself weakening. His shoulder was throbbing, but knew he couldn't give up. Fallon would kill Katie. He couldn't let that happen.

Fallon groaned as Jake twisted his wrist and held it with all the strength he could summon. Jake slammed the man's arm across his knee. Once, then again. Fallon still managed to hold on to the knife. He came at Jake with a left hook. It connected with Jake's jaw. He stumbled backward and sank to the floor.

Kaitlyn's heartbeat tripped as Jake fell and Fallon pounced on him. The gun was a few feet away, by the foot of the bed. She grabbed for it as the two men wrestled. She aimed it, but couldn't risk a shot. She was apt to shoot Jake. His forearm was bleeding where Fallon's knife had sliced his skin. Finally Jake had Fallon's wrist pinned to the floor. He slammed his fist into the man's face. Again. And again. Fallon's hand went limp. The knife fell from his grasp.

Jake raised his fist again, then stopped. Fallon was unconscious. Katie was safe. Jake looked around for her, spotting her next to the bed, kneeling on the floor, the gun aimed at the man who would have killed her. Her eyes were still full of fear. She held the gun trained on Fallon as if she couldn't put it down.

"Katie, it's over." Jake sat beside her, gently pried the gun from her stiff fingers and laid it on the floor.

"You're hurt," she said, her voice a mere whisper. She was trembling.

Kaitlyn reached for Jake's knit shirt, the closest piece of cloth she could find. She had to stop the flow of blood from his wrist. The cut went from his thumb, across his wrist and up his arm a short way. More blood seeped from a scratch on his chest, and the fight had torn his stitches enough that his bandage was turning red. Hands shaking, she wrapped the shirt tightly around his wrist.

Movement... She caught a flash of motion out of the corner of her eye. Fallon. He had come to and was sitting up. She whirled for the gun.

Instincts on alert, Jake grabbed for the weapon. He pointed it at the other man. Fallon shook his head as if he were still disoriented, then in an instant he had the knife in his hand and was charging at Jake. Jake shoved her out of Fallon's path, then fired. Eyes closed, Kaitlyn heard Fallon's body hit the ground.

More men burst through the door. Someone whisked her out of the room and settled her on the sofa. Star, hearing more commotion, increased her frantic barking and scratching at the basement door.

"Hang in there, Red," Steele said, squeezing her shoulders.

She struggled for a deep breath. "Where's Jake?" she asked, looking around the living room. He was gone, leaving her alone.

"Max is taking him to the hospital. A few more stitches and he'll be as good as new," Steele told her.

She tried to nod to show she believed him, but couldn't pull it off. All she could think about was how lonely she would be without Jake. He'd left without saying a word to her. Left her in the care of others he trusted to look after her in his place. Very unlike him where her welfare was concerned. She had a feeling he wouldn't be back.

"It's a good thing Jake could call us when Fallon first showed up," Steele was saying, probably in an attempt to calm her.

But she needed Jake, she realized. Needed him to be with her. Without him she felt very empty and very much alone.

"Can you take care of Star before she hurts herself?" she asked Steele. "She knows you."

"Sure. I'll put her in my car. She'll be all right there."

The house was filling up with people in uniforms and suits, she noticed dimly as Steele walked away. They drifted in and out of the bedroom, stood talking in small groups. Two officers at the front door made sure only authorized personnel came on the crime scene.

Kaitlyn sat on the sofa, watching the activity and wondering where Jake was. Had he made it to the hospital yet? Were the doctors concerned about the cut on his wrist? How much damage had Fallon's knife caused?

She longed to be with Jake, but knew he wouldn't want her there, not until she could promise him forever. She needed time. Time to see how they dealt with each other. Time to be sure she could handle his protectiveness, his authoritativeness. But Jake wanted his answer now.

"Chin up, Red."

Kaitlyn blinked past her threatening tears, and Steele's face came into focus. He knelt in front of her, pulling a handkerchief out of his pocket. When she raised her chin, he dabbed at the smudge of drying blood at her throat.

"Looks like it's just a nick," he said, studying the tiny cut. "A small bandage should be sufficient." He glanced at his watch. "Jake should be getting sewn up by now. They would have taken him back right away."

She nodded. He gave her a reassuring smile, then walked over to chat with one of the uniformed cops. Kaitlyn didn't know how much longer she sat there, lost in thoughts of

Jake, before someone touched her arm. She looked up to see Rob Donovan sitting beside her, his gaze full of concern.

"How are you doing?" he asked her.

"Fallon. Is he…"

"He's dead. He can't hurt you anymore. It's over."

Over, Kaitlyn thought, letting out the breath she'd been holding. The nightmare was finally over. But so were she and Jake. He would have no reason to come back to her until she could give him the commitment he wanted.

"Jake said it was a justifiable shoot," Rob told her softly.

She nodded again, closing her eyes as she thought of the knife stained with Jake's blood. His courage and strength had saved them both. But now he was out of her life.

"I'll have to get your statement," Rob continued, "but I can do that later. Right now, Shelly's here."

"Shelly?" Kaitlyn opened her eyes and saw her friend waiting by the front door.

"I called her when I saw them taking Jake out. She'll drive you to our place while I deal with everything here."

Steele handed her a card. "My cell phone number is on that. You call if you need anything at all. As soon as I hear about Jake, I'll phone Shelly's place and leave word."

Kaitlyn merely nodded once more and let Rob lead her to the door. She paused on the small porch to gaze back inside for a brief moment. There was nothing here for her now, she thought. Without Jake, there never would be.

The day was dragging by like all the others since Jake had left, Kaitlyn thought, sitting at her desk Thursday afternoon. Four days and not a word from him, other than Steele's phone call from the hospital assuring her they'd sewn up all Jake's wounds and he was on the road to recovery.

She'd spent that first night after the attack with Rob and

Shelly, at their insistence. They hadn't wanted her to be alone, to have to deal with the bloody carpet left behind and the nightmarish memories. She'd been unusually quiet and withdrawn that evening, but they'd assumed she was still in a state of shock over Fallon's attack and had left her to herself.

In truth, Kaitlyn had been trying to deal with Jake's leaving her, wondering if she would ever see him again, ever hear the sound of his rich and rough voice again, ever look into those incredibly dark eyes of his again.

She'd stayed there with Rob and Shelly because she hadn't wanted to be alone in the condo, alone with her thoughts. After that first night, though, when Jake didn't phone her, she'd had to accept that he had meant what he'd said and that she would have to pick up the pieces and get on with her life—without him.

She had to face the reality that he wouldn't be there when she came home from work in the evening, wouldn't be there to ask her how her day had gone as he cooked dinner for them both, wouldn't be by her side as she walked Star in the morning. Wouldn't be there beside her when she woke up. There would be no middle-of-the-day phone calls from him. He wouldn't be there to take her to lunch, wouldn't show up at her office with a tuna sandwich from her favorite restaurant.

The nights were the worst. Hour after sleepless hour of tossing and turning in the bed where she and Jake had made love. After one night of that, she'd moved to the sofa. Star hadn't dealt well with the change, either. She would pace the floor for a long while, then finally lie down, only to get up and pace some more.

When Kaitlyn would at last fall into an exhausted sleep, she would dream of Jake holding her, loving her, then walking away without a backward glance. She would awaken to the emptiness that was her life now.

"Shouldn't you be on your way to your mother's apartment?" Mary asked, poking her head through the doorway.

"My mother's?" Kaitlyn repeated blankly.

"You know," Mary prompted, handing Kaitlyn her purse and steering her toward the door. "She's going to help you pick out your new carpet."

At least she wouldn't have to explain the bloodstained carpet in the bedroom to her mother, Kaitlyn thought, getting into her car. Steele had come by the house the day after the attack to return Star and had kindly offered to help her remove the carpet and haul it off—at Jake's urging, she suspected. That was the closest thing to communication between them, though.

And it would be the most contact she would have with him, she had to acknowledge. He wanted total commitment from her and he would stick to that.

If only she could make him understand how very afraid she was to surrender to his demand. If she gave in this time, on such an important issue, how could she maintain her independence in the future? She wanted Jake in her life, but at what cost to herself?

"You've become a very strong woman, Kaitlyn," Gloria Adams said, running her thin fingers over a plush hunter green carpet square. "I've long admired that about you."

Kaitlyn glanced up from a rack of beige carpet samples, a little surprised at this sudden change in the conversation. Or was it sudden? She'd been so lost in her own thoughts about Jake that she'd paid only minimal attention to what her mother was saying during this shopping trip.

"You've never told me you admired my strength," she said.

"I do." Her mother gave her a small smile. "But sometimes I'm afraid you've become too strong."

Too strong? Did her mother have any idea how hard Kaitlyn worked at being able to stand on her own, how she often struggled with her doubts and fears? She'd come a long way, but still felt she had so very far to go.

"You don't need anyone, Kaitlyn. I'm not sure that's a good thing."

Seeing a salesman approaching, Kaitlyn took her mother's arm. She obviously wanted to have a rare serious discussion and the carpet store was not the place. Kaitlyn led her to the car, then drove to a nearby diner. They found an empty booth and ordered coffee and a cola, Kaitlyn stirring the soft drink with a straw for a long moment and staring out the window. Now that she was here, she wasn't sure she wanted to have this conversation. How could she tell her mother that she was afraid of ending up like her, broken, disillusioned and depressed?

"Mother, people walk all over someone who is needy and dependent. I don't want anyone to have that kind of control over me...."

"The way your father controlled me, you mean?" Gloria asked.

Kaitlyn regretted the pain she saw in the other woman's eyes, wished she could erase all the hurtful memories. "Us," she said. "The way he walked over us, controlled us."

"But you would rebel," Gloria said, her smile returning. "How you would rebel. I was secretly proud of you."

"Sometimes I thought you were actually encouraging me," Kaitlyn said, recalling the occasional sly nod she would get, or the rare times her mother aided and abetted in her daughter's schemes.

"I was. I wanted you to be able to stand up to him, to anyone. To not be beaten down, the way I was. I wanted you to be strong where I couldn't be."

"Isn't that a form of strength in itself?" Kaitlyn asked. "You had your own bit of defiance."

"I suppose you're right." Her mother's eyes warmed. She laid her hand over Kaitlyn's. "Darling, the point I'm trying to get to is that you are not me. And Jake is not the least bit like your father."

Kaitlyn frowned into her soft drink. "I know that, Mother."

"Do you, dear? Your father was a bitter man. He was extremely demanding and even more critical. Nothing ever pleased him."

"Tell me about it." How often had she tried her damnedest to meet his impossibly high expectations, only to have to endure failure and his criticism and wrath? "Perfection wouldn't have been good enough for him."

"He took a cruel pleasure in beating me down." When Kaitlyn looked up in surprise at the declaration, Gloria nodded. "I'm learning quite a bit about myself, and him, in therapy."

Kaitlyn breathed a small sigh of relief at this sign of how well her mother was doing, of how far she had come. Perhaps she would finally find her way out of the depression that had plagued her for so long.

"Jake, on the other hand," Gloria said quietly, "only wants you to lean on him a little. He wants to be able to take care of you."

Kaitlyn frowned. "Lean on him?" she asked. "Mother, it sounds as if—"

"Jake has come to visit me a couple of times," her mother admitted.

Kaitlyn should have guessed he wouldn't walk away from his friendship with her mother, and she was grateful he hadn't. "It isn't only the leaning," she said. "He's so bossy."

"Not the way your father was, darling. Jake has a kindness your father totally lacked."

He did, Kaitlyn mused, sipping her soda. He was thoughtful, sensitive, tender, caring. She remembered how he'd stayed with her at the hospital when she feared she might lose her mother. Remembered the headache he'd nursed her through, and the bout of nausea. Recalled how he'd wanted her to be very certain of her feelings before making love with her.

And of how he'd demanded she marry him.

"Mother, you don't understand—"

"Yes, darling, I do. More than you realize. For all these years you've had to be strong enough for both of us, and now you're so strong you can't bend even a little. Bending and breaking are two different things, you know."

"Not in my book," Kaitlyn muttered.

"Then you should read from another book. Breaking people was your father's style, not Jake's," Gloria pointed out firmly.

Perhaps. But what was to keep that from changing? Kaitlyn wondered. One demand was sure to lead to another. Where would it end? With her fighting him every inch of the way to maintain her own strength?

She couldn't live the rest of her life that way. Nor could she live giving up the strength she'd finally gained after all her struggles.

"*Compromise*, Kaitlyn, is not a dirty word," Gloria insisted as she reached in her purse for money to pay their bill.

Compromise *was* difficult for her, Kaitlyn realized, and sometimes just as difficult for Jake. But on this issue there was no middle ground, no halfway. If she couldn't make the total commitment, he would put them on hold until she could.

With a sigh, she followed her mother out of the restaurant. Somehow she had to sort through her thoughts and feelings—before the wedding rehearsal tomorrow night. Jake would be there. She had to know what she would say to him.

How long did it take for a woman to come to her senses? Jake wondered morosely, staring into his half-empty beer mug. To the other three men at the table, the beer mugs were half-full, but that's not the way Jake saw things lately. Four days without Kaitlyn had him in a funk—worse this time than the last.

After the attack, he'd gone home from the hospital to his empty apartment. Though he'd known Katie was safe and with Rob and Shelly, he hadn't been able to stop worrying about her, stop wondering whether she was worried about him, whether she felt as lonely and desolate as he.

He could have ended his own misery right then, he knew. Still could. But this time he had to be sure of Kaitlyn. Had to be certain she wouldn't walk out on him at the first sign of trouble. She'd left him devastated the last time. He couldn't risk that again. If they were married, she would have to deal with him, work conflicts out rather than pack her bags and leave. He needed that.

Consequently he'd been going through his days and nights barely able to function. Thanks only to his top-notch staff, the business had run smoothly. He sure hadn't been involved in anything. Ninety percent of his days had been spent staring out his office windows, wondering what Katie was doing. Was she thinking about him? Was she missing him? Wishing he were there with her?

Did she remember their lovemaking? He could still recall every wonderful detail. When he closed his eyes, he could still feel her touch, the satin of her skin, the heat of her as she lay next to him. He still wanted her, ached for her, still dreamed of her at night.

Nights. Without her they were exercises in torture. Each one was longer than the last, stretching on for endless hours as he longed to have her in his bed. Longed to hold her, touch her, take care of her, hear her calling his name as he made love to her. Hell, he would be content just to see her face, hear the sound of her voice.

She would be at the wedding rehearsal tomorrow evening, he remembered. What would she say to him? Would she even speak to him? What should he say to her? If she wasn't ready to commit to their relationship, there could be no future for them. Could he bear that?

Jake blinked as someone gently cuffed his right shoulder. "Damn, Jake, this is a party for Rob, not his funeral," Max said from beside him.

"You're all pitiful," Dallas said, shaking his head. "Max is married, Rob is getting married and Jake is miserable because he wants to be married. You're all crazy, if you ask me."

In unison the other three said, "Shut up, Steele."

"You don't know what you're talking about," Rob said.

"Look at you guys," Dallas insisted. "Each of you is letting a woman—one woman—run his life. The women have total control. You don't do what she says and you're the ones who're miserable," he said, pointing his finger at Jake, then at Max and finally turning it on Rob. "You're next, Copper. Mark my words."

"One day," Max warned. "One day it'll happen to you. You'll be in love."

"Yeah," Rob said, echoing the sentiment. "You'll fall so hard and so fast you won't know what hit you."

The way he had, Jake thought. All over again. Despite all the things he'd told himself to the contrary, all the warnings, all the holding back. He'd fallen in love with Katie Adams all over again.

"Put your money where your mouths are," Dallas was demanding. "Fifty bucks says I make it to fifty unattached and unbrokenhearted."

"You're on," Jake said, figuring if it could happen to him when he'd gone into things with his eyes open, it could happen to any man.

"Yeah, you're on," Max and Rob said, nodding in agreement.

Dallas wasn't bothered by the fact he was so outnumbered. "I turn thirty-five next May," he told them. "Fifteen years from that date, we meet in the office and I collect."

"It won't be fifteen years and you won't be collecting," Rob said. "You'll be in love and doing whatever it takes to make your woman happy."

Dallas arched an eyebrow. "Whatever it takes?" he scoffed. "Like Jake here? Red wants to take things slow and Jake's rushing her."

Rob laughed. "He's not there yet. Me, I think of Shelly and of all I'm gaining and I don't mind giving in."

He could give in, Jake thought. Had given in on so many other points. This time was different, though, the point too important. He had to know Katie was as committed to them as he was, and there was no two ways about it.

But when he was back at home, alone, unable to sleep, missing her more than ever, he had to remind himself how important this was to him. He couldn't live in a constant state of uncertainty. He wanted it all—marriage, kids, the PTA, grandkids—and he wanted it with Katie.

What if she didn't come to him?

He knew she cared for him, but how deep did her feelings go? He was learning that his own went to his very soul. He knew that she was afraid they wouldn't be able to work things out. Gloria Adams had explained how Katie had had to fight her way through her growing-up years just for a chance to stand on her own. He understood she didn't want to do battle the rest of her life. She pictured marriage as a possible war zone.

It had been that way between them before. Could he convince her they could do it differently this time around? Convince her he understood her need to be strong and would do all he could to support her?

Chapter 14

Kaitlyn lay in the darkness. Alone. Unable to sleep in the bed without Jake beside her. With the dog following behind her, she wandered to the front-room window and peered out at the starry night sky.

What was Jake doing? Was he sleeping peacefully? Or was he, too, awake and lonely? Perhaps missing her?

She thought of this afternoon's conversation with her mother. Kaitlyn had always prided herself on not needing anyone. She never wanted to be that vulnerable, that open to hurt.

So she'd shut Jake out.

Her breath caught at that thought. She recalled his last words to her and realized she had been unconsciously planning for their separation all along. She'd figured they would fail again, just as they had the first time, and hadn't given them a chance.

She thought again about Jake and all they'd been through. Of the times she'd gone head to head with him and of how they'd resolved the issues that had come up, each giving a little. Of the way he'd taken care of her when the headache and nausea had incapacitated her. Of how surprisingly wonderful it had felt to have him there holding her, comforting her, doing whatever he could to ease her pain.

Absently petting the dog behind the ears, she noticed the Riley Security Services car do a slow drive-by, still checking the condo though Fallon was out of the picture for good. She smiled to herself, realizing Jake was still taking care of her, protecting her from a distance. Odd that it didn't upset her as it once would have. In fact, instead of making her angry, it gave her a definite sense of security.

Jake wanted a woman who would lean on him, let him take charge. Kaitlyn had fought so long and hard to stand on her own, had worked to succeed and achieve. It wasn't in her nature to relinquish control of her life. The risk of devastation was too great.

Yet when she had given Jake control of her life for the few weeks that fear had her unable to function, he'd given it right back to her. She'd leaned on him heavily, depending on him for nearly everything, and he'd practically forced her to stand on her own—getting her a guard dog, signing her up for self-defense lessons, making her stay in the house alone.

Was that a fluke? Something he'd done because of the dangerous situation she'd been in at the time? Was it a one-time occurrence? Or perhaps a glimpse into the future?

Jake threw back the covers and got out of bed. He was losing count of all the sleepless nights he'd endured lately. This one was worse than all the rest. This time he couldn't just lie there feeling desolate. His mind raced with what he would say and do tomorrow.

Tomorrow evening he would see Katie for the first time since Fallon had attacked them. Jake hadn't contacted her since that night, figuring her decision about them was one she had to reach on her own.

Did she know she held his future happiness in the palm of her hand? Did she know he wouldn't be able to survive without her? The feelings were much stronger this time around. He'd fallen much harder and deeper in love than before.

Sitting on the balcony, drinking a cup of decaf coffee, he thought of his life without her. Long days and longer nights of endless loneliness. Never to hear her laugh, see her eyes light up with desire. Never to hold her, make love to her. Never to wake up with her beside him.

She was the one woman he would love with his heart and soul. She loved him, too, he thought. Why was it so difficult for her to admit it?

She wasn't the type to lean on him, but in the past few days he'd come to realize he didn't want that as much as he once had. He realized he wanted her strength, her independent nature. He wanted someone to share his life and that someone was Katie. It always had been and always would be.

Kaitlyn parked her Honda next to Jake's Town Car in the church parking lot, shut off the engine, then wiped her palms on her denim skirt. She wanted to get this meeting over with, and yet she wanted to put it off for as long as she could. She wasn't ready to face Jake again. Wasn't sure she ever would be ready.

She'd hardly slept last night, knowing she would see him today. Hour after hour she'd struggled to sort through her feelings. She missed him, wanted him in her life. Somewhere along the way she'd realized she loved him. Loved a man she might not be able to live with. If that wasn't a recipe for disaster, what was?

He'd kept her safe from Craig Fallon and would always go to the limit to protect her. The problem was he tended to go overboard. Then there was his method of operating—making decisions without consulting her, giving orders.

She couldn't live with that. Yet how could she live without him?

That's the way it had gone all night and all day today, and still she'd come to no definite conclusion. She couldn't have it both ways. It was either life with him or life without him. The first could be a series of battles. The second would be a bleak and lonely existence.

With a sigh she got out of the car. Birds chirped merrily in the trees that lined the parking lot. The early-evening sun shone down brightly. The air was warm, but not uncomfortably hot. It was a perfect evening, and tomorrow's forecast was for more of the same. A good sign for Rob and Shelly's wedding? Kaitlyn sincerely hoped so.

The church smelled of flowers and beeswax candles. Kaitlyn stepped inside and paused to let her eyes adjust, and to give herself time to get composed. Soft voices and quiet laughter drifted from the altar. She spotted Jake standing beside the groom and the priest, tall and silent, unsmiling.

Her heartbeat did a rough flip-flop. She longed to be able to see Jake's face clearly, to read his expression, to know what he was feeling. Was he dreading this moment? Was he anxious to have this wedding over so they could get on with their lives?

Shelly saw her at the back of the church, excused herself, then walked briskly away from the others. When she was a few feet away, she paused to search Kaitlyn's face for a long moment before taking her arm and leading her back to the nursery the church kept for children of the congregation.

"I thought you'd never get here," she said, shutting the door.

Shelly was radiant, Kaitlyn noticed, positively glowing with happiness. This marriage was right for her and there wasn't a doubt in her mind. Kaitlyn felt a stab of jealousy. Why couldn't her decision concerning her own love life be so cut-and-dried?

"Aren't you supposed to have a case of the wedding jitters or something?" she asked her friend gently.

"The only thing I'm nervous about is your fainting during the ceremony, and you look as if you just might," Shelly said in an urgent voice. "You and Jake both look as if you haven't had a good night's sleep in days. What's going on with you two? This is more than the deal with Fallon."

Kaitlyn's heartbeat tripped again. "Jake looks as if he hasn't slept?" Hope flared to life. Did he miss her, then? Truly miss her?

Shelly let out a quiet groan. "He looks awful. Dallas said this is the first time in three days that Jake has shaved and he wouldn't have done that if Dallas hadn't reminded him."

Jake had let his appearance go? That could only mean he was upset. Miserable, perhaps? She hated that. Never had she imagined he would be going through this kind of agony. Never had she dreamed he would be hurting as much as she.

"Kaitlyn, what's going on between you two?" Shelly asked, taking Kaitlyn's hand. "Is there something Rob or I can do to help?"

How could she explain? Kaitlyn wondered. She needed to deal with the sudden numerous questions that raced through her mind. Why was Jake so unhappy? What was tormenting him? Always she'd pictured him waiting stonily for her to come to him. So many questions. So much uncertainty.

"How do you know?" she asked Shelly. "How do you know so definitely that Rob is the man for you?"

Shelly smiled broadly. "Ask me something hard. Kaitlyn, Rob is my soul mate. My other half. I feel complete with him and completely lost without him.''

Soul mate, she mused for a moment. "But what about the problems? How do you know you can deal with them?''

"Communication.''

Kaitlyn sighed. Could the answer be that simple? And yet how complicated that was when it came to her and Jake. Or was it as complicated as she was making it?

"Look, Kaitlyn, we don't have all the answers. No one does. There just aren't any guarantees in life,'' Shelly said, squeezing Kaitlyn's hand briefly. "Rob say he loves me and he'll stick by me. The rest I have to take on faith. Now, come on, the natives are getting restless up there.''

Kaitlyn followed Shelly up to the altar, wondering how to take Jake on faith. She didn't do that with anyone. How could she rush into something so very important—even with a soul mate—on faith alone?

From the left side of the altar she chanced a glance into Jake's eyes. The anguish she read there took her breath away. Was this distance between them tearing him apart, too? Did her decision mean so much to him?

Jake saw the fatigue in Katie's eyes. Fatigue that no amount of makeup could conceal. What was he putting her through? He wanted to go to her, pull her into his arms and demand she let him take care of her. But that wasn't what she needed from him.

He'd steeled himself for this moment when he would see her again, but he hadn't been prepared for the way seeing her torment would hit him in the gut. How could he do this to her? There was a weary and defeated slump to her shoulders. Her face was pale under her makeup. She looked thinner. She hadn't been eating, he was sure, and just when he'd finally managed to get her interested in food.

Father Allen ran them through their paces, with Jake paying minimal attention to the details. Frequently he would catch Katie's gaze on him. Even across the aisle he could read the longing in her eyes. It was nearly his undoing. It unleashed all the needs he'd been trying so desperately to hold in check.

He wanted her. Needed her. Loved her to the point where he couldn't think of anything—or anyone—else but her. He had to have her back in his life again.

But could he live on her terms, afraid that one day she would leave him? What could he do to keep her by his side?

Someone nudged his arm, bringing him back to the rehearsal with a jolt. Rob stood with his arm outstretched, palm open, waiting. Jake stared at him blankly, then quickly searched his pockets, coming up empty.

Rob rolled his eyes. "It's a rehearsal, Jake. You're supposed to pretend to pass me the ring."

Shelly sighed loudly. "Kaitlyn's just as bad. She's going through the motions, but I doubt she realizes that right now she's supposed to be taking my bouquet so you can put the ring on my finger."

"Sorry," Jake said, realizing Katie had mumbled her apology at the same time.

Did she know they were meant to be together if they were this brokenhearted apart? How could he convince her? He had to get her alone, he decided as the rehearsal continued. He wouldn't have time before the dinner party tonight, but as soon as it was over...

What if he'd pushed her too hard, though? What if he'd driven her away? She hated being backed into a corner, and that's just what he'd done.

"Enough," Shelly said in exasperation. "Neither of you is paying one bit of attention to this."

Jake glanced up to see everyone staring at him, Katie included. Her gaze, though, held so much sympathy and concern. She cared, he knew, but was that enough? Could he take a one-day-at-a-time relationship with her? Did he have a choice?

When Shelly snapped her fingers under his nose, he blinked in confusion. He hadn't even seen her come up to him.

"You've done it now, my friend," Rob muttered without a trace of concern for Jake.

"The nursery," Shelly commanded. "You, too, Kaitlyn. Let's go."

Obediently the two followed her to the back of the church and into the children's nursery. Shelly gently shoved Katie in first, then Jake. He took a step into the room, then waited, suddenly very uncertain of the woman he loved. If she said she didn't love him he would never be able to pick up the pieces.

"I don't know what's wrong between you, but neither of you comes out of here until you've solved it," Shelly ordered. "The rest of us will finish this rehearsal, then we'll go to the restaurant."

"But—" Kaitlyn began.

Shelly held up a hand to demand silence. "Take as long as you need. We'll go on to dinner without you, and Rob and I will fill you in on what you're supposed to do later. Tomorrow, if necessary. Just don't either of you move from this room until you've settled everything."

Shelly walked out, closing the door behind her, leaving Kaitlyn alone with Jake. Her stomach knotted. Her mouth went as dry as desert sand. Her mind raced with fear. What was he thinking, feeling? She didn't have a clue.

"Why don't you sit down," Jake said, watching her. She looked as if she were about to fall down. He figured if she started pacing, she wouldn't last five minutes on her feet.

To his surprise, she did as he asked. Hands in her lap, she twisted at her purse strap and bit her bottom lip. He sat beside her, a foot or two away, wondering what to say, where to start.

"How are your stitches?" Kaitlyn asked, noting the

flesh-colored, square adhesive bandages on the inside of his wrist.

"They're fine," he said. "The doctor said there was no permanent damage."

She nodded, relieved. "I was worried about that."

"Were you?" Jake asked softly. Was that all that had kept her up at night—worry about his cuts? He needed to know, but was afraid to ask.

"Of course I was worried. Jake, you saved my life...."

Is that all she felt? he wanted to demand. Gratitude for what he'd done? He wanted a lot more from her than gratitude. What about the love they'd made? Hadn't she shown she cared for him? Hadn't she said as much? Had she changed her mind?

"Saved your life," he repeated flatly.

"Yes," Kaitlyn said, puzzled at the lack of emotion in his voice. "I was afraid Fallon might have hurt you...might have done some lasting damage."

"Oh," he said, flexing his fingers for her benefit. "Well, you don't have to worry about that."

He got up and walked to the window, his back to her. Kaitlyn frowned. He was turning away from her and she didn't understand why. He was so difficult to read. Was this the same man who had said he loved her? He was, she admitted to herself, the man she loved. And she was losing him.

"Jake," she said, her voice shaky, "I get the feeling I'm saying all the wrong things."

He turned to study her for a long moment. "There's no right or wrong. Just say what you feel."

Her feelings were a jumble—worse than ever with him looking down at her with that unreadable expression. She sighed and attempted to sort through them. Outside the room she could hear the sounds of the others leaving the church and heading for their cars. Inside the room the silence stretched on.

"I'm feeling scared," she finally managed to say.

Jake whirled around, amazed at how those three words could bring out his protective instincts. He wanted to slay all her demons, but he was learning he couldn't. He had to give her room. He couldn't push her into love. Her eyes were wide, her gaze expectant.

"Afraid of what?" he asked.

She lowered her eyes, bit her lip, twisted her purse strap again. If ever he wanted to go to her and hold her, it was now. But he had to let her struggle with this on her own, no matter how it tore at him to stand there and do nothing.

"Of making a mess of my life," she said after a long moment. "Of making a mistake."

Jake's breath caught. What was she saying? "You think we're a mistake?" Is that what she meant?

Kaitlyn raised her chin and squared her shoulders. Now that she'd begun, she knew she had to continue. Regardless of what happened, there were issues that had to be resolved.

"We were," she told him.

But that was then, Jake wanted to protest, as he had at the engagement party and so many times since. Five years ago, they'd both been younger, more quick-tempered, less inclined to give a little. Didn't she see that? Hadn't he shown her he could be flexible? What more could he say or do to make her see that this time was different?

"Katie, you're remembering the past."

She liked hearing him say her name, Kaitlyn thought. Liked it a lot, especially when his voice was husky with passion. She studied his strong features—the firm line of his jaw, the angle of his chin, the curve of his full mouth.

She thought of his smile and how it would soften his face and crinkle his eyes. Somewhere along the way she'd committed it to memory, never to be forgotten. Wherever she went she would always remember the thrill of his kiss, the pleasure his hands could give her, the tenderness in his lovemaking.

"We had some major fights back then," Jake continued, "but this time wasn't like that."

"No," she agreed softly. "This time was…"

"Different?"

"Nice. Better…" Much better. Ecstasy, in fact. The feelings were much stronger this time. There was so much she wanted to experience again. She was beginning to realize that she would not make her mother's mistakes, would not make the same choices. Realize that in dealing with Jake she would be dealing with a kind and reasonable man.

"Better until I said I wanted marriage or nothing," he noted. "Until I tried to push you. I hardly gave you a chance to tell me what you needed. I tried to bulldoze you in the direction I wanted you to go."

Kaitlyn nodded. That was the issue in a nutshell. "I'm afraid our lives would be a battle—you pushing and me pushing back."

Jake ran a hand over his jaw. "Last night I thought long and hard about that and saw how stupid I acted when I all but demanded you marry me. I know how that 'we do it my way' approach works with you. You dig your heels in and don't budge."

True, she thought, but that wasn't what she was doing in this case. Or was it? Was she going to blow a chance at happiness out of sheer stubbornness?

"So I've decided I'll take whatever you can give me," he told her.

"Whatever?" she asked. Was he saying… Could he mean…

He nodded. "I was a fool. I love you, Katie, and I've been unhappy without you. I want you in my life, and if all you can offer me is one day at a time, I'll take it gratefully."

He would do that? Make the ultimate compromise? He was putting her needs ahead of his own, as he had when he'd made her face her fears and take back control of her life. Showing her that he could work with her, that he understood her.

"You would do that?" she asked. "For me?"

"For us." He gave her the hint of a smile. "I do have an ulterior motive. I want us to be together."

"So do I, Jake." She meant it. With every fiber of her being.

Her heartbeat quickened as he pulled her into his arms. She closed her eyes and savored his nearness, his strength, his tenderness. She'd wondered if she would ever be in his arms again. This was where she was meant to be, she knew for certain. Where she wanted to be.

"Jake," she said, taking a deep breath, "will you *ask* me to marry you?"

"Honey, I said I wouldn't push you—"

"You aren't. I figure I love you. Completely. I want to spend the rest of my life with you. That's about as committed as it gets. I'm bound to you in spirit and I want to let everyone know it."

"No more uncertainty?" he asked, his heart racing with happiness. She loved him. She would be his—forever. All he'd ever hoped for, everything he'd feared he'd lost, was his.

"I'd be foolish to think we'll have smooth sailing all the time, but last night I thought of the past few weeks and how we've dealt with each other. No screaming, no shouting."

"We've talked, worked things out for the most part."

"At first I thought it was a fluke...." She laid her hand along his jaw, needing to touch him. "You're still pushy and probably still overprotective at times."

"But you're strong enough to reason with me this time."

"And strong enough to lean a little every now and then."

Jake stared down at her. "Do you mean that? You'll let me take care of you—occasionally?"

She smiled. "As long as you don't go overboard. I've

found I need you, and I like having someone to share the load. Ask me to marry you.''

It was his turn to smile. He released her to get down on bended knee. This time he would do it properly.

*   *   *   *   *

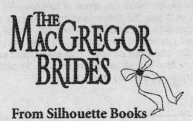
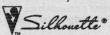

Take 4 bestselling love stories FREE

Plus get a FREE surprise gift!

Special Limited-time Offer

Mail to Silhouette Reader Service™

3010 Walden Avenue
P.O. Box 1867
Buffalo, N.Y. 14240-1867

YES! Please send me 4 free Silhouette Intimate Moments® novels and my free surprise gift. Then send me 6 brand-new novels every month, which I will receive months before they appear in bookstores. Bill me at the low price of $3.34 each plus 25¢ delivery and applicable sales tax, if any.* That's the complete price and a savings of over 10% off the cover prices—quite a bargain! I understand that accepting the books and gift places me under no obligation ever to buy any books. I can always return a shipment and cancel at any time. Even if I never buy another book from Silhouette, the 4 free books and the surprise gift are mine to keep forever.

245 BPA A3UW

Name	(PLEASE PRINT)	
Address	Apt. No.	
City	State	Zip

This offer is limited to one order per household and not valid to present Silhouette Intimate Moments® subscribers. *Terms and prices are subject to change without notice.
Sales tax applicable in N.Y.

UMOM-696 ©1990 Harlequin Enterprises Limited

The Stars of Mithra

**Three gems,
three beauties,
three passions…
the adventure of a lifetime**

SILHOUETTE·INTIMATE·MOMENTS®
brings you a thrilling new series by
New York Times bestselling author

Nora Roberts

**Three mystical blue diamonds place three close
friends in jeopardy…and lead them to romance.**

In October
HIDDEN STAR (IM#811)
Bailey James can't remember a thing, but she knows
she's in big trouble. And she desperately needs private
investigator Cade Parris to help her live long enough to
find out just what kind.

In December
CAPTIVE STAR (IM#823)
Cynical bounty hunter Jack Dakota and spitfire
M. J. O'Leary are handcuffed together and on the run
from a pair of hired killers. And Jack wants to know
why—but M.J.'s not talking.

In February
SECRET STAR (IM#835)
Lieutenant Seth Buchanan's murder investigation takes
a strange turn when Grace Fontaine turns up alive. But
as the mystery unfolds, he soon discovers the notorious
heiress is the biggest mystery of all.

Available at your favorite retail outlet.

ELIZABETH AUGUST

Continues the twelve-book
series—36 HOURS—in
November 1997 with
Book Five

CINDERELLA STORY

Life was hardly a fairy tale for Nina Lindstrom. Out of work
and with an ailing child, the struggling single mom was
running low on hope. Then Alex Bennett solved her problems
with one convenient proposal: marriage. And though he had
made no promises beyond financial security, Nina couldn't
help but feel that with a little love, happily-ever-afters really
could come true!

For Alex and Nina and *all* the residents of Grand Springs,
Colorado, the storm-induced blackout was just the beginning
of 36 Hours that changed *everything!* You won't want to miss a
single book.

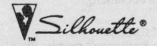

SILHOUETTE WOMEN KNOW ROMANCE WHEN THEY SEE IT.

And they'll see it on **ROMANCE CLASSICS**, the new 24-hour TV channel devoted to romantic movies and original programs like the special **Romantically Speaking—Harlequin™ Goes Prime Time.**

Romantically Speaking—Harlequin™ Goes Prime Time introduces you to many of your favorite romance authors in a program developed exclusively for Harlequin® and Silhouette® readers.

Watch for **Romantically Speaking—Harlequin™ Goes Prime Time** beginning in the summer of 1997.

If you're not receiving ROMANCE CLASSICS, call your local cable operator or satellite provider and ask for it today!

ROMANCE CLASSICS

Escape to the network of your dreams.

See Ingrid Bergman and Gregory Peck in *Spellbound* on Romance Classics.

Welcome to the Towers!

In January
New York Times bestselling author

NORA ROBERTS

takes us to the fabulous Maine coast mansion
haunted by a generations-old secret and introduces
us to the fascinating family that lives there.

Mechanic Catherine "C.C." Calhoun and hotel magnate
Trenton St. James mix like axle grease and mineral
water—until they kiss. Efficient Amanda Calhoun finds
easygoing Sloan O'Riley insufferable—and irresistible.
And they all must race to solve the mystery
surrounding a priceless hidden emerald necklace.

Catherine and Amanda

THE Calhoun Women

**A special 2-in-1 edition containing
COURTING CATHERINE and A MAN FOR AMANDA.**

Look for the next installment of
THE CALHOUN WOMEN with Lilah and Suzanna's
stories, coming in March 1998.

Available at your favorite retail outlet.

Return to the Towers!

In March
New York Times bestselling author

NORA ROBERTS

brings us to the Calhouns' fabulous
Maine coast mansion and reveals the
tragic secrets hidden there for generations.

For all his degrees, Professor Max Quartermain has a
lot to learn about love—and luscious Lilah Calhoun is
just the woman to teach him. Ex-cop Holt Bradford is
as prickly as a thornbush—until Suzanna Calhoun's
special touch makes love blossom in his heart.
And all of them are caught in the race to solve
the generations-old mystery of a priceless
lost necklace...and a timeless love.

Lilah and Suzanna
THE
Calhoun Women

**A special 2-in-1 edition containing
FOR THE LOVE OF LILAH and
SUZANNA'S SURRENDER**

Available at your favorite retail outlet.

Share in the joy of yuletide romance with brand-new
stories by two of the genre's most beloved writers

DIANA PALMER

and

JOAN JOHNSTON

in

LONE STAR CHRISTMAS

Diana Palmer and Joan Johnston share their favorite
Christmas anecdotes and personal stories in this
special hardbound edition.

Diana Palmer delivers an irresistible spin-off of her
LONG, TALL TEXANS series and Joan Johnston crafts an
unforgettable new chapter to **HAWK'S WAY** in this wonderful
keepsake edition celebrating the holiday season. So
perfect for gift giving, you'll want one for yourself...and
one to give to a special friend!

Available in November at your favorite retail outlet!

Only from

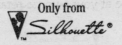